Unravelling Lives

Janet Jones lives and writes in Somerset. She has
written a number of prize-winning short stories, now
in a collection entitled Time and Tide, as well as
another novel – We Are Unknown.

Unravelling Lives

Janet Jones

Watersmeet Publications

© Janet Jones 2024

All rights reserved

This book is dedicated to Peter, with
love and thanks - for introducing me to your
Somerset homeland, and for giving me the time and
space to write about it.

PROLOGUE

2010

A mere handful of people are gathered at the church on the hill. The voice of the solemn clergyman booms and reverberates off the cold stone walls; there is too much space for his words to hang in the air, and they fall quickly to the ground.

'We are here today to mark the life and passing of our sister and fellow parishioner, a life that was unknown to most of us. Not all lives are able to produce that rich tapestry which some achieve. But they are no less precious for the fact that they have been filled with only the simplest of tasks …'

A solitary bee has found its way into the holy space and settles on the small wreath of flowers adorning the plain coffin. The cleric's words have briefly ceased, as though an unfulfilled life is also a life barren of commentary or description; but the insect, buzzing gently as it nuzzles up inside the chrysanthemum petals, seems to prompt the colourless man, and he winds himself up to speak again.

'She was, of course, in some small way, a woman of the great outdoors. She loved her garden and indeed kept several hives for many years, sharing her honey produce with members of the community.' He pauses again, pondering perhaps why he himself has not been a recipient. 'She loved to walk, to take in the wonderful scenery with which we are blessed in this small corner of the country; and it was that walking which sadly …'

His words blend with the droning of the bee, forming a meditative chant, and despite the chill of the church, the small congregation find themselves closing their eyes, sinking into the words and the pews, forgetting for a brief moment the reason why they are sitting in this place.

Until. Until …

THE LITTLE PLACE NAGGED AT HER

How had she never noticed it before? In all her tramping of the coastline she was sure she had never seen this small wooden building. And yet, there it was, perched at the end of the beach, adjacent to its pastel-coloured companions, and so obviously part of the long-established landscape. Perhaps the dullness of its sun-bleached, wind-whipped wood had given it camouflage, allowing it to hide amongst the rocks and sand? But nevertheless, it was different enough to be the dowdy wallflower overlooked at the village dance.

Martha had taken to walking when the grey emptiness of the house had threatened to starve her of breath. It had burrowed inside her head and swamped her thoughts until one day she had rushed from the door, gasping, crying, trying to find some solace in a small patch of sunlight.

Every day she would criss-cross the grid of her neighbourhood streets, taking little notice of the Edwardian houses and their newer companions until she met up with the shoreline. Some days the tide would be in and she would have to satisfy herself with a stomp around the curve of the harbour, watching the boats as they jumped the swell of the waves before sliding back to their moorings. She liked it best though when the tide was out and she could walk on the beach, searching among the pebbles for sea-glass or staring into the rockpools for signs of life, or simply standing, mesmerised by the push and pull of the waves, endlessly churning. But even this hadn't been enough, and she had pushed herself to go further – sometimes for the weariness it brought to her limbs, something which might bring her sleep. Sometimes it was the nearest thing she could find to a spoonful of exhilaration; mainly though it was to prolong the moment when she would have to return home.

Curiosity got the better of her and she sauntered over to the hut, passing a hand over its dry faded coat as she circumnavigated it. Her fingers reached out, as if of their own volition, and tried the rusting bolt. She looked around. There was no-one about, no-one in sight for at least a hundred yards. The bolt was stiff, salt-coated, but with her gentle encouragement it shifted, little by little, until the door space yawned open and she could step inside.

The room was shaded, but not grey like her own house. Someone had seen fit to drape sacking over the small windows and it gave the space the tones of late honey, warming and calm. There was a small table in the middle of the room and a tin mug, a spoon too large to stir its contents, and a penknife, folded, unready for action. She peered around, looking for a seat where she could rest herself and think.

But as she did so, a clattering on the roof shook her from her daydreaming and she pushed at the door and ran out, rattling the latch, not checking whether it was fully closed or not. She realised, as she looked back from the safety of the other brightly coloured huts, that it had simply been two seagulls, jumping heavily on the small roof, arguing over a stolen chip or a crust of bread. But her heart was still skipping and she had no inclination to return – not today anyway.

But the little place nagged at her. For two days Martha forced herself to stay away, walking huffily to the other end of the bay, but by Friday she was back, pulling on the bolt once more, slipping in through the dark doorway and taking the place for herself. This time though, she went straight to the small windows and pulled back the sacking, tucking it in on itself so that a slab of light could join her inside.

There was nothing else to be seen on the table apart from the items she had previously noted, but there was a chair – the sort with a severe upright back and no cushion on its raffia seat. She lowered herself gingerly, unsure whether the tattered fibres would support her. They moaned and groaned but they held their place and after a few moments Martha relaxed, tipping her head to take in the rest of the secluded room. There was fishing equipment, long past its catching best, and ropes neatly coiled and stacked, but her eye was drawn to the back wall where, incongruously, a carefully carved bookshelf was attached to the uprights. Three volumes, curled by winter dampness, sat on the bottom shelf sentried by stones, but on the top ledge was a piece of driftwood. It was like Medusa's hair, creeping in and out of itself, bending and curving and knotting into a tangle that would never be undone.

Martha stretched, but there was no reaching it. It was an inch beyond the furthest tip of her fingers, no matter how much she strained and snatched. She dragged over the chair, hesitating as she imagined her foot plummeting through the raffia, but unable to stop herself nevertheless; she had no idea why, but she had to lift the wood from the shelf.

She struggled to keep her feet on the edges of the wooden frame, the chair wobbling and swaying on its rickety legs, but she steadied herself and waited for it to stand motionless once more. Finally, it submitted and she was able to reach out, lifting the tangle of wood from its dusty shelf, cradling it as she stepped clumsily down.

Martha couldn't stop her fingers from running themselves around each curve, following the hard strands until they disappeared inside the knots of wood, losing all track of time as she turned and followed every last pathway. It wasn't until, reluctantly, she was about to return it to its home that she noticed the snippet of paper which her dragging of the wood must have pulled to the floor.

The scrap was a piece of something, with a scrawl of faded ink; "*…have you ever…*" were its only words, and they left her standing, impatiently waiting for more.

For a moment she didn't move, but then, with the compulsion of finding a missing jigsaw piece, Martha clambered back onto the chair and began searching for more. She ran her fingers along the dusty shelf and a snowfall of paper fluttered to the ground, collecting at her toes.

It was only as Martha gathered them all into her hands – considerably more pieces than she had been expecting – that she noticed the light had dimmed. She stuffed the pieces into her pocket and slipped out of the hut, this time making sure that the bolt was firmly shot home.

The pieces prickled her curiosity as she made her way back along the emptying streets. Lights came on in bundled terraced houses and once-grand 1920s villas alike. Rooms appeared through uncurtained windows, and Martha longed to be inside - that room with the children jumping on the garish blue cushions, or that one with the couple laughing at something in a newspaper. But those happy scenes threatened to dampen her spirits and she pushed on, surrounded by the evening, until she got to her own front door. For once, slipping the key into the lock and lighting up the hallway wasn't as daunting or as melancholy as it had usually felt.

EDGE PIECES FIRST

Martha threw her jacket over the worn newel post and scooped the papers from her pocket, heading for the kitchen. She was ready to spread out the pieces, eager to resurrect their message, but as she flicked on the light she stood in bewilderment, as if putting on new glasses and seeing her home clearly after years of shortsightedness.

The table was spread with such an assortment of bowls and spoons and cups and knives that there could be little left in the tall oak cupboards. She glanced over at the sink, which was similarly stacked with pans and lids and implements; the chaos hit the backs of her knees and she dropped onto one of the smooth oak chairs. She had never been the greatest of housewives – he had always teased her about that - but she had usually managed to keep sufficiently on top of things so that the place had at least a veneer of cleanliness. It would never have passed her mother's fingertip test, but her home had always been presentable. Now Martha realised that for each of the numbing days which had passed she must have pulled a bowl from a shelf, allowed a fluttering of cereal to fill it, must have emptied the bowl as she stared at the abandoned garden where he seemed to have spent so much of his time. Soup must have been tipped from tins, an egg had presumably found its way into boiling water, but the aftermath of these untasted meals had been beyond her; she had evidently pushed every utensil to one side, and wandered off, allowing her mind to settle on happier times, until the clock had dictated that she should sleep or eat again.

She looked down at the fistful of paper pieces clutched between her fingers. She wanted to winkle out their secrets but she didn't even have a surface to put them on.

'Right.' Martha spoke aloud to herself as she often did these days, walking back into the hall and replacing the pieces inside her jacket pocket. 'Not even a peek until this is put right.' It was as if she were talking to the girl she had once been, the girl with unruly plaits dancing on her back, red ribbons tethering the ends in place; the girl who had pulled a face at every task allocated by mother or teacher and requiring completion before she was allowed to play. But the method would suffice again, she thought, as a system came to her fingers and her mind barely entered into the proceedings at all. Bowls were stacked, plates ranked beneath, cutlery standing to attention inside a jug. She pulled gingerly at the dishwasher door as if some unknown creature might jump out, wondering why she hadn't seen fit simply to conceal everything inside. She stacked and arranged and re-arranged until nothing more would fit then turned her attention to the sink. There was something soothing about hot soapy water, the clarity it brought to murky glasses, the way it cut through week-old grease and food scraps. It took three tea towels to dry the china mountain, and Martha absentmindedly turned on the radio as she worked, just as she had once used to after Sunday lunch or Christmas dinner, working her way through mindless tasks while someone told her stories or read news items or gave her the reasons for everything.

When she was finished, her hand went to the kettle and it occurred to Martha that this is what happened in normal houses when the tasks were done. The water boiled and the tea was made and women would sit around the table with biscuits or cakes to sweeten their words. She was now bereft of such companionship, having allowed – encouraged - friends and colleagues to slide from her turbulent life. But for once she didn't resent her solitude, because now she could enjoy the treat she had postponed.

Martha returned to the jacket hanging untidily on the post, and slid her hand once more into the pocket. It was all still there, the raggle-taggle cluster nestling between her fingers as she took it in both hands like an injured bird and carried it through to the kitchen.

'Edge pieces first,' her mother had stridently instructed the young Martha, every time a new jigsaw had emerged from the Christmas wrappings.

She laid the pieces on the table and spread them with her fingers, anxious that not a single shred should escape, moving them until no piece overlapped another. She could see a word here, a full stop there, but she averted her eyes, not wanting to get to the end of the story before she had made the beginning. She moved each straight-edged piece to the top of the table, and then looked for the corner stones. Three. The three corner pieces made her heart sink, because already the fragments were telling her that some of their number were absent.

'One step at a time, no rush,' she said, sipping at her tea, examining the crooked lines of the pieces for links and similarities. There was no picture to follow, no instructions other than the torn edges, but somehow, like the dishes, Martha began to take comfort and enjoyment from the sheer repetitiveness of the task.

The clock in the hall, the one which Richard had spotted on one of his delivery jobs, and had insisted on buying from the antique shop across the bay, geared itself up to strike. Martha assumed it must be eight o'clock, but as she listened she counted, surprised to reach ten – no eleven o'clock. She checked the mother-of-pearl watch on her wrist and saw that she had been sitting at the table for almost four hours.

She looked down at what she had achieved. One quarter, perhaps less, of the pieces were in place, and finally she allowed herself to take in what they were telling her.

There was a date – "29th June", but no year.

There was a "dearest", but no name.

And there was a "nothing without …", presumably missing its "you".

Five words seemed very little reward for her evening's work.

NOTHING WOULD SETTLE IN ITS RIGHTFUL PLACE

The persistent pounding pressed its way into her dream.

Martha's eight-year-old self had been watching the Changing of the Guard in her best lilac coat with matching hat, clutching the black palace railings as she pushed her face tight for a better view of the scarlet uniforms and the marching boots, until the boom disturbed the rhythm of their steps. She had looked up at her mother, her soundless mouth asking questions amidst the hollering and stamping outside the palace walls.

The guards seemed oblivious as the onslaught continued, and she tugged at her mother's coat, trying to drag her away from the cannon fire, looking anxiously over her shoulder for the next battalion of soldiers who should be marching up The Mall to take command.

She touched her own shoulder and it was cold, and she realised as she turned, that she had tugged the covers from her sleeping body. As she drifted away from the pageantry of the palace and moved forward some thirty-five years into the greyness of her current day, the thudding continued to disturb the air.

Martha reached for her dressing gown, untangling the belt as she swung her legs out of bed and slipped her feet into her waiting slippers. As she dropped wearily down each stair the colours of the stained-glass window in the front door jumped and changed. There was movement on the other side, causing the yellows and the blues of the geometry to reassign themselves like a kaleidoscope. She stopped, wondering who, of all her rejected companions had decided to make one final assault on her house, hoping it was only a postman or hawker who she would have to expend no time in speaking to.

The letterbox rattled but it was not a letter.

'Martha. Martha – I know you're there.'

Her sister didn't need to announce herself. The harsh staccato notes of her voice did that for her.

'I'll break the glass, Martha. I'm not leaving until you …'

She pulled open the door, leaving Laura's hand to jump back from the opening.

'I've been knocking for ages.' A woman with sleek hair and co-ordinated outfit, and, incongruously, a wicker basket, stepped over the threshold. She paused and took a deep deliberate inhalation. 'I thought so,' she said, breathing in the staleness of Martha's life. She took the basket from her arm and scowled at Martha.

'This can't go on. I'm not going to allow it.' She turned, heading for the kitchen. 'It affects one's mental health – there have been studies you know ….' By which Martha knew that a discussion on Radio 4 had wheedled its way inside her sister's head. 'And I knew this place would be … Oh.'

Laura had pushed open the kitchen door and was stopped in her tracks.

'Oh – well, I thought …' By which Martha guessed that her sister had managed to push through the warped garden gate in some moment when she had been absent, and had peered through her windows. 'Yes, well, I thought – I just thought you might need ...' Her fingers ran over the cleanliness of the nearest worktop.

I'll make some tea.' Martha gazed at her sister's open mouth, noticing for the first time that Laura's jawline was uneven, and that she had the beginnings of what her father might have called a turkey neck.

As she turned though, her arrangement of the torn papers caught Martha's attention. One had fluttered at her movement, and found itself a place beneath a chair; another had crawled across the table and teetered on the edge.

She looked from her sister back to the scrubbed wooden surface. 'Why don't you go into the front room – I'll bring the tea.' She reached for a tea towel as camouflage, but realising that it would cling and pull at the pieces like a stubborn sticking plaster, she looked around afresh. A newly scoured baking tray was all that was within easy reach and she placed it precisely over the part-formed letter, just as her sister's voice shot through the air.

'I knew it. I knew you weren't managing.' The kitchen door opened again, a moment too late to whisk the shreds of paper into the air. 'There's not even a space to sit. Anyone would think you'd been in this house six weeks instead of six years.' Laura brushed her hands together, discarding the grime she assumed had already collected there. 'I'll do it for you – help you at least. We'll have this place shipshape in no time …'

Martha was about to justify, to protest at the delight in Laura's voice, but she glanced at the mottled face of the baking tray hiding her secret. She would give her sister her moment of pleasure and later on she would have her own.

They sat themselves in the high-ceiling room, still adorned with its Edwardian fireplace and bell pushes. But Laura couldn't hold herself down on the worn blue armchair, even once Martha had cleared it of a bowl and two jumpers and a chocolate wrapper. She bounced, and touched and flittered, moving and replacing; she sipped at the too-hot tea, peering into its darkness as if to cool it more quickly so that she could release the cup and pick up a duster. She had already pulled back the curtains at the bay window and, even in the weak sunlight, motes of dust were twirling in the air like snowflakes, deciding on which surface they might best settle.

'You know you really can't carry on like this Martha.' Laura spoke eventually. 'I know this whole thing has hit you like a hurricane, but at some point you're going to have to get back to some sort of normality. I mean, the bookshop have been brilliant – allowing you this extended leave – but they won't be able to carry on with that indefinitely. At some point you will have to think about returning to work. And it might actually be good – getting some sort of structure back in your life…'

Martha gave the barest of nods, recognising that her sister was right, but knowing that this still wasn't yet the time. Laura nodded too, acknowledging perhaps that small steps were going to be needed.

They picked up and put down their tea cups in a random choreography accompanied by Laura's attempts at more neutral conversation – recounting programmes she had watched and purchases she had made and cakes she had baked. As she half-listened to the random selection of words which could be reformed and hung out to dry in a dozen new sentences, each time making no more sense than the first, Martha tried to coax her dark curls – as unruly as her sister's were orderly - into some sort of compliance using her fingers as combs. But her hair, like her life, seemed unwilling to come under her control.

'Perhaps once we've finished this,' Laura was saying, 'We could make a start on …'

'One room at a time – that'll be fine.' Martha watched her sister's lips begin to form in protest and then to relax in resignation. She had got this far; she would come back.

It was a bare ten minutes, but Laura could restrain herself no longer. 'Better make a start – it'll take a while,' she said, rattling the tea tray towards her and beginning to pile it with all the detritus she could reach without even needing to take a step.

Their tasks eventually completed, the two women headed for the front door. Martha was unsurprised to see Laura's neatly parked car waiting in the driveway. Her sister's home was on the edge of town, nearer the moors than the sea; a walkable distance, but Martha knew that Laura would always find reasons for needing to drive. Today it was the rubbish bags which she was bundling forcefully into the boot, still offering strands of advice even as she slid into the driver's seat and pulled away.

With her sister's leaving, Martha stood, back pressed against the front door and closed her eyes. Laura had somehow disturbed the balance of things; the air fluttered, and the light through the windows quivered, and nothing would settle into its rightful place. It was as though a bedsheet had been shaken and refused to lie flat, regardless of the hand reaching out to smooth it.

Martha went through to the kitchen. She had longed all morning to get back to the paper pieces, but now she too was unsettled. And as she looked down at the uncovered shreds, the why of it all seemed to overtake her more than the what. Why some unknown fingers had seen fit to tear the message word from word – and yet had not sent them into oblivion, but had placed them up on the wooden shelf in that timeworn little hut?

And the thought of the shaking hands which might have destroyed the letter dovetailed into her own memory, and as she dropped into the chair at the kitchen table, she watched herself for the umpteenth time, tearing apart the details of the past few months.

A TANTALISING GLIMPSE

He hadn't been there. And to Martha's eternal regret she had taken no notice. Instead, she had savoured the minutes and hours that she was able to hoard to herself, gorging on them until the light dimmed. And it was only then that she had begun to take stock, to consider whether all was as it should be.

Yet even so, she had been distracted, thinking about the chicken casserole which had been bubbling for too long. Should she eat her share, or leave it to cool and put on her coat? And if she put on her coat, where would she go? Richard had spent so much time away, delivering to every nook and cranny of the British Isles, that when he was home, he didn't usually want to go out. He wasn't a pub-goer or a club member; he enjoyed friends coming to their house, but was reluctant to accept the invitations of others.

Martha had eventually picked up the phone. Richard was renowned for forgetting to have his own mobile switched on, and most of the time his battery wouldn't be charged. But she had been sure that this time he would pick up, that he would joke that she was checking up on him and tell her that he would be home in ten minutes; she had pressed his number, but it had gone straight to voicemail.

She remembered scrolling other numbers, thinking who she might call. But it was ridiculous; what would she say – that it was seven o'clock on a Saturday and Richard hadn't turned up? Anyone in their right mind would laugh at her, she knew, and so she had done nothing. Not for another two hours at least.

She was angry with him then, and yet more furious with him now. Why, she could only think, was he selfish enough to have put her in this predicament?

But she could only rifle through the bones of her own story so many times. She could try to arrange and re-arrange the elements of herself and Richard, but the results would always turn out in the same way. And she would be left, looking at the remains of her life, but bringing herself no peace. She sighed heavily, shaking her head.

Someone else's life had to be a better proposition, she thought, bringing herself back to the present. She wondered, as she grasped the edges of the baking tray, if the pieces would still be in place or whether she would need to start again; but they all sat silently, the best parishioners in their rightful pews. She took one small pile of unplaced fragments and spread them out once more. Three pieces immediately had their obvious homes in the uncompleted puzzle – why had she not seen that yesterday? And then, by twisting and turning she managed to place another five pieces. But all they succeeding in doing was filling some of the blanks – the spaces between the words. She tried the other pile of pieces and had no success for another ten minutes; she began to think that the whole exercise had been a waste of time. Why was she bothering to recreate something which might as easily have been in the rubbish bin or feeding the embers of a fire? But as she moved a triangular piece beneath her index finger, round the table like the message from a Ouija board, it came to her. Surely that *was* the point? Someone hadn't thrown them away, and somehow they had been stored on the shelf, deliberately or otherwise. Martha knew that even that might be of no consequence, that she was as likely to end up with the items required on a shopping expedition to the nearest city, but there was something about the whole thing that she just couldn't leave alone.

Her stomach complained, and Martha realised that it was already three o'clock, and that once more she had been entranced by the pieces, whisked into a space where time seemed to have its own dimension. She reached for the cupboard and was glad that she hadn't turned away the fresh loaf her sister had thrust on her, or the wedge of Cheddar which graced the newly cleaned fridge. She had dismissed as nagging Laura's endless comments on her appearance "you're too thin; you're a shadow of your old self", but Martha realised now that this was the first time in ages that her mouth had watered at the prospect of the food; she cut two ungainly slabs from the crusty bread and filled them with equally inelegant slices of cheese. She devoured the sandwich within minutes and repeated the exercise, the whole episode reminding her of the appetite which appeared from nowhere when you had been out walking or cycling, and the desire for the food made it all the more flavoursome.

Sated, she slumped back in her chair, allowing herself to slide down the years which had polished the wood. But as she did so, she realised that bread had scattered itself across the papers; crumbs of cheese too were wedged between the pieces and she would need to pick them out one by one. The difficulty of trying to keep everything in order and not stained by the patterns of life was evident; she needed a better way of holding the story together if she was ever going to find her way to the end, and so she cast the net of her mind across the rooms of the house, fishing for a possible solution.

A catch eventually landed itself, and she rushed upstairs to the box bedroom. Like the rest of the house it had been abandoned by her, but the disorder here was one of longstanding. Unwanted boxes and books had been left to amuse themselves while she and Richard had put to one side decisions about their destiny. She ran a finger along a shelf, and then bent down to the floor, straining to see what lay at the bottom of the bookcase. She pulled out one volume and then another, until she found the one she had been thinking of.

It was a stamp album, one of Richard's waxing and waning interests which had needed more time and effort than he had been prepared to expend. But the mere act of holding his book in her hand made Martha wish she'd had some hint of the state of mind which might have explained his actions. But just that thought brought the weight of a rock to her chest. She hadn't the strength to deal with it though, and so she opened the pages and snatched each of the regular gummed squares from the strips of holders, dropping them deliberately to the ground. She clutched the book to her, *her* book now, and took it to the waiting table.

Each small piece was transferred into the waiting rows of pockets, and now, sitting as neatly as Victorian schoolchildren, they began to take the shape of a real letter.

She noticed that a panhandle-shaped piece had started the year appearing, and she was convinced that it was a 19 rather than an 18 – so maybe the letter was not as old as she had at first anticipated. But it was pen and ink – no biro here – and so she began to imagine a "20" or a "30" on the end of the date. When had people stopped using fountain pens? She had briefly used one at school, but how long for? She couldn't remember the transition, just that her handwriting had never been quite the same once the ink bottle and nibs had been resigned to a desk drawer.

And now she looked again there was a tantalising glimpse of a word after "your". What she had presumed to be "yours" – sincerely or faithfully – might actually be "your ever-loving"; which would put a very different perspective on things. She sighed, checking that there were no other pieces which should be in the book. Sadly, none of the others could be found a place, and so she took a tin from the shelf – one that had contained French chocolates in a very different chapter of events – and made space for the gaggle of displaced pieces still to find a home.

A drawer, full of plastic bags and cake candles and serviettes for different occasions, all of which had once seemed pertinent to her life, was emptied into the bin, and wiped and cleaned, and there was a new home, a nest, for her gestating letter in its book and the tin of pieces yet to be. She closed it in for the night, and then pulled the drawer open once more, confirming in her own mind that she would return to the beach hut to seek out more pieces.

AWAITING THE ARRIVAL OF THE MAN IN BLACK

EVA

The old woman wakes in that nether state, drifting between reality and some other world, anxiety wrapping itself around her with the tangle of the bedclothes and she has to fight for her freedom.

As she lies back, calming her breath, Eva drags to the forefront of her mind the scenes which have been taunting her as she comes to the surface of sleep. There had been blue skies, unbroken by a single cloud. There had been the quietness over the empty moor, orchestrated only by the percussion of the wind, and the high-pitched call of a smaller woodwind - the eek-eek, monotonous and mournful, of a bird, she thinks, as she drags her aching legs from the mattress. A bird which circles, calling, swooping in spirals before pulling itself back up, a skilful pilot riding the thermal waves.

She has seen them often on her solitary walks up on the hills - buzzards, reminding her of vultures circling, although she has been assured that they had nothing of the viciousness or callousness of their African counterparts.

As she pulls herself into a dressing gown, looks from the window at the new day, Eva has no idea why this scene has unsettled her. She feels as though something has happened which needs to be undone, but she cannot bring to mind the what or why or when, and the more she thinks, the more the dream gets away from her.

Downstairs she watches as the honey drizzles from the spoon, the special spoon with a name which eludes her for the moment. It puddles on her toast – thin white processed toast, which she hates. But then she doesn't get to do the shopping any more. 'You needn't,' they say, 'Needn't bother with all that queuing and trolleys.' But they don't mention the "M" word. She knows her memory isn't what it was; although what had been, was exactly what her memory was these days; she can remember her childhood, her wonderful times as a young woman – they are all as clear as day. But then she gets sidetracked, starting off quite happily down one lane, only to find that someone or something has beckoned her off down a side road.

But not today. Today she knows what she wants to do. It's cooler this morning, and she can think straighter when it's cooler. She calls out to the young girl to get the solicitor. The girl is from next door – Mary Buckley's child, who needs money but doesn't want to work for it. She's supposed to dust and tidy, neither of which she's any good at.

'What solicitor?' the young girl snaps, taking the knife from her, dragging the honey across the toast, forcing it into four ragged squares. The old woman wonders why she has to be so difficult.

'Just get me the phone book.'

Jodie rolls her eyes. 'We don't have phone books no more – haven't had them since I was a kid.' She picks up the cup of tea, skin on the cold surface and tuts at the waste of her efforts.

'No – not the big book.' In her head the old woman is saying "directory", but big book will do. 'My book,' she says, meaning her address book, with all her numbers in. 'The blue one.' And she mimes a writing action, so the girl will know she means the one she uses for her letters.

'Well why didn't you say.' Jodie unearths the book from a pile of newspapers and slaps it down on the table. She gathers yesterday's plate and a magazine and sweet wrappers from around the room, and her wittering gets into the old woman's head, like a trapped fly. Nevertheless, she picks up the book and begins leafing through. Eva struggles to recall the solicitor's name, the one who has already drawn up the paperwork, so she starts at the first page again and looks down every list, the crossings out meaning mainly that they have died – no forwarding address. She must have chosen a solicitor with a late-alphabet name, she concedes, because it's some time, amongst the side-tracking of old friends, until she finds "Whittaker and Webster". She reaches for the phone, asking for one of the partners to come and visit, to take note of the amendments to her instructions. Then she sits, like Miss Haversham, awaiting the arrival of a man in black, picturing him still with quill pen and ink, ready to take down her wishes.

FIVE BOB A LESSON
EVA

The solicitor has come and gone, but now that she has set out on this track there is more to be done, another visitor to be summoned.

Despite the years, Eva recognises Martin the moment he appears at the door. He looks so like … she closes her mind to the thoughts which are about to rampage, forcing herself to concentrate only on the here and now. His skin is too pale, too pink, he is sweating, everything too tight; his body is fighting with his clothes, as though he might burst from his skin, and a little bit of him – the real him, secreted and folded - will be exposed to the world. And for an instant, she feels sorry.

He glances at her then stares at the floor, not moving from the place where he has first halted. 'I brought what you asked for,' he mutters, as though it has taken all his will. She is unsure if it is the task itself, or the coming to visit which he finds so distasteful; he has a sourness about his thin unhappy mouth.

She beckons to him, knowing he would rather stay in the doorway. He wavers, half-turning as if to go, then he sighs. She gestures again, and he slinks across the room, running a finger round his sweaty collar.

'Is it all done?' she asks.

Martin nods, holding out a large brown envelope; the duty which this bundle of legal requirements has placed on him heavier in his hands than the paper it contains.

'Put it on the desk,' she says, her arthritic fingers directing him. 'Over there.'

She wants to call the girl, but the wretched name has gone from her again. 'Tea!' she screeches, louder than she intends. 'Get her to make some tea … come and sit down where I can see you,' she says. He is perplexed; her multiple instructions and his strong desire to be gone all fighting for precedence.

He speaks to the girl then slides the envelope onto the crowded desk; backs onto the edge of the armchair, perching like a pigeon on the worn cushion.

'We never met much, did we?' Eva says, staring, remembering him as a small red-haired boy tossing conkers, attempting to juggle, in a room very like this one. 'Why was that, do you think?'

He looks up, puzzled, evidently not the conversation he has been expecting.

'Did they used to tell you what a selfish woman I was? That I didn't care about anything or anyone but myself?'

He shakes his head, still silent.

'Cat got your tongue?' she says, beckoning the scowling girl who is pushing through the door, huffing with the weight of the tea things. The loaded tray is put down carelessly, almost dropped, and a puddle of brown splashes from the pot. She hovers by the table. 'Do you want me to pour?'

The old woman shoos her away, knowing that it's nosiness and not concern which has fuelled her offer. She waits for the door to close then points to the pot and the cups, indicating that he should take over what is beyond her increasingly useless fingers.

As he places a cup in front of her, Eva catches his eye. 'I've asked a lot of you … all this taking over my affairs nonsense,' she says, indicating the brown envelope. But he stares into his own cup, watching the trails from the swirling spoon. 'It should have been your father; that was always my plan. But he's gone, and so who else …?' She looks at him, but he has no more of an answer than she does. 'I should tell you the whole story. You deserve that much at least.'

Now he looks up, alarm in his eyes; a desire to know but not to know fighting within him.

'You know my memory's not what it was …' She points to the envelope, and he nods briefly. 'Some days it has more holes than a fishing net …' she laughs. 'But today it's all here.'

She picks up the cup, and it rattles against the saucer, shaking all the way to her mouth. She sees him twitch, lift out of his seat, then sit again, not knowing what he should do.

'Have you never speculated?' the woman asks, managing to dock the cup back into its place. 'Never wondered about the family situation?'

He runs a sweaty hand through his thinning sandy hair. She has read somewhere that the red hair gene is usually overpowered by brown or black, but in her experience it always outs. She realises she is clenching her fist, and drags her thoughts away from there.

'When I was a young girl, I wanted to fly.'

Martin snatches a look at her as if she has drifted into foolishness.

'Bear with me,' she says. 'I need to start at the beginning.' She takes another breath. 'We used to come to this part of the world on our holidays, every summer, and every year I'd see buzzards, up on the hills and watch them soar and glide. It looked so wonderful, so free, that that was all I wanted. Of course, as I grew up, it faded into a childish dream, but then I read about – you know – what's her name, flying all over and breaking records everywhere she went, and my desire to be up there,' she tilts her head skywards, 'Came back to me. I found out about lessons, behind my parents' back of course, but they were well beyond my reach. Then one day, I saw an advertisement in the newspaper, "Five Bob a Lesson" it said. It was like one of those – what's that word?' She looks at him, wanting him to find the word "serendipitous", but he shakes his head. 'Anyway, it was one of those moments.'

'I looked at that advert a dozen times a day, until I knew it by heart. But it didn't bring the possibility any closer. Because you see, even though they were only asking five bob, it might have been five pounds or five hundred, because I still didn't have that sort of money.'

'I thought about asking David – your father. He always seemed to be flush – goodness knows how. But every time, I lost the courage to ask. Then one day we were out in the garden; he'd been doing some digging for Dad and I was raking up the grass mowings, and the words just tumbled out.

'"What!" I remember him saying, shocked and laughing at the same time. "You know Pa will go absolutely crazy, don't you, Sis? And Ma'll have a fainting fit. You must be completely barmy …"

'But I could see he was excited. Maybe it was just the thought of Mother and Father getting themselves into a state, but I think that maybe I was doing something he wished he was doing himself. Either way, he agreed to let me have the money. Goodness knows how much of a debt I ran up with him – pounds and pounds probably, but he didn't seem worried. "Go for it, Sis", he said, handing over another pound note to me. And I was glowing with pride, because I'd found something I was good at, and there was no way back once I'd got that far.'

He has been staring at her for the past few minutes, as though he has been watching some far-fetched film, a storyline too outlandish to be taken seriously.

'This is only the beginning. You'll see the sense of it all …' she tries to reassure him.

He opens his mouth, closes it again. 'I'll come back,' he says eventually.

A HOLE WAITING TO BE FILLED

She could see it before she got to the door. The tired grey wood of the hut was as it had ever been, just more so today. But there, hanging like a vagabond's earring on the hasp below the handle, was a small, very new, padlock.

It stopped Martha in her tracks.

It was a hand being held up; it might as well have been a barbed wire fence.

She turned on her heel, then stopped. She ran a hand through her halo of dark curls as she tried to summon some idea of what she might do. In her mind the place had already become her sanctuary, an escape from her sister and from her problems, but now it had been taken from her like some mistaken gift.

'Lost sommat?'

Martha looked round. She could easily have conjured the voice from her musings, and felt ridiculous, seeking out something which might exist only in her head.

But a man who could have been fifty or ninety, paintbrush in hand, was gazing at her.

'No – no, it's fine.' She looked back at the hut then took two steps away.

'He was here t'other day,' the man said, eyes still searching her face. 'Sorting things out, he said.' He looked down at the paintbrush, as if only now remembering that he was holding it. 'S'pose he's going to sell it.' He waved the brush at the little building. 'Worth a fortune these days.' He stepped away and began painting the wall of his own hut, peppermint green.

She followed, watching his hand move rhythmically, bringing new life to the faded colour.

He stopped again, dipping the brush in the paint pot. 'Did you want him? Andrews they call him.'

She hadn't thought about a real person owning the hut, spending time in it. To Martha it had been abandoned; hers for the taking.

'Is he the owner?' she forced the question out.

'Nephew or some such, I believe,' he said, not looking up. 'Didn't seem too bothered 'bout the hut – just what it's going to bring him,' he said, rubbing his thumb and index finger together.

They continued in silence, him brushing the dry wood, her watching the transformation, like green shoots appearing in a bare field.

'You need to get in there?' He still concentrated on his work.

Martha nodded. She didn't know why; she had no right to be there, there was nothing of her own belongings in there, her life would still carry on if she didn't enter the hut ever again… but there would be a hole there, waiting to be filled. And she didn't want another gap in her life, which had, she realised, more holes than content at the moment. Here was one space that she might be able to fill, and which might help her to darn and patch her tattered existence as well.

'Nail file? Or scissors maybe?'

She frowned, his words seemingly as useful as a dandelion clock in a storm.

'Either might work…if you were to wiggle them inside the lock maybe? If you just happened to have something like that in that bag of yours?' He glanced up briefly, nodding at the tapestry bag on her shoulder. 'I need to be somewhere else for a few minutes,' he said, and might have winked as he wandered off, brush and pot in hand.

Martha glanced around her. There were people, but no-one who looked as if they would give a damn about her and her actions.

She rooted through her bag, with no idea what might be there at the bottom. It was the style of bag which kept accepting more, with no need to remove any of its previous occupants, and it had been a lifetime away when Martha had last been bothered about clearing and sorting handbags. But she was sure there must be something.

After what seemed too long – too long at least for the painter to still be turning his blind eye – her fingers touched on a small plastic case. She knew the contents without looking, knew that she had found what she needed.

She removed the nail file and walked over to the hut. Did people always feel they were being watched when they were doing something they oughtn't, she wondered. She didn't look round, didn't want to see who might be looking, but grabbed at the padlock before she could change her mind.

It was too easy – inserting the metal point into the lock, turning, and then the smallest of clicks as the lock sprang its clutches, and she realised that it wasn't a proper lock at all, just some cheap importation, bought at a pound shop no doubt. But it was done, and she was pulling back the juddering door of the hut and stepping inside and casting an eye round what she now considered hers.

After what the painter had said, she had expected everything to be changed – tidied, swept, put away. But nothing was.

It was exactly as she had left it, and she rushed forward, keen to gather whatever was left to be collected, eager to find the rest of the pieces of the letter, before anyone – Andrews or whoever – might close off this little space properly and forever.

Just as before, she lifted the driftwood away and ran a finger along the shelf. Nothing.

And then she used her whole hand, up to the elbow, pulling the dust and the pieces of broken wood and the dead flies with it. Now something fell from the shelf. To anyone else it would have been simply more detritus, more rubbish to be cleared; but to Martha there were missing pieces to be reunited, to be savoured, to be interrogated for their story.

She stuffed them into the pocket of her jeans and then got down on her hands and knees, checking for what she had missed. Six more pieces had been hiding, but were now found out. She stood looking for more, a drunk hoping for abandoned dregs in the darkest corners. Two more pieces under the table, another caught between the frame of the chair and the seat. And finally, as Martha lifted the driftwood to replace it on the shelf, she saw a piece folded into its curves, concealed beneath a thick matted cobweb.

A final glance around. She wanted to stay, not to open the door back into the real world, but she could hear whistling outside – a television theme tune she couldn't immediately place. She pulled herself away, and slipped out of the door, into a watery sunlight.

The painter was back at his work. 'Maybe just – you know…' he said, pointing at the hanging padlock with his brush.

She turned and clicked the lock together. 'Will he want much for it?' she asked, without knowing that she had been going to.

'For that?' He nodded towards the hut. 'They're going for thousands these days, my lovely. But you know – poor condition, needs money spending … all that sort of thing.' He carried on with the peppermint paint for a while. 'Maybe there's a deal to be had – isn't that what they say?' And he smiled as he turned back to his work.

SOME SORT OF SALVATION

Martha drifted along the seafront for a while, lost in thoughts of present and future, with very little past being allowed to infiltrate. She only realised that she was back at the town end of the promenade when two children, squawking relentlessly for treats from their harassed mother, interrupted her daydreaming. She walked quickly to escape them, and then, as if her feet were acting independently, she strode through the streets until she found herself outside the estate agent's office. At first she did what all holidaymakers do, allowing her glance to flit across the windows, taking in the stuff of dreams - the vibrant gardens, the fitted kitchens, the sea views. And then, before she could stop herself, she opened the glass door and slipped inside, looking directly at a suited woman with extraordinary red lipstick.

'Beach huts,' Martha spoke firmly, ignoring the fact that she was probably looking dishevelled and unworthy of serious attention in comparison. Her shorts were hanging loosely, and her tee-shirt had been part of her wardrobe longer than she cared to remember.

'Well, they are extremely sought after.' The woman stood, the better presumably to demonstrate her superiority. 'They don't often come up, so when they do – well, there's always what we call a "feeding frenzy".' Her sarcastic smile contorted her face, stretching it sideways, so that she appeared to have two blood-red streaks severing her cheeks.

'There's one now,' Martha's words were crisp, her thoughts suddenly precise. 'Just down on the seafront. Could you let me have the details, please.'

The woman turned resignedly, her sales techniques ground down like a cigarette end. Martha noticed a bee on the window while she waited, buzzing but not angry. It flew up and circled as the woman returned with a single sheet of paper.

'We've only just received it.' She seemed to have recovered some of her haughtiness. 'Haven't even had chance to finalise the details. You will need to be quick though. As I say, they …'

'Thanks. I'll be in touch.' Martha left, the ping of the doorbell adding a full stop to their conversation.

She itched to unfold the sheet, to see what the price was, but she made herself wait, made herself walk calmly through the streets, then through the house and out into the back garden. The sun had come out and she rolled up her tee-shirt to expose her pale belly. No-one could see her here, and she needed to let the meagre breeze trickle over her skin.

The paper shook in her hand as she skimmed down, past the incomplete descriptions to the bottom line. Recalling the words of the painter and the estate agent she had been expecting an amount which was way beyond her reach, an amount which would put the hut into the waste paper bin along with the property details; what Martha saw was something which made her smile, a smile which curled itself into a melody so that she was soon laughing out loud. Something she hadn't done in months.

She had no idea why the urge had overwhelmed her – to make the insignificant little building her own; just that the beach hut seemed to represent some sort of salvation. And now that she had seen it was within the realms of financial possibility, she needed to move along that path.

But as she went back into the house, Martha realised that the affordability of the property hadn't actually made it hers, and so she picked up the phone and called the number on the paperwork.

It wasn't the red-lipped woman but a younger voice, a man's, who seemed surprised that she had the details, accusatory almost, as if she had crept through a back door and spirited them from the estate agent's system.

'I'll put your offer to the vendors,' he said, recovering himself. 'I'll let you know what they say.' His tone was doubtful.

'It's the full asking price,' Martha pointed out. 'Do you think it's likely they'll refuse?'

'I'll be in touch.' He seemed almost to cut himself off, in his haste to be free of her.

When Laura called later that evening, Martha had opened an anticipatory bottle of prosecco, and was looking at the world through thoroughly different glasses.

'Have you been drinking?' Laura's teacherly words were interwoven with disapproval.

'Just feeling a bit more cheerful, that's all.' Martha wasn't going to allow Laura to splash water on her newly painted watercolour of life. And she certainly wasn't going to mention the beach hut and the estate agent.

WHAT POSSESSED YOU?

What in God's name were you thinking of?'

Martha had, for the first time in untold months, felt the flutterings of long-abandoned joy in her heart. The uncared-for beach hut had awakened something in her, and she had wanted desperately to share the news of its impending purchase with someone who would be lifted with her, like kites soaring and interweaving. But every friend she might ever have had was long since gone; they hadn't abandoned her, but instead had been washed away, like flotsam on a rising tide, by Martha's increasing insistence on isolation. Now there was only Laura, at the end of the phone.

Her sister, joyless as a pebble, allowed no time for answers. 'I mean, that money – Mum and Dad worked so hard to put savings in the bank, not to mention Grandpa and Grandma. They all desperately wanted to have something to pass on to the two of us …' Laura paused, working up another head of steam.

Martha picked up a newspaper, displaying a myriad of pictures of Prince William and Kate and their blossoming relationship; the phone though was still clamped to her ear through some sort of ingrained good manners, some distant voice of her mother's urging her to "Pay attention, Martha – it's rude not to listen when someone's speaking …"

She missed Laura's next words, a gap in transmission as she gazed at the royal couple, ambivalent to their obvious happiness and the press speculations about a possible engagement.

'…You're forty-something, not fourteen …what *possessed* you?' Laura machine-gunned on. 'Something must have got into that mad head of yours to make you go and blow all Dad's money on a … a *shed* …' Even as children she had stretched her two-year seniority over Martha until it was more like eight or ten; but Martha side-stepped it all.

'It's a beach hut,' she said. 'And anyway, it was Mum's money as well. She's the one who had three jobs so that we could go on holiday every year – she would have loved a beach hut.' Martha paused, recalling her mother tipped at a strange angle in a deckchair on the sands at Caister-on-Sea, skin the colour of nectarine peel, happily fighting a newspaper in the breeze. 'She would have been in her element – I'm doing it for her.' The words only became thoughts as they left Martha's lips. 'I'll get a sign,' she added; 'Put her name over the door,' she said brazenly, thinking what "Beryl" might look like, painted in pastel shades of thrift and sea holly.

'You just get more impossible every day,' Laura uttered. 'It's not worth even wasting my breath on you.'

The phone went dead, and Martha placed it down on the table. Laura had always done that – abandoned a conversation when it wasn't going her way. But now Martha had conjured the idea of a sign she pulled paper and pencil from the drawer and began sketching a design. Perhaps the painter would be able to make something for her, she thought, visualising the rugged hands of the man wielding the peppermint paint.

But when she arrived at the seafront the next morning, somewhat breathless from her impatient walk through the streets, there was no painter, just the squawking of the gulls, arguing over who would christen his handiwork first… And a "For Sale" board, being hammered impatiently where her "Beryl" sign should have been.

'What's happening?' Martha demanded of the shaven-headed youth who was swearing at his uncoordinated fingers. 'I've put in an offer – it's not for sale any more…'

'Dun't mean it's yours though, does it?' He carried on, dropping a shower of nails to the floor as he tried to impose his will on the errant sign.

Martha could feel the heat rising in her face. She had no defence though – the boy was right. The property wasn't hers yet, and she had no right to venture inside, but it didn't stop her wanting to tear both workman and sign from their posting, and cast them to the sea.

There were letters on the mat when she returned home, the majority addressed to Richard – still - even though he hadn't been there for months. She turned them on their faces, abandoning them on the worktop, and reached instead for the kettle, mindlessly taking the album from the drawer and opening it to look at the paper scraps as she flicked the switch. She had done a pretty good job at blending the pieces, but something wasn't quite right. She noticed it now, with the full scope of daylight, and carried the book nearer to the window.

Now that she looked, it was obvious. There were two different papers – not massively dissimilar to be fair to herself – not even different brands probably, but different tones of the same shade, as if one sheet might have been left in the sunlight of a window, and the other tucked away in some forgotten drawer. Martha ignored the bubbling demands of the kettle and began to separate out all her work into the different shades of paper. Too late she realised that she should have taken a picture on her phone of her original attempt, just in case that turned out to be the correct solution after all. A month ago she might have stewed with irritation at this lapse in judgement but now she just shrugged and took the paler of the two piles and began her sorting process over again – corners, straight edges, anything that looked as though it slotted together.

Now she was getting somewhere. There were definitely two letters – it was so obvious that she ridiculed herself for not having seen this before.

She stopped the sifting and sorting only when her stomach growled, but the kitchen cupboards yielded only the tail-end of supplies. She smothered a dry crust with bobbles of cold butter, then found a chocolate bar well past its best, sultanas from a time when baking had been a factor, a wrinkled apple. Eventually Martha came to the point where she felt not just sated but gorged almost to sickness; she flopped down on the sofa and cried.

She had no idea what she was crying about – her inability to solve the puzzles, her so far unsuccessful bid for the beach hut, her rollercoaster appetite … or the lack of Richard in her life. But she wallowed in the emotion until gradually the sobs subsided and she began muttering to herself.

'It doesn't matter, any of it – the letters, the beach hut … Richard,' she yelled at the empty room, punching a cushion at every word. 'It doesn't matter – not one bloody bit of it.' She scraped a sleeve across her running nose. 'Everything is what it is. You bawling and moaning and feeling sorry for yourself will make not one iota of difference…'

And then Martha began to laugh as she snivelled; laughed until her belly ached. Because she sounded exactly like Laura. 'Well, now you're well and truly up shit creek, if you're turning into your sister.' She wiped her face with her hand once more. 'So just bloody well *get on* with things.'

It felt good, allowing everything to grind relentlessly to the farthest reaches of her feelings, like an outworn steam engine facing a near-impossible hill. Now she was there she could begin to see the view of what was to come.

Nevertheless, the tears had left her exhausted. She knew that, despite the early hour, if she didn't drag herself up the stairs at that very moment, she would never make it as far as her bed.

The next morning the sun was shining, and Martha set to, clearing the previous night's detritus from the kitchen, momentarily ashamed of the amount of rubbish she had managed to consume, pushing the evidence to the bottom of the bin. But with the last few wrappers still in her hand the puzzle tugged at her attention once more.

One letter was clearly addressed to "My darling E…" and, by tipping her head one way then the other, she could see that the other appeared to be from "Your loving J". Well, at least she thought it was an "J", but the tear in the paper had left only the most minute hints of the capital letter. It could just have easily been an "T" or at a push an "I".

Frustrated, Martha put the letters to one side and began to make coffee, and while she did so she checked her phone. She had missed a call from the awful woman at the estate agents and she pressed the button to return the call immediately.

'It's Martha Townsend – you were trying to call me.'

'Yeees.' The voice drawled, as though the woman had far more important things on her mind… or more likely that she was applying another coat of the melodramatic lipstick while she tried to remember who Martha was.

Martha was determined not to be drawn into the woman's games. She uttered not a word, until the silence was as tight as an overblown balloon.

'Oh, yes.' The woman eventually pricked the tension, letting her words pop forth. 'The beach hut. Well, against all expectations, the vendor has decided to remove it from the market.' She paused, perhaps waiting for Martha to erupt, but something about the woman's manner left Martha wondering about the ambiguity of her words. She tried the silent treatment again, and it worked.

'Yes … well, it appears they feel your offer is more than reasonable – and have therefore decided not to proceed with any further possible purchasers.' The words were wrapped in disdain, as though the owners were completely out of their minds, and had stolen any inflated commission from her to boot.

'Well, that's good news.' Martha tried to play down her excitement. 'Of course I'll need to double-check my finances …'

Before she could finish, the woman was intercepting, a vulture ripping the innards from her prey. 'But you said your money was immediately available, that this would be a straightforward cash transaction. I can't possibly delay things at this point …' And so she went on, for a full thirty seconds, while Martha held the phone under her chin and searched the newly-arranged cupboards for the biscuit tin.

'I'll be in touch very shortly,' Martha slipped in when eventually a chink appeared in the woman's wall of the words. She enjoyed squashing the woman's slick superiority, but she knew that she would only be able to keep away from the phone for half an hour at the most. There was something about the hut, something about its abandonment and its small secrets which had given Martha a surge of energy. Her emotions over the past few months had swept her into a perpetual storm – sometimes with the wind behind her, pushing her forward into tidying and sorting and planning; at other times the tornado was in front of her and it was all she could do to stand up straight and catch her breath. Both states were exhausting, but the beach hut had given her a sense of direction – a port in her emotional storm, and she longed to have the keys in her hand.

Whenever she had a moment she would fiddle with the slivers of paper, arranging and re-arranging, and arranging again; it became evident that some pieces were still missing, and Martha had to hold herself back from further visits to the beach hut. Her solicitor had warned her that the owner was aware the property had been entered, and had "taken steps" as he put it, to prevent further intrusion. The threat of jeopardising the sale loomed over her, and so she played with what she had, writing out the versions she could make, taking photos on her phone, making sense here, creating yet more knots to unpick there.

THIS IS NADYA
EVA

'You need proper help,' Martin says, looking around the room. 'She's not up to the job – nothing more than a schoolgirl.' There is a reluctance on his face – as though he knows now that his hoped-for single visit will never be enough. He jerks his head towards the kitchen where the girl is clanking dishes so that they will know she's earning the twenty-pound notes which the old woman gives her.

'She's all right – she's from next door,' Eva says. 'She does what's needed. I don't want a fuss, it's nothing.'

'It's not *nothing* when some stranger has to bring you home because you've gone out and can't get yourself home again.'

She wants to say that the man isn't a stranger, that he lives nearby; but she has no recollection of the man's name. 'I wasn't lost, I just turned right instead of left …'

'Why were you so desperate to go out anyway?' he butts in, giving no credence to her explanation. 'He said you'd gone to post a letter … why didn't you get *her* to do it?' Martin inclines his head again towards the kitchen, disapproval written across his pale face. He's agitated, not happy to be in the house, or to be having this conversation. 'If I've got to do this - look after your affairs - I'm going to do it properly,' he says, pulling himself to his full, but not lofty, height.

And the military stance, brief though it is, betrays his father, she thinks, sending a shiver down her aching back. She's concerned, about what might be to come, what she has set in motion. 'Whatever you think, I'm not going to one of those places,' she says quickly. 'You won't get me out of that door – not upright, anyway.'

He looks at her critically, the beginnings of a staring match. But she saves him the trouble and turns to look for something on her table. 'It'll cost too much – you'll have to sell this place. There'll be nothing left.'

He glances at the piece she's torn from the newspaper, which she's now waving at him.

He sighs, walks over to the window. The fact that he hasn't even looked at the cutting telling her that he's already looked for himself.

'Anyway, I was going to tell you some more – about the family,' she says, knowing she should change the subject.

He sighs, nods half-heartedly. 'This doesn't change anything though,' he says, easing himself into the chair.

She wonders if he's got piles; it's on her lips to ask, but he butts in.

'I'll make some enquiries – about some help,' he says.

She can see the set of his shoulders, the determined angle of his mouth. He's more stubborn than she'd expected, standing his ground instead of heading for the door. Maybe he's got more of his mother in him than I'd expected, she thought.

'You had flying lessons.' Martin's words are abrupt. 'Tell me what happened next.'

'I got the letter, asking me to go for an interview at the aerodrome – Hertford, Hampstead … something like that.' She keeps scratching away for the name, but nothing comes. 'I'd been pestering the poor woman in charge for months, writing, telling her how good I was and that I'd be perfect for the ATA …'

'The ATA? I don't know what you're talking about; I've never heard of it …' He looks at her as if she's making the whole thing up.

'The Air Transport Auxiliary – you must have.' She gets into her stride, could tell the story in her sleep. 'You see, they'd realised that there weren't enough RAF boys to go round – you know in the war … to fly their missions *and* deliver planes to the places where they were needed, once they came off the production lines.' She sees that his wartime knowledge is less than she's given him credit for but she's too far into the story to stop for explanations. 'So they got women to do the job – the delivery. Just a handful to start with, ones who'd been flying for a while of course. But the whole thing was growing by the week, and they needed a lot more experienced flyers to take care of the deliveries so that the Brylcreem Boys – that's what we called them - could get on with the war. It was obvious to me that it was what I'd been born for – why I'd gone through all those lessons.'

There's a crash. Not just a single cup, but what sounds like a cupboardful of plates and dishes and servers.

The old woman tries to push herself out of the chair, but the suddenness of her movement drains the blood from her head, and she sways unsteadily.

Martin takes her shoulders, more gently than his ham hocks of arms might suggest, and steadies her back into her seat. 'Stay there – *I'll* go.'

She waits for the raised voices, the swearing; he'd been like a chained dog since he'd stepped through the door, but there is just the low hum of his words. She can make out nothing, but as he comes back, she can hear the broken crockery being pushed around by a broom.

'She'll stay until we find other help,' he says, picking up his anorak. 'In the meantime, no further expeditions.'

His face is agitated as he opens the door and makes his way out, leaving her with the rest of her story hanging by a thread in her mind.

'This is Nadya,' he says, pointing to a thin little thing with a face as pale as the cheap bread which is foisted on her. They have wound forward - the number of days Eva is not sure – and a young woman has accompanied Martin into the house.

Although she remains behind him, she is not shying away; she has the stance of someone who has encountered far worse than him, or Eva herself for that matter.

Nadya steps forward, holds out a hand to be shaken. The old woman ignores it and looks into the girl's eyes. She can see straightaway who is going to be in charge here.

'I am pleased to meet you.' The girl's voice is heavily accented, not what the woman was expecting. 'Can I call you Eva?'

'Mrs Bonfield will be fine,' she says, turning to look at Martin. 'Who is she?'

'Look, we've talked about this,' he says. 'I said I would sort something out – get some better help for you. You know we agreed about Jodie.'

You can only agree if both of you decide the same thing, she thinks, but the words stay in her head.

'She'll stay in the spare bedroom,' he goes on, moving newspapers from a chair so that he can sit down; sees the girl watching, makes space for her to sit too.

'I don't want her staying – I'm fine on my own.'

'She'll do the same things as Jodie …' Eva tries to butt in, but he carries on, overriding her words. 'Nadya will do the same things, but she'll do more – she's experienced, qualified. She can deal with more than Jodie.' He looks directly at the old woman for the first time. 'And she's starting tomorrow.'

"Bugger" she wants to say. She wants to say a dozen things. Instead, she leans on the arms of the chair and pushes herself to stand, but her stick is nowhere to be seen. She looks out to the garden, then to the door into the hallway. She would give anything to march out in stately silence, to leave the two of them shrugging at each other, but her body is unwilling.

'Pass me that,' she snaps, pointing to the stick which she has just noticed is beside the young woman's chair.

Nadya turns and picks up the stick. She hands it over with a smile on her face. 'See you tomorrow, Mrs Bonfield,' she says.

NOT REALLY A JOB FOR A GIRL
EVA

There's a word for it – they use it on the television all the time, but it isn't in Eva's head at the moment. But the gist of it is that if she agrees to "see how it goes" with the girl, then Martin agrees to listen to more of what she wants to tell him. And she needs to tell it all to him, or the important bit will make no sense.

'What did I tell you about before?' she has to ask him though.

'The organisation …. The ATA, was that what you called it? You wanted them to write to you …' She can tell he wishes he could flip a few pages forward, speed up the process, but he doesn't know the half of it, so he'll just have to plod through the story at her pace.

'Yes, that's it.' She pauses for a minute, trying to find her thread.

'I couldn't believe it when I got the letter.' He opens his mouth to interrupt, and she realises she might have said this bit before, but she needs to explain – how she'd been writing regularly, asking, pleading for them to let her join, but there'd always been a reason why not. 'That morning I woke up early because the sun was so bright through my bedroom window, and I'd got myself ready to go out walking, to take my mind off things. As I went down the road, Billy Wilkins the postman was coming towards me. He had letters in his hand and he waved them at me.'

'You're popular today, Missy,' he says, handing me the whole bundle. I could see there was one from Maisie who'd already signed up for the WAAFs – I'd have known her writing anywhere, and one from my aunt; but the one which took my attention was type-written.

I might have even blown a kiss at Billy, I was in such a daze. I ran down the lane, then up the hill to my favourite little hidey-hole in the trees, but that morning it only got a quick glance because I was desperate to see what was in the letter.

```
Dear Miss Andrews,
Further to your recent enquiries
regarding   the   Air   Transport
Auxiliary team, we are pleased to
invite you to an interview to
assess your suitability.
You    should    attend    Hatfield
Aerodrome  on  Monday  15th  June  at
10.00a.m.
Yours Sincerely,
Patricia Gould (Mrs), Operations
Officer
```

Eva remembers it as if it was yesterday. Reading it and rereading it, until she knew the contents off by heart, checking that she hadn't got it wrong, that it was her they really wanted. 'And then, on the way home, when I realised I'd have to show the letter to Mother and Father, I was sick in the hedgerow.'

'Oh Eva,' Mother said. 'You can't – it's not really a job for a girl, is it?'

'Father was obviously divided. He looked as pleased as punch, but I could tell he wanted to back Mother up as well.'

'She'll be fine Betty,' he said in the end. 'It's not as if she going to war, is it? She'll be in England the whole time, just too-ing and fro-ing from one airfield to another. What harm's going to come of her doing that?'

She hadn't told him that the planes had no instruments. That you just had to use any landmarks there were, to find your way, just as if you were driving a bus or a lorry, and tough luck if there were clouds or rain to block your view. She hadn't mentioned either that there was no radio contact; that if things were looking dodgy there was no way of letting anyone know. 'And I definitely didn't tell them the story I'd heard about Joan Regis, coming down in a field only the week before, and barely getting out of it alive.'

He looks at her. It is obvious that he doesn't believe a word of it.

'It's all true.' Her cheeks are red with indignation. 'But I did have to get through the interview first.'

NO NOOK UNTOUCHED

On Tuesday morning, at last, the call had come. "Everything's complete – you can collect the keys at midday." The prospect of the red-lipped woman had long since ceased to worry Martha; she'd got what she wanted despite the woman's attitude, but she still felt nervous as she walked down the street at 11.55, trying to pace herself so as not to arrive early and have to stand around superfluously.

Inevitably, the woman wasn't there and it was the inept young lad who made the simple job of handing over keys even more simple. He might have been offering her a mint, or the loan of a pen. Martha hurried out of the building before anyone could call her back, but then tried desperately to stop herself from running like a child to the seafront. She had prepared for this moment, had packed up her favourite china cups, bought celebratory macarons in pastel shades which matched the row of beach huts; and so she walked back to her car, gave the keys their own seat, and drove slowly down the tourist-filled road to the beach.

'Moving in day?' The fisherman she had met previously called across to her, casting an eye over the pile of boxes growing on the pavement from the back of her car.

Martha blushed, embarrassed now she came to look at her collection, at the amount she was investing in this hut.

'Need a hand?' he said, strolling across the sandy grass verge towards her.

'No – don't let me interrupt your work … I'll manage …'

'It's okay, I'll get Carl – he can carry it all for you.'

Martha hadn't noticed the younger pair of hands working on the peppermint paintwork of the neighbouring hut, but he turned at the call of his name and laid down the brush.

There was paint on his overalls and he sported the rubber boots worn by most of the fishermen; he brought a faint odour of the sea with him.

'Give this young lady a hand,' the older man said, motioning to her belongings.

The younger man scanned the pile, took two boxes under each arm and walked off. He needed no instruction to leave them at her door and repeated the procedure without a word until it was done.

'That's really kind – thank you so much … Carl, isn't it?' Martha said, holding out a hand.

'S'okay,' he muttered, turning back to his painting task.

Martha looked between him and the older man, trying to read the situation.

'Man of few words, is Carl.' The old man followed him, picking up a net from the veranda of the green hut and was beginning to weave a cord through a hole as she passed by.

Martha, still unsure of the situation, was nonetheless keen to get the key in the door. *Her* door. 'Well, thanks again, anyway. Pop in for a cup of tea some time.'

She'd been desperate to open up the hut, legitimately this time, and to clear and sort and install herself, to see what else might be sitting in the shadows, but now she felt awkward. Was there a problem with her taking over the hut? Had she trodden on someone else's dream? She looked across from her doorway to the two men, both entangled in their own occupations, acknowledging neither her nor each other. Perhaps the sorting should wait, she thought; perhaps she had bridges to build. She found mugs and biscuits and brewed strong tea, emptying a cardboard box to carry it all outside.

Both men accepted her offering, stopping their tasks to enjoy the break. Carl stood awkwardly, gripping the mug, as if he might squeeze a few words from it, but the older man propped himself against the wall of the hut and chatted of everyday nothings.

Martha had the words ready to ask about the previous owner of the building, and what he might know of them. Would they have been contemporaries? Probably not, Martha thought. The wind and the weather had probably aged the man beyond his years, but he might still have known the woman – or know someone who did. She smiled at a fishing tale he was relating, awaiting her moment, but as she did so, she became aware that Carl was staring across the scrubby grass area towards the roadway. The old man sensed something too and stopped his tale.

'Is that him?' Martha asked.

They were all looking now at a stocky late middle-aged man who in turn was staring at the three of them.

'Ay. Martin Andrews, they call him.' They all looked again at the man. 'He's the supposed nephew who's sold out on the old lady.' The fisherman sniffed and folded his arms.

'*Supposed* nephew?' Martha's short experience of her new neighbour was only of kind words, and his scorn brought her up short. 'Don't you believe … who do you think …?'

'Let's just say there are those who have their doubts.'

Martha looked back across the road, but Martin Andrews was no longer there.

The door shut behind her. She had expected the grey aging walls to be of little protection against the outside world, that inside she would still hear the gulls and the children shrieking at each other, the distant chatter and clink of glasses from the harbourside pub; but everything was muffled, like a landscape under freshly fallen snow. Inside the warm woodiness of the hut she felt a childlike comfort, and for several moments simply sat in the stillness, surveying her new kingdom. The battered table and chair had been left behind, but it was evident that the room had been swept; there were no cobwebs now and the accumulated dust and leaves which had gathered in the corners were gone.

Martha sat upright. The final missing pieces of paper which she had been hoping to unearth, the snippets which would reveal the remaining words and story to her were presumably gone. There was no nook untouched in which they might now hide. She jumped up and went to the shelves; the piece of curling driftwood remained, but the shelf beneath contained only the tell-tale marks of a brush drawn across the film of remaining dust. She looked around, pulling open a battered cutlery drawer in the kitchen area, tugging at a dilapidated cupboard door but there was no sign of anything remaining. Martha kicked out at the wicker chair, causing it to judder and jolt before it tipped on its side. She didn't want to return to the darkness of her previous pointless existence … but where would she go from here, if she could find no further pieces of the lovers' story?

Martha propped open the door absentmindedly as she wavered between thoughts and actions. Eventually, the shushing of the sea and the shriek of the birds calmed her frustration; she lifted the chair from the floor and reset it by the table. She began to unpack, looking for places to put her belongings, realising she would need more shelves or cupboards, but her head was still filled with the dissatisfaction of the unfinished puzzle.

As she stacked mugs and plates, Martha attempted to conjure images of the people in the letters which had brought her to this point – not just of being in their beach hut, but actually owning it. She wondered whether they might still be alive. But she realised she had no idea how old they might have been at the time – and so whether there was even the vaguest possibility of them still being around. She would re-check the dates, she thought, dropping her mother's apostle teaspoons into the drawer, cursing herself for having left the pieces of the letters back at the house.

Martha drifted through decades, adding and subtracting what might be possible, doing her best to ignore the jingle telling her that a message had arrived on her phone. She didn't want to be brought back to the present before she was ready; it was only after it had sounded a third time that the thought came to the forefront of her mind – that she had taken photos of the snippets of paper in their various different arrangements - and that they were of course waiting there, on her phone.

"29th June 1943" was the date on the letter. Martha found notebook and pen and started working out the possibilities. Assuming that "Dearest E" had been relatively young when the letters were written, so would've had to have been born in the early 1920s – which would make them possibly into their late eighties by now. Martha thought of herself at twenty, and the fact that no-one had been writing *her* love letters at that age, that no-one had been feeling anything like the passion for her that seemed to be lying between the sheets of those letters. She thought of Richard, casting around in her mind for scenes of their time as a couple. They had been married for ten years, the Millenium having seemed at the time a memorable enough event to coincide with, but had their relationship been similarly momentous? Had he ever *really* loved her, she wondered?

They had "rubbed along" – that was the phrase her mother would have used. They had been for weekends away, and had shared the washing up and the cooking, and he'd done the heavy work in the garden, and she'd planted daffodils. But did that count as love? When he'd failed to return home on that Saturday night, how had she truly felt? She'd been panicked and distraught, that was for sure. And devasted that she might have been abandoned. And yes, she conceded, there had been an aching in her chest that only Richard could have calmed. She remembered fighting the sense that her life was teetering on the edge of an enormous chasm, and terrified of what that would mean and how she might cope. Recalled too, that in the end she had taken her phone from her pocket and clicked on Laura's name.

Laura had come, of course she had. Had barely got through the door before she was looking in understairs cupboards, checking rooms. When Martha had asked, she had said, 'Well, we'd look pretty stupid if we call the police and Richard was here all the time, mending a fuse or doing some DIY in the box bedroom wouldn't we?'

'Why would we call the police? Surely it's not … he's only gone … he's probably …' Martha had stopped, realising that she had no idea at that moment of Richard probably being, or probably doing, anything.

Instead, Laura had given her chapter and verse on police procedure – presumably gleaned from television or radio - and how they wouldn't want to know for 24 hours, because Richard was an adult, and not vulnerable in any way.

'Michael's already done a once-round of the town,' her sister had added, checking the messages on her phone. 'He says he'll try the railway station next, and the bus station; and Martha had wanted to say what about the hospital, but at the same time not wanting to know. Of course, she hadn't wanted to think about him being extricated from a car accident or writhing in the aftermath of an assault. But at least she would have *known.* Unlike the past months, she thought, and the not knowing, not understanding – the where or the why of Richard's existence. That was the hardest part.

As she sat in the beach hut, emotions began to build in Martha's chest, the pain so real that she clutched at it to make it stop. She didn't want to go to that place again. She had spent too much time there, hurting and despairing, and she couldn't – wouldn't - return to the blackness. She swallowed hard, pushing away the tears that threatened to engulf her;

closed her eyes and willed herself to think of something else.

She would concentrate her thoughts on E and J – much safer ground. Martha contemplated the possibility of one day meeting up with them, discussing the letters and finding out the couple's real story. It was a longshot, their being alive; and even if they were, there was the possibility that, at ninety, they might no longer be compos mentis.

Nevertheless, Martha tried to conjure a picture of them, not as they might be now, but as they would have been, as young lovers. The thought occurred that she might be sitting in the very place where the letters – or at least one side of the correspondence – had been written; in what could have even been the couple's trysting place, and she let her fingers drift across the wooden walls, as if the touch of her skin might bring their story to life once more.

A WHOLE LIST OF QUESTIONS

She could easily have stayed in the hut all night, wrapped in her daydreams and the spotted woollen blanket she had brought with her. But eventually Martha acknowledged that she had to get up, push herself out of the door and back into the real world. For one thing, Laura was coming to dinner. She had foolishly allowed herself to be bullied into making the invitation as repayment after the cleaning spree – and she had to put together at least the appearance of a reasonable meal, otherwise there would be more lectures, more grim words from her oh-so-sensible sister.

The thought of cooking something from scratch was, though, one step too far, and Martha called in at the supermarket and bought stuffed chicken breasts and sautéed potatoes and a range of vegetables, and melting chocolate pots for pudding; no-one – not even Laura – could be crotchety after chocolate pots, she thought smugly.

'How is it then?' Laura had managed to contain herself until they had at least sat down at the table.

'Your new "property"?' The disapproval in her voice was tangible.

'It's wonderful. I love it. I might move into it completely and sell this place,' Martha said, indicating the house around them. She had no intention of doing this – well not for the time being at least – but it was worth saying, just to see the look on Laura's face; her sister almost choked on the chicken.

'You can't … what would … it's not …' she paused, trying to push her words into some sort of comprehensible assembly. 'Well, you just can't Martha. It would be like … like living in a – a – caravan!' she spluttered, as if this was the worst possible fate which could befall anyone.

'That's what I like about it actually.' Martha was calm, surprising herself that she had only just begun to consider what she herself really thought of the whole situation. 'Anyway, I'm thinking of doing some research, and the beach hut would be just the place to shut myself away from interruptions.'

There was silence as they sat, both contemplating the fact that really Martha had no interruptions at all in the rambling empty house in which they were currently sitting, but neither wanting to point this out to the other at that moment.

They carried on eating for a few minutes, allowing reality to suspend itself like the cobweb swaying on the ceiling.

'What sort of research?' Laura forced the words out as Martha brought in the chocolate pots.

'Well, I'm not even sure what there is to find out at the moment, but I wanted to know a bit more about the previous owner of the hut.' It sounded very thin, now that she had spoken it out loud, and of course, without mentioning the letters, it seemed to have no basis in reality. But she knew that Laura would take over instantly if she showed her the pieces of paper. As it was, she could already see a whole list of questions building on Laura's face.

'It seems that the old lady who owned it – well she didn't have children, and some man seems to have come forward - supposedly her nephew, but seems to have taken over her affairs and is selling everything in sight, and … well, I just wanted to know a bit more…' The bright energy of her words fizzled like a flickering sparkler and then went out.

'Hhmm.' Laura sighed, licking the last of the chocolate from her spoon, looking over her glasses at her sister. 'Well, it seems like a complete wild goose chase if you ask me – you'd be better off spending your energy getting this place spruced up a bit...' She cast a disapproving eye around the dated décor.

'Well, it's something I …'

'But, I *was* going to add,' Laura interjected forcefully, 'That at least it has brought a smile to your face, which no-one or nothing seems to have been able to do since – since …'

She didn't finish her sentence, for which Martha was grateful. For the second time that day she was desperate to drag herself away from remembering the events of the past few months. 'Enjoy that?' she said, indicating the remains of the meal on the table.

'Delicious, my dear – we should do this more often.'

That was not what Martha had in mind, but she was amazed to see a genuine smile on the face of her sister, and even more surprised to see her running a finger around the rim of the chocolate pot, searching out the last remains of the pudding. Please don't offer to help me with the research, Martha suddenly thought.

'Perhaps it would be a good idea if I helped?' Laura looked up, smiling.

SHORTHAND NOTEBOOK AND TWO COLOURS OF PEN

How many ways were there to say "no"? Or more accurately, how many ways could you embroider a "no" into something which wouldn't offend your sensitive sister? Martha wasn't sure that she'd managed to achieve either – that her sister had taken no for an answer or that she had been unoffended - and as she pitched between sleep and wakefulness, like a skiff in a storm, Martha searched her head for a small task she could give Laura just to pacify her; or maybe a long arduous time-consuming task was what was required she thought, sitting up in bed and switching on the bedside light.

She found a notebook on her bedside table, hidden under six novels, none of which she had progressed further than the first few pages. She scribbled at first, doodling flowing patterns, adding lines and swirls as she let her mind wander along similar routes. It was something Martha had returned to over the years, either when she needed to empty her mind, or, like now, when she needed to harvest whatever was blossoming in her head, and make some sense of it. The swirling stopped and she allowed the pen to start making a list –

    1. *Talk to* … it occurred to her that, despite sharing tea and biscuits, she didn't know the fisherman's name … *"talk to fisherman – find out what he knows about previous owner"*

    2. *Track down Martin Andrews.* She had little faith that she would be able to do this, but it needed to be on the list. Perhaps this was one she could pass to Laura, she thought – she had the tenacity to follow rabbits down ferret holes, their mother had once said. She put an asterisk by this idea as a "Laura possible".

    3. *Solicitor* – The solicitor who had dealt with the sale of the beach hut for her would surely still have the paperwork, and probably amongst the mountain of sheets he had stuck in front of Martha for signing would be a vendor's name… and did beach huts have deeds, like other houses? Surely that sort of thing would reveal some information about a previous owner?

    4. *Museum – worthwhile speaking to someone at museum and visitor centre about what was happening in the area in 1943?* At least that would put the letters into some sort of context? Martha liked this one – thought it had more about it than some of the others; she'd keep this one for herself.

> 5. *Once full names established – look at Census or other records.* Again, Martha fancied this one for herself. She'd seen television programmes where people traced their relatives, uncovering interesting stories of past lives and indiscretions. She revised the asterisk system, and instead put initials alongside each item on the list – MT for herself, and LW for Laura.

Martha jolted awake, realising as she peered at the fluorescent figures of the alarm clock that she must have dozed off – for at least an hour. She craved more sleep, and so allowed the book and pen to drop to the floor, and closed her eyes again before the comfortable drowsiness could leave her completely.

When she awoke for a second time the room was light and there was a thumping, echoing somewhere; the front door, she realised, groaning, leaning back against the pillows, unable to fully open her weary eyes.

'No – I am *not* "sliding back" into my old ways,' Martha was indignant, determined to make coffee whilst trying to clutch at the dressing gown which had lost its belt; endeavouring to issue comprehensible words while blinking her eyes into a state of openness. Her sister, sitting at the kitchen table with brand-new shorthand notepad and two colours of pen, was evidently keen not to let any more of the day slip by without serious investigative work having been carried out.

All Martha wanted was to get down to her beach hut, sneak inside and relax into its cocoon-like warmth while she contemplated stories and nibbled her way through the remains of yesterday's macarons. She slid onto a chair at the kitchen table, spilling some of the coffee in her uncoordinated inelegance.

'Oh, just give it to me.' Laura grabbed the coffee jug from her and in one movement got it to the sink, grabbed a cloth, mopped the table, reset jug and cups and conjured toast, seemingly from nowhere.

The coffee and buttered toast brought Martha some way back into the reality of the day, and as she drained her cup, she was finally able to recall at least one item from her nocturnal list.

'Well, if you're really sure you want to help …' but Laura already had her blue pen poised over the pristine page. '…I did think of something which would be ideally suited to your skills.' Martha paused and saw a brief smile cross her sister's face. 'It's something which I'd probably struggle with to be honest, but …'

'Oh just get on with it, Martha, I've got plenty of time on my hands until the new term starts, and even then it will be a while before my private tutoring really gets started again, so, just tell me what is it that you need me to do - while I've still got time to do it.'

Martha could see that her sister was eager to be occupied. Laura had retired from full-time teaching - "it's become far too onerous" - and then appeared to immediately regret her decision. She had ricocheted between various volunteering posts until a friend had asked her to tutor their wayward son, to get him through his GCSEs. Word spread, and before she knew it, Laura's termtime evenings and weekends were filled with reluctant teenagers pushed forward by anxious parents. But the long empty summers always made her restless.

And so Martha explained about Martin Andrews, staring across at the beach hut, and presumably her, and of the fisherman's comments. 'So, if you could just try to find out a bit more about him – you know, his relationship with the previous owner, where he fits into things, that might throw a bit of light on the situation.'

Laura was packed up and out of the front door before Martha could rouse herself, and as she stacked the cups and plate in the sink it occurred to her that the task she had given Laura would keep her at a good arm's length from the letters and the need to reveal that part of the story. 'Bit of luck,' she smiled to her image in the hall mirror as she brushed crumbs from her mouth.

NO IDEA REALLY

She was torn now. She had her own notebook ready, had checked the opening times of the museum, but it was one of those days when the sky was impossibly clear, ridiculously blue and seemed determined to stay that way for the entire day. So different from a few months ago, when the Icelandic volcano had decided to cover the whole world in ash clouds, Martha thought, musing on the metaphorical similarity between weather conditions and life. But today she hated the idea of being indoors when the weather was so obviously enjoying itself, and the prospect of a fusty museum most definitely did not entice her.

And then of course there was the question of Laura, which had started to nag at her. She knew she was probably being ridiculous – that Laura was a match for anyone that Martha had ever met – but there had been something about that man when he had lingered by the beach huts, the way he obviously felt it was okay just to stand and stare, that was making her slightly regret sending Laura off into the unknown.

Martha lifted books and clothes and eventually found her phone.

Her sister, who normally answered after one ring, wasn't answering.

She ended the call, stared at the phone and re-dialled. She was just getting ready with her message when Laura picked up. 'What? What is it? I'm right in the middle of …'

'I was just checking you were ...'. To say "okay" sounded ridiculous, when Laura was being so obviously and normally her usual self. '...Just checking how you were doing …' she mumbled.

'Well, I'd be getting on a lot quicker if I wasn't being continually interrupted.' There was a rustle of papers.

'Are you still at home?' Martha asked.

'Well, unless you expect this Mr Andrews just to appear when I click my fingers, then yes. Research, Martha – that's the only way to do this sort of thing efficiently.' Laura stopped, perhaps realising her abruptness. 'I'll let you know when I've got more information,' she said.

'Well, take care then ...' Martha began, but the call had already been ended.

She was still feeling delicate from lack of sleep. Perhaps then just an hour or two down at the beach hut? And anyway, Martha thought, as she pulled on sandals and packed some lunch in her bag, she could just as easily make a start on her list down there.

As she approached the colourful line of huts with a bag full of intentions, the area seemed deserted. Of course there were children playing, running in and out of doors in various combinations of rubber rings, snorkels, multi-coloured swimsuits – but there was no sign of the fisherman. Martha abandoned her belongings in her own hut and went back out, shading her eyes, searching both sides of the beach for any sign of the man's rotund silhouette. There was nothing, but she noticed movement over at the nearby hut.

'Morning Carl,' she waved.

There was no response. She strolled over to him, and for a moment he looked like he might turn his back. 'Do you know where …?'

'Out in his boat.'

The voice was low, unwilling.

'Oh – thanks.' She wondered how he'd known what she'd been about to ask, but supposed it was a reasonable assumption to make. 'Will he be out all day?'

Carl had moved to the back of the beach hut and was levering open the paint tin. He muttered something but didn't look up.

'Sorry – I didn't quite catch …'

'Dunno.'

She waited, and he shifted awkwardly. 'Usually back lunchtime – no idea really.'

'Oh that's a shame – but thanks anyway.' Martha paused, deciding to ignore his reluctance. 'Umm Carl, I don't suppose – it's just that I was going to ask … sorry I don't know the other man's name …'

'Ted.'

'Oh right, yes – well I was just going to ask Ted if he knew anything about the person who used to own my beach hut, you know, just in case I find anything …' She was rambling, and to anyone else it would have been obvious that she wasn't being entirely up front. But Carl seemed oblivious. 'I don't suppose *you* know anything …?'

He was quiet, already dipping the brush in the pot, applying a second coat with meticulous calming strokes, backward and forward. She watched him work, forgetting for a moment that she had asked him a question. She was somewhat taken aback when he suddenly spoke.

'Don't know nothing really. Been empty as long as I can remember …'

And that was the end of it. He moved round to the next face of the hut, taking his paint and brushes with him, and Martha was left looking at a blank wall of pale green, drying in the breeze.

PREPARED FOR TAKE-OFF
EVA

He's back. And immediately she can see that he's not going to be the best of company – even more so than usual. He's not just solemn, he's obviously unhappy, she can see it written in the lines of his face. He runs his hands up and down his legs, as though he's preparing for a race. Does he want to leave, Eva thinks, even though he's only just got here; or does he want to say something? If he does, he's struggling to get the words out of his mouth. His fidgeting is making her uncomfortable too, but she wants to get on with her story.

Martin sees Eva looking at him, nods. 'I'll make tea then you can tell me what happened next,' he says.

But even before he returns with the tray, she has transported herself back to the aerodrome.

'I told you, didn't I, that they called me for an interview?' she says, as he pushes his way back through the door. He nods, but nothing more, as if to say, don't go through all that again; please don't repeat it all.

'Well, just the sight of the Chief Flying Officer made my legs jitter, I can tell you. The other girls had told me all about him – Mr No Nonsense, they called him. 'Don't bother trying to give him any excuses, either – he'll see straight through that.' His face was deadpan when he called me over. He strode out ahead of me across the airfield to the Tiger Moth – I had to skip along to keep up; then he stood back, making me take the lead. It took all my effort to hoist myself into that cockpit – not that I hadn't done it a hundred times before, but this time I was … what's the word – legs wouldn't move, scared. I just wanted him to smile, to say "that was excellent, Miss Bonfield", for the whole thing to be over with and me already part of the ATA. But I knew that none of it would happen until I'd got through the test.'

Martin wants to stop her, to point out that she wasn't a Bonfield at that point. But that would mean repeating and backtracking, and he just wants to get it done, so he drains his cup instead.

'I mean, it wasn't as if I couldn't fly.' The old woman is in full flow, and he lounges back in the chair, allowing her words to wash over him. 'I'd clocked up I don't know how many flying hours by then, but so much was riding on that test. I knew there were more of us women pilots than there were ATA places, someone had told me that. Do you know that even Amy Johnson was turned down first time…'

He sits up at the mention of the name, a name he recognises, wondering at the woman's random ability to pull such information from her head when she struggles sometimes to know what she has had for lunch.

'… but I tried to put all that out of my mind, telling myself this was just another flight, just with a passenger along for the ride this time. It didn't stop my hands shaking though, as I prepared for take-off.'

Eva looks over at him. He's perched on the edge of his seat again, but this time his face is livelier, less like he's desperate to get out of the door. He gives a nod of encouragement, and she's keen to carry on while it's all in her head, while the plane and the airfield are still as clear as day in her mind's eye.

'The Tiger Moth – you've heard of them, I bet - it had an open cockpit, draughty at the best of times, and especially when there was a cross wind … and to start with they wanted us girls to wear skirts to fly in!' She smiles at the madness of men. 'Anyway, I followed my procedures, keeping her steady as she skipped up from the ground and into a clear blue sky. The officer asked me to do a few – you know …' and she spins her finger in circles '… round the airfield, and that gave me a bit of my confidence back. Then he barked at me, wanting me to demonstrate a few spins, just to show I could get myself out of them again, I suppose. I just kept telling myself "Don't stall, whatever you do", but I managed it, tipping us upside down then flipping us back the right way again. I'd been holding my breath, but then I started to enjoy it.'

Eva stops, her mouth dry, and sees he's looking down at the floor; at what she had no idea, or even if he's still listening. He realises she isn't talking, looks up, makes a deal of refilling their cups, asking if she wants a biscuit. 'Don't interrupt,' she wants to say, because she might lose the thread, the story might be gone. She grasps the handkerchief in her lap, twisting it this way and that, as though the action might help her squeeze out a bit more of her tale.

'The next bit was cross-country,' she gabbles on. 'You know, where you have to follow a railway line, or a river, or use the edges of the fields.' She looks over to see if he's impressed; chuffed to see that, despite himself, he seems to be. 'They even called it Bradshawing – using the train schedules to plan a route, but anything that would give you an idea where you were. A church spire, little groups of houses – I did tell you we had no instruments, didn't I?'

That makes him look up. He's got an expression on his face, as if he wants to say "are you sure?". He's half out of his chair, looking as if he'd like to go and find a book – to check what she's telling him. But she carries on. She might be rusty on what happened yesterday, but this she can remember with ease.

'I really liked that bit – finding my way. I was really good at it. I was almost sorry when the flying officer told me to go back to the airfield.' Eva looks up. 'I knew he wouldn't be able to fault me, but it didn't matter how well *I* thought I'd done, did it? It was still down to him and his decision. I got myself in a bit of a state as we headed back towards the aerodrome. What if I got it wrong on the last knockings, I kept thinking, what if I damaged the plane, or worse still the officer; what if I smashed into the runway?'

'Anyway, I made myself concentrate, lined up the plane ready to come in to land. But as I did so, I could see three men on the aerodrome roof. RAF boys, they must have been, and the sun was shining off their binoculars. They'd must have been watching me, and as we came down I could see that one of them had his hand to his mouth, shouting something to his chums. You know that even though the ATA was doing such an important job, and that they might not have had planes to fly if it wasn't for us girls, some of the men didn't like it. They thought we were a liability, that we hadn't got the brains …' She taps a finger to her head. 'That we should be at home polishing floors or cooking the dinner… Anyway, the flying officer looked out at them, and scribbled something on his clipboard then waved me on to land. I bet they got a good old dressing down for that,' Eva laughs.

'The wheels hit the runway, and I brought the plane to a stop. And that was it. He was saying something to me, the flying officer, but I missed it because I was concentrating on pushing open the cockpit door and trying to get down as elegantly as I could, not wanting to fall flat on my face at the last hurdle. Then he just nodded and walked away, and I still had no idea whether I'd passed his test or not.'

Eva sits back in her chair, tired, the story having sucked away her energy, but still smiling at the memories.

'That's some story,' Martin says eventually. He still looks like he doesn't believe a word – as if she's just recounting something she's seen on television.

There's more,' she says, making an effort to sit up, hoping he'll agree to her carrying on. But he looks at his watch, stands up. 'Next time,' he says, and goes to the kitchen to speak to Nadya.

ON THE TRAIL

'There you are – I've been waiting ages.'

Martha straggled along the last few yards of her driveway. She was ready for a long soak in a steamy bath, but there on her doorstep was her sister, clearly itching to tell her story.

'I'm tired,' Martha said, searching for her keys, irritated by Laura's critical look as she checked her bag then her pocket then her bag again.

'Well – I can come back tomorrow,' Laura snapped, clasping her notebook to her chest.

'No, no – come in now you're here. I'll put the kettle on.'

Laura took over immediately, collecting cups, warming the pot, while Martha searched for biscuits. She needed a shot of energy if she were going to have to listen to Laura for any length of time. She slid into a chair as Laura brought everything to the table, tilting back her head, closing her eyes.

'Well…' Laura made a fuss of making herself comfortable, arranging her notebook and pens. 'Don't you want to know what I've got?'

Martha pulled her head forward, opening her eyes and reaching for a chocolate digestive. 'Measles?'

'Very funny. I thought you'd be dying to know …?'

When Martha nodded lethargically it was all the invitation Laura needed.

'I've found him,' she gushed. 'Martin Andrews – well not him exactly, I haven't met the man himself, well not yet anyway, but I'm on the trail …'

Despite her sister's "Miss Marple" act, and the fact that she'd had an unproductive afternoon herself, Martha couldn't help but be stirred. 'So, what have you found then?'

'Well, I thought - when you gave me the job – where would *anyone* begin looking for anyone? So of course I Googled the name. You won't believe how may "Martin Andrews" there are in the world – one's a professor of Criminal Psychology at City University in New York, another's a ballet dancer …'

'Just get on with it Laura,' Martha sighed, taking a third biscuit.

'Well, no luck there – it would have taken me a lifetime to go through all of those. So I thought I'd try Facebook. And there he was, large as life.'

'How did you know this one was the right one?' Martha sat up, peering at her sister. 'There must have been just as many "Martin Andrews" on that website, surely?' She had shied away from social media in much the same way she'd shied away from the real world in the past few months, and had no real desire to know how the whole thing worked, but logic told her that one worldwide list of people would surely be much the same as another.

'Aahh, but on Facebook you see, people give a snippet of their details on their Profile page – where they grew up, what football team they support, what school they went to, that sort of thing.' Laura gazed into space, as though remembering many a lost beau whose details she might have tracked down in a similar way. 'Anyway,' she said, coming back to the present. 'There were a couple of entries that mentioned this part of the world, and then one that mentioned Moyon's Quay. He's got something to do with that Enterprise Park – you know, over towards Taunton.'

That easy. Well, maybe Laura might be an asset after all, Martha thought. 'So, we could find him there?'

'I went along actually – well, I had all day, so I thought I might as well. I just strode up to the reception desk of the company he'd mentioned, and asked for him; surprised myself actually,' Laura laughed with the sort of fake modesty which Martha had never seen on her sister before. 'There was a bit of a madam at the desk; you know the sort, all nails and coloured-in eyebrows; "Not here today" she chirps from under her ridiculous false eyelashes. I gave her one of my teacher looks and she managed to add "Doesn't actually work here – just a consultant …". Sulky little madam. And she couldn't tell me when he'd be back – "only works part-time, semi-retired" she said, doing those ridiculous quote marks in the air. But at least we know where to find him now.' Laura sat back, sipping her tea, looking satisfied with herself, despite not finding the man in the flesh.

Martha was taken aback at the new aspects to her sister which she was seeing; for someone who would always walk the long way round when she saw a "Keep Off The Grass" notice, Laura had been remarkably bold. 'What would you have said to him – if he'd been there?' Martha asked, mainly because she had no idea what she herself would have said – would say – if and when she met him.

'Hadn't thought that far ahead to be honest. I was quite glad when the girl said he wasn't there. At least it gives us chance to have a think about it…and I did get a work phone number for him.'

Laura at last reached for the biscuits, munching enthusiastically, as if the relaying of her tale had given her an appetite. 'What do you want me to do next?' she asked, reaching for her notebook and turning to a new page.

Laura's revelations had rather shaken Martha. She hadn't considered the reality of this road she had started out on - that real people would be involved, not just names on pieces of paper. She pondered for a moment on any future meeting she might have with Martin Andrews and what she would say to him, hoping that that encounter might be more successful than the way she had spent her afternoon. Gradually she became aware of a clicking, of Laura sitting beside her, snapping her pen on and off, on and off, awaiting instructions.

'I don't know,' she said, reaching for another biscuit and then pulling her hand away. 'To be honest I hadn't really thought this all through …' The words were out of her mouth before she could stop them, and she braced herself for a barrage of reprimands from her sister. But the room was remarkably quiet and still. She glanced over to see Laura doodling on her pristine pad, apparently caught up in her own contemplation.

'Perhaps you should go back a step,' Laura said, still staring at the paper in front of her. 'Think about why are you so keen to find all this out in the first place? What is it that you really want to know … and why?' she added, looking quizzically at Martha.

Good question, Martha thought, realising that it had never taken much for her sister to see through her. The whole thing had started out as a distraction – the pieces of paper, the letters; it had certainly pulled her out of her emotional mire and set her off on a new road, and for that she was grateful. But did it really matter if she never found out who the two letter writers were, or where Martin Andrews fitted into the story? Except that something didn't appear to be quite right about the Andrews situation, and even if she was just able to get to the bottom of that, it would be something. And the story of the two letter writers *did* intrigue her, even if it was just a bit of entertainment, some escapism from her real world. She found herself blurting all this out to

Laura, and eventually telling her the whole story – the bits of paper, the letters, the whole thing.

'Well, that puts an entirely different light on things. I can see exactly why you're intrigued,' Laura said, pushing the doodles to one side, 'But it is just …. well, just being nosey at the end of the day, isn't it?'

Martha began to clear the tea things away, to look in the fridge to see what oddments she had there that might be able to make a meal. 'Will Michael be expecting you?' she asked, realising that Laura hadn't mentioned her husband once.

'Probably hasn't even noticed I'm not there,' Laura mused. 'Let me make you an omelette and you can get all the bits of letter out to show me,' she said, but she was smiling, not her usual bossy self.

A few days ago, Martha would have done anything to keep the details away from her sister. But now, as she watched Laura busying herself with ingredients, Martha felt some sort of affinity – yes, maybe even sisterliness, she supposed.

It wasn't until they had finished eating that Laura looked up, stirring her coffee deliberately. 'And anyway, how about you?'

For a moment Martha thought that her sister was delving into the rabbit warren which was her current emotional state; she was about to claim a headache of convenience, not wishing to venture into that abyss, but her sister was already continuing.

'Well, you were going to do a bit of investigating yourself, weren't you? You haven't mentioned a single word about how you got on.'

OTHER PEOPLE'S LIVES

The morning had drifted away along with the outgoing tide while Martha had arranged and re-arranged as much as she could in the beach hut and was beginning to think about lunch. She'd brought with her some local cheese – from the man at the small cheese shop in town, the one with the café, who was always willing to recommend and to provide tasters to sway a choice. She'd intended to gather up all the odds and ends she hadn't found a home for and tidy them away into the cupboard under the kitchen sink for now, but as she forced open the ill-fitting door it was evident the space wouldn't take anything more. There were garish bottles of half-used detergent, and soap powder long since hardened into cheaply perfumed rock. But most of the space was occupied by a wooden box. She pulled it towards her and out spilled the unlikely contents – old-fashioned shoe polish tins and brushes and dusters, cascading across the floor. Martha swore, having set her mind on lunch, but leaned across to gather everything back into its home; it was something she would sort out another day. But as she tried to push everything home the box refused to take its original position. She stooped, seeing that a paper bag had slipped down, blocking the back of the cupboard. She reached out and grabbed it, but with no chance to think about what it was before there was a tapping at her door.

'Come in,' she called out, trying to stand on legs which were now fired with pins and needles.

There was no opening of the door though, and Martha eventually managed to pull herself up and hobble across.

Ohh – Mr – Ted. How are you?'

'Carl mentioned you were looking for me – something wrong?'

'No – no, everything's fine,' she said, looking over her shoulder at the bag. 'It was just – Carl didn't say anything then?'

'You know Carl – wouldn't waste a word unless he needed to.' The old man grinned, wiping midday perspiration from his face.

Martha was eager to look inside the bag, but she couldn't really leave the poor man sweating on the doorstep.

'Come in, out of the sun. I'll make tea.' Martha fussed about, pulling the wicker chair from the top of the table where it had been relegated while she cleaned. She resigned herself to the fact that the bag was going to have to wait; and anyway, she might get some useful information from the old man if they sat and chatted for a while. 'I was going to make a sort of ploughman's lunch – would you like some?'

The old man, held up a hand, but she could see him eyeing the freshly baked bread spilling out of the bag on the counter. 'It's no problem – I've got plenty.'

And so they sat in the shade by the open door, munching their feast, talking politely about the weather and the town and the tourists.

As they took their last bites, Ted turned to her. 'So, what was it you wanted to know?'

Martha related again her story about wanting the previous owner's details in case she found any belongings to return.

Ted looked out to sea. 'I'm sure there's more to the old lady than meets the eye, but I've never heard any stories – and you usually would, in a small town like this.' He paused, watching as a windsurfer tried for the third time to hoist himself back onto his board.

Martha wriggled in the silence. A dozen questions tangled themselves on her tongue, as she took on board that the owner had been a woman. She was still deciding what to ask first when Ted beat her to it.

'Eva, I think they call her. Andrews is the name of the nephew or whatever he is, but whether that's the old lady's name … I thought it was Benford, Barford, something like that. I'm terrible with names …' Ted appeared to plunder his memory, but came back empty-handed. 'Didn't you get anything from the solicitor – you know, in the sales paperwork and everything?'

'No – I – well, you know what solicitors are like, there was so much paperwork that I just kept signing wherever he told me to. I didn't really take much notice – one form looked much like another to me.' Martha realised she that she sounded scatterbrained, irresponsible even. 'I just wanted to get the formalities out of the way as soon as I could …' Her voice drifted off, her excuses floating on the air.

'Hmm.' Ted looked back out to sea. 'Is it important… knowing who the owner was?'

'Yes - no – not really, I suppose.' Martha didn't want to go through the whole story again, about discovering the letters and why she wanted to find out more. 'But I just thought …'

Ted nodded, running his tongue over his lip. 'Other people's lives are sometimes easier to deal with than your own – is that the way of it?' he said, batting away a seagull with a greedy eye on the remains of his lunch and daring to come closer.

'Something like that.' Martha wondered how someone who appeared to have such a simple grasp on life could be so astute; he'd only met her a couple of times but he seemed to have got the measure of her already.

'Last I heard, she was still in a house up on the hill.' He waved vaguely in the direction of the wooded hill which stood guard over the harbour.

'What? You mean she's still alive? Still living here in Moyon's Quay?'

'Well, can't guarantee she's still with us, but the gossip has it she still has a place up there, alongside St Michael's.'

Martha glanced up at the distant church standing proudly half way up the hill, its pale stone shining in the afternoon sun.

'Just up there … I can't believe she's been there all the time,' Martha laughed, wondering what Laura would make of all of this.

'Ay well, she might not still be there – although I've seen nothing in the papers to say otherwise.' Ted nodded sagely again, presumably the type who checked the obituaries every week to see who, of his contemporaries, was still with him and who had moved on.

'D'you think I'd be able to visit?' Martha's mind was racing, three steps ahead of herself.

'Mebbe.' Ted paused. 'But don't forget about yon man – Andrews. He might not be so keen.'

And with that, Ted picked up his mug and plate and took them to the table, tipping his hat to Martha as he sauntered off into the afternoon heat.

PETRIFIED TO CHANGE DIRECTION
EVA

By the look on his face, he's done some homework, Eva thinks as he takes the tray from Nadya and settles himself into the armchair. Doesn't look such a Doubting Thomas, more relaxed, and Eva wants to say 'see, I told you it was all true.' But that might make him scratchy again, she thinks, and she knows that before long time will run out – either for his patience or for her memory. So she has to make hay – while the sun shines, as they say.

'I didn't have long to wait,' she begins. 'Before they let me know that I'd passed. I was jumping round the room like a child, whooping at the news. Mum and Dad weren't so thrilled, of course, but David managed to conjure up a new pair of nylons from somewhere as a celebration present for me. And then the time came for me to leave home.' She looks at him, sees him thinking that this will be where the story ends, that she opted out and stayed with her parents. But he doesn't know her, doesn't know that wasn't how the story went at all.

'I loved it – every minute, even when I was lost and sick with panic, not wanting to be the first one who had to come back and admit they'd pranged a Hurricane. Of course, they started me off with the Oxfords, which were about as basic as you could get for a fighting plane, so it was like going back to infant school, but my dream, like all the other girls, was to fly a Spitfire. It seemed to be just a lucky-dip – who got to fly what – but I'm sure that Marian Monkson, who was in charge of us all, kept a secret tally, trying to share out the good stuff amongst us.'

'I worked for months and months, with hardly a break – just an endless merry-go-round of arriving at the airfield, getting instructions, flying off, delivering, trying to find space on a crowded train to get back to base, then starting the whole thing over again. It was only once in a blue moon that we were allowed an overnight stay.'

Her throat is dry from all the talking, and as she turns to pick up her cup, she sees that she has caught his attention; that, just for a moment, she's not a demanding old woman but someone who might have actually done something interesting, the sort of thing you might read about in a book. He seems to have forgotten that there is any purpose to the storytelling other than her being able to reminisce. And she also knows that, by rummaging around in the detail of the story, she's just playing for time, putting off the moment when she'll have to tell him what really needs to be said.

'Anyway, enough of all that,' she says abruptly, watching him jerk upright, as if someone has turned off the film before the end. 'I'm telling you this to explain – so you'll know how it all came about.

Now, where was I?' She sits in silence, trying to pull from the cluttered cupboard of her mind the detail which will allow her to proceed; but she struggles to extract anything from the untidiness.

'You were saying …' Martin speaks after enough moments have passed that they both feel uncomfortable. '… that it was relentless – the work, the flying …'

'Yes – that was it – so much work. We were all exhausted, but we just carried on.' She stops again, noticing his fingers beginning to drum on the arm of the chair. 'Sorry – I'll … yes … Well, one day they wanted me to drop off …a Wellington, I think it was, at Chivenor and then take a Lysander they no longer needed back to Filton. They often did that, shuttling planes from one place to another, and it was a route I'd done before, so I wasn't worried. On top of that, they'd given in and given us girls proper flying uniforms by then – boiler suits and flying boots instead of skirts and shoes, so I was comfortable in my little cockpit. I was on the return journey, with a good clear view of the route up the Bristol Channel, and I was singing to myself – I can't remember what now, but I was singing at the top of my voice, happy in my own little world, when suddenly it was as though someone had turned the lights off. What had been a clear summer blue sky was suddenly grey and dark as winter. I was used to flying in all weathers mind you, so I didn't take much notice at first.'

Martin is watching her now, intently, his cup rattling on the saucer in his hand.

'But the clouds just got thicker and thicker, and before I knew it, I was surrounded by a heavy sea mist. It rolled over me, as if someone had thrown a blanket over my head, and I couldn't see a thing. The plane had no instruments – did I tell you that? So I had no idea of what might be coming up, and worst of all I had no idea of my – what's it called – height … you know …'

'Altitude,' he mutters, but she's already carrying on.

'Yes, altitude, that's it – no idea at all. I knew I'd been flying along the North Devon coast before the weather started to come in … so I thought to myself, if I just stay on this course I'll still be following the coastline – more or less. And then as soon as I'm out of this awful fog I can correct myself. To be honest, I was petrified to change direction, but scared not to as well. I knew that there were hills below me, and that they began to rise further along the bay, but I had no idea, in that fog, whether that point was right beneath me or a mile off. Being deprived of your …' she points to both her eyes, '… it does strange things to you, you know, and to be honest, I had no idea which way I was going …'

And she is there – sitting in that cockpit once more, and her hands are gripping the edge of the table, until her knuckles turn white; until a terrible trembling moves through her body.

She feels a hand over her hand, another on her shoulder.

'Stop.' It is almost a whisper. 'You don't need to tell me any more – it's upsetting you.'

She fights away his grasp. 'No – I have to, I have to tell you – you need to understand.' She is crying now, but with frustration, annoyed with herself for not completing what she has set out to say.

'There'll be another day,' Martin says quietly, putting on his jacket.

'But I might not remember another day,' she weeps.

'You will – you'll remember well enough.' And with that he leaves, as if this is the only way he can bring an end to her upset.

THE DAMNED PLANE
EVA

With Martin's departure Eva is left with the quietness of an almost empty house. The girl is doing something in the kitchen; she has the radio on, music, but low, and the hum of it closes Eva's eyes. She rests her head on the cushions of the armchair and she is back in the plane.

My mind is dark. Someone has shut out the lights – goodnight and God bless. Except that this is no blessing. I am welded into my seat, only my left arm moving, my legs not at all. There is silence. Silence except for one invisible bird, chirping brightly to itself, oblivious to me and my predicament.

I squirm in my seat, trying to find another part of me which might move. The muscles in my backside are still in some way alive, twitching to my command, but having no effect whatsoever in getting me out of the jam I am in. The straps which are supposed to cradle me in safety are holding me prisoner, shackling me to my seat. The only blessing is that they are away from my face and I can breathe.

The bird again. I try to twist my head, to move the angle of the landscape, but I see only trees. Trees with such an abundance of greenery. I can't tell, from my narrow line of vision exactly what has happened, can only assume that my wing has caught the top of one of those magnificent hills, that its waving arms have flipped me like an acrobat, but I obviously haven't landed gracefully.

I try not to panic, try bringing to mind pictures of mother and father, and David who would all be shouting instructions, encouraging me to find a way out. But nothing will move.

For some bizarre reason, a song comes into my thoughts. All Things Bright and Beautiful. I begin to sing, realising that all the words of my infant classroom are still in my head. I come to the end and wind round to the beginning again. If these are to be my last moments, with no-one to take my hand, then singing will at least be a companion.

I grow tired of Bright and Beautiful, try to find the words of something else. But I can remember only first lines, and the songs evaporate. I crane my neck, searching for any sign of life, but there is only the bird. I try a feeble call for help. I try again, louder, not caring whether I sound frail or stupid. But my words seem to evaporate into the air, refusing to go any further than a few inches from my mouth.

Maybe I black out. Because when I open my eyes, the sun has moved. And two faces are staring at me from an odd angle, on the ground somewhere. They looked more scared than I feel, because at that moment I am just relieved that someone else is there – someone who can take over, make the decisions which need to be made.

'It's alright lovely, we'll have you out of there in no time.'

They talk, quickly, quietly, and I catch the odd scrap, something about fetching help. I don't see either of them going anywhere though, but someone must go to raise the alarm because then they are back at my side, and while they wait, they chatter. I'm content to listen as they discuss the weather and their work, and how difficult the war is making things – their voices are soothing, like a balm; in my head telling me that there is no immediate danger to be concerned about. I gather they are both sheep farmers, but that they have turned over strips of ground to potatoes and carrots and whatever other vegetables they can raise. They supply the local shop they tell me, eventually remembering that I am a silent party to the conversation. 'And the neighbours – there's plenty for them too. No need for coupons here,' they say.

'You need a cup of tea?' One of them, the one with the battered hat, looks at me directly for the first time. 'I could get my missus to bring something over?'

I'm parched, I realise. I can't see my watch, but it seems like hours since I sat down with the other girls and tucked into slabs of toast and big mugs of tea. I nod, suddenly angry that this will all be put down to the fact that I'm a woman, proving we're incapable. Yet at the same time, feeling very sorry for myself - perhaps because I can see no way that the man might transfer my needs to his wife, and I sniff loudly at the impossibility of the whole thing. But the man in the hat has already stepped away, and I hear him whistle, loud and shrill. For a moment nothing moves; even the bird seems to have disappeared. But then, as I try to still the panic in my stomach, the sound of feet thudding on impacted soil reaches me. I can't turn enough to see, but the man is calling out instructions to someone.

'Roy, get your ma to make a flask. Run it back down here – soon as you can lad.' He pauses, and I'm guessing that the boy is transfixed by what he is seeing. 'Come on, quick sticks lad – this poor lady is dying for a cup of tea.' As though it's the most normal thing in the world to be ordering drinks for a pilot who is wedged at an angle in a crashed plane – and a woman at that. 'Oh, and Roy, tell her to wrap a bit of that cake she's been keeping – the one she thinks I don't know about!' He laughs, a strong satisfied laugh and moves closer to me. 'Won't be long, maid, he'll be back afore you know it.'

The two men walk away from me, but their voices are still within hearing distance. They seem to be assessing my situation, and I can feel the plane lurch as they lean on one of the wings; my stomach lurches with it, at the thought of the whole thing sliding further down the hill, or going up in flames, but they seem unfazed. One of them must have found a log, perhaps, or a bit of old fencing, but something big enough, strong enough, to stand on. Because the next thing I know, he has stepped up, closer to my face, and begins pulling and pushing at the cockpit door. 'How does this work then?' he asks. 'Does it need a lever moving or a button pushing?'.

'It's just here,' I say, trying unsuccessfully to point with my chin. 'But I can't reach it.' A tear runs down my cheek and I am furious. Some of the RAF men insist that ATA stands for "Always Terrified Airwomen" and now I've damn-well proved them right. I am angrier still that I can't even sweep the tears away.

'Don't you fret miss,' the man says, turning away, looking at a bird soaring over our heads – and another tear, two, run down my face at his touching tactfulness. 'Help'll be here before you know it.'

And it is. No sooner has Roy returned with the flask and the cake, than there is a commotion of voices, calling and breathless and running and shouting orders. I sit, as helpless as a cow in sand, while they push and hack and pull – both at me and the plane. At some point they move enough of the bodywork to get proper access to me, and drag me painfully from the wreckage.

I lay on the ground, breathing heavily, yet nonetheless squirming with embarrassment, wanting to be anywhere else. Not here, but not back at base having to explain what has gone wrong, and why I haven't delivered the precious plane like I have a dozen and more times before. I want to hide my face in my hands but I can't even do that. My left hand, now that I can see it, is turned like a broken branch, away from its true line, and won't move anywhere near my face, no matter how much I will it.

A stretcher appears, an old sagging canvas, held precariously on two poles. They lift me, surprisingly gently, onto it, and four of the rescuers, including my two men, carry me to a waiting van. I feel like a Post Office package, a parcel to be delivered, with my destination already decided. I close my eyes, hopelessly trying to avoid the barrage of questions which is coming my way.

'What's your name then dear?' A woman, the only one amongst this band of men, leans in and speaks, efficiently, brusquely, but not unkindly.

'Eva,' I manage to squeeze out. 'Eva,' I can only repeat.

'Well, Eva, we'll get you patched up in no time, don't you fret.'

But I am more worried about the damned plane than my own battered bones.

A GOOD OLD SORT

Martha paused as she crossed from the promenade and onto the scrubby grass between town and sea. A figure was standing close to the beach hut, but just far enough away from her to be indistinguishable. It wasn't the fisherman, Ted, or even Carl, she decided, as she screwed up her eyes, trying to focus on the detail. The thought jolted her that it might be Martin Andrews; and despite the plan – desire even – to talk to him, to find out more, Martha felt a bird's wing of panic fluttering in her chest. Perhaps he had sought her out so that he could demand to know what in God's name she and Laura were doing? She pictured his face, thrusting an inch from hers, the spit of his threats spotting her skin as he warned her against stepping in where she wasn't wanted.

The image reined in any desire to speak, and she continued to watch from across the street, fingers fiddling blindly with the handles of her bag.

The figure was dressed in a shapeless waterproof jacket, a faded navy blue with streaks of mud adorning the back and sleeves. Despite the mildness of the day, the hood was up, making it impossible to see a face – or to establish whether the wearer was male or female. Whoever they were, they were pacing up and down, stopping every few moments to look along the row of huts.

You can't stand here all day, Martha told herself. Either go home or go and face the music.

She decided to face the music.

Striding across the grass, she nodded good mornings to holidaymakers and a dog walker, as if she hadn't even noticed the figure until she was almost at the door of her hut.

'Morning,' Martha called out casually, as if it were just another sightseer, taking in the views of the hills and the harbour, admiring the beach.

'Ms Townsend, isn't it?'

The familiarity from the stranger jolted Martha, and she snapped a glance directly into the face of the visitor. It was a woman, although the leathery brownness of her skin and the tattered straggles of salt-set hair could have passed her for either sex.

'Yes…' Martha hesitated, not sure that she liked the disadvantage of being known, but not knowing the stranger. 'Is there a problem?'

'Saw you moving in t'other day. I was walking my dog.' The latter words were quickly attached, like a tail to the others, as if Martha might have otherwise thought that the woman was pestering her.

'I was, yes.' Martha was reluctant to say more.

'I hear you were trying to get in touch with the previous owner.' She nodded towards the beach hut. It wasn't a question but a statement of fact.

Martha felt a tingling on the back of her neck, that the story might be creeping forward in some, as yet unknown, way.

'Do you know her?' She played for time, trying to work out why this woman was asking.

'Friend, of sorts. Family friend, suppose you'd say. More mother's than mine. Haven't spoken for some while. Wanted to catch up – old times, that sort of thing. But that carer of hers, giving everyone the cold shoulder, you know …' The woman looked directly at Martha for the first time. 'Something important you needed to discuss with her, was there?'

Martha stretched herself upright, irritated at the interference, but the woman continued.

'Maybe we can help each other. See if between us we could get to speak to the woman…'

Martha was confused by the stranger. Her manner seemed to dart like a dragonfly from abrupt to conciliatory. 'I'm sorry, I don't really …' she hesitated, wanting to ask what business it was of this stranger's, but realising that Eva was none of her own business either. 'Can I ask why? Why do you want …?'

The woman butted in, jumping ahead of Martha's thoughts. 'Questions. Mother left more questions than answers when she … well, family history, can't say more yet.' She hesitated, apparently considering where to go with the conversation. 'Things need sorting, story to get to the bottom of. Now's the time, before it's too late.' The woman took in Martha's confusion.

'Alzheimer's. Getting the better of the old lady. If we don't talk soon...' She allowed the words to be caught by the breeze, as she gazed out to sea. When she looked back at Martha, she was holding out her hand. Martha reached forward on a reflex, but her fingers almost recoiled as the woman thrust a filthy scrap of paper at her. Martha was about to drop it, disgusted by the stains, but noticed the number scrawled across it.

'Let me know when you're ready, we'll get a meeting set up.' And with that the woman walked away.

Martha fiddled around with the lock on the hut; her hands were shaking. What the hell had just happened? A complete stranger was offering to help her; and she didn't even know the woman's name she realised, as she looked again at the revolting scrap of paper.

She slumped into the wicker chair, shaking her head. Nothing made sense, and just for a moment she wished that Laura was here. 'But she's not,' Martha spoke out loud, 'And *you* need to get a grip'. She pushed herself up and collected coffee and milk and made herself a large mug, taking it out onto the narrow veranda which edged the grass-strewn sand.

'You okay there?'

Martha had been miles away, trying to unpick the tangle of threads in her mind. She smiled as she saw Ted, holding his own cup of something, gazing out to sea as he spoke. He wasn't one for eye contact she had noticed.

'Yeah. Yes - sorry – I'm fine, thanks. Just got a lot going round in my head.'

'Not much luck with the old lady then?'

Martha frowned, lost for words. 'Not exactly,' she began, but Ted was already continuing.

'Saw Hilly Farrant here a while ago.'

Martha looked up, struggling to find words about the woman that might not be offensive.

'Good ol' sort is Hilly,' he went on. 'Don't you be put off - looks like she's been through more than one hedge backwards,' he laughed. 'And she's not best friends with her bath either, is she? But she's okay, is Hilly. She'll see you right.'

And with that he wandered off, checking the paintwork which Carl had previously undertaken.

SOMETHING MORE SUBSTANTIAL

Martha went back into the hut. 'What on earth is going on here?' she muttered to herself as she rinsed out the mug. She felt like she was in some sort of time-slip where everyone was on a completely different page of the story. She couldn't help but laugh to herself at all the characters who had suddenly come into her previously solitary life, as she searched for the tea towel. And then she remembered the bag.

She scrabbled under the sink, pulling out the old box and reaching back. The bag rustled between her fingers as she dragged it forward. She took it to the table and tipped out the contents.

What she had been expecting were more pages of letters. But she could feel inside the bag something more substantial than the torn pieces she had previously discovered. What she got instead was a small bright-yellow folder. It seemed to Martha a long time since anyone had needed to take rolls of film to the chemist to be developed, and the little wallet brought back childhood memories of waiting impatiently for holiday snaps to materialise.

She eagerly flipped open the folder in her hand and removed the contents.

There were several pictures – not of the same set, evidently, for a couple had deckled edges while another was straight-cut. That one was larger, the others only a few centimetres of white-bordered picture. But it was obvious that they belonged together. A young woman, sitting on the slope of a sand dune in a tight-waisted summer dress; a man in a too-large shirt, posed self-consciously on a rocky outcrop; a picture of the two people together, strolling on a promenade.

This was them; Martha was sure of it. And the thought that these were the people whose voices she had been trying to reconstruct from their written words made her skin prickle. Here they were, looking up at her, and she could feel her pulse racing. She gazed at the images until she was lost in them, scanning the backgrounds, examining every detail of their faces, trying to find a clue which might tell her more about these people and the letters they had written. But there was nothing. Reluctantly Martha slid them back into the yellow paper wallet and put it into her bag. She tipped up the paper bag to see if there might be anything else – but no; all of the treasure had been in the folder, and for the moment she had to be content with that.

As she put the box back in the cupboard, she wondered if they had been in their hiding place the whole time … but could think of no other explanation for their presence. Someone – the someone who had brushed and swept the cobwebs in the small hut, before handing they keys over to the estate agent – had presumably been unaware of their existence, otherwise they would no doubt have taken them away, or thrown them straight into the dustbin, having no idea of their significance.

But the thoughts kept coming – if the photos had been here all the time, since the 1940s, then what had happened to the beach hut in all that time? Had no-one else used it in sixty-odd years? And why hadn't the old lady been here in all that time herself, to recover her belongings?

NO NONSENSE

Martha's thoughts were interrupted by the sudden sound - a drumming, like marbles in a tin. Rain. It hadn't rained since she'd had the hut, and Martha had never heard noise like it. She sat for a while, enjoying the sound, taking some comfort from the world continuing to do what it had to do, despite what was going on in her own small life; but eventually she became restless, casting around once more for something she could do until the showers passed, and she noticed again the scrap of dirty paper which had been thrust upon her.

Hilly. Strange name; short for Hilary she guessed, although the woman looked nothing like a Hilary. She was one of those women who had forsaken all modern concerns – appearance, clothes, make up – who seemed completely comfortable in her own version of the world, even if that involved unwashed hair or mud-streaked coats. Martha found women like her disconcerting; larger than life, no-nonsense, no sympathy. But she *had* been sympathetic, Martha remembered, about the old lady, had shown concern about what was happening in the woman's life.

She grabbed her mobile phone on an impulse and input the number from the scrap of paper. It rang for so long that Martha was about to cut the call off, but just as her finger hovered the ringing stopped.

'Yes?'

'Oh, sorry – is that – um - Ms Farrant?' There was silence at the other end. 'This is Martha – Martha Townsend – we spoke earlier, at the beach huts…'

'Yes. Fine. Had some funny callers of late. You wanted to meet?'

Martha was taken aback by the abruptness, but pushed on. 'Yes…yes please.'

And so they arranged that Martha would visit Hilly's home, up on the moor. "Less interruption up here," Hilly had said, and for no apparent reason the words had brought a frown to Martha's face. She decided immediately that Laura would have to go with her, although what Hilly would make of her sister, and vice versa, she had no idea.

ROOT OF ALL EVIL

'You're far too rash,' Laura snapped, striding out onto the concrete driveway where her car was parked. It was obvious, in her mind, that there was no question of taking Martha's, still full of empty boxes and rubbish.

'What on earth did you agree to that for?' She slammed the door, and fixed her eyes on Martha; in the close proximity of the car the glare disturbed the air between them. 'And more to the point, why rope me in as well? Although I have to say, if you're going to visit a madwoman …'

Her diatribe continued, all the way along the street, up onto the main road, and was still with them, trailing along with the trees and the bushes on either side, as they climbed the steep road up onto the moors. Martha had switched off; her sister's voice was just a wasp's buzz in the back of her mind. She was thinking about the old lady, and about what she would say to her when they eventually met; about whether Hilly would be an asset or a liability, whether Laura and Hilly would destroy each other before the day was out.

'Surely this isn't it?' Laura's voice interrupted her thoughts, and Martha looked in the direction her sister was indicating. In front of them stood an old farm building which had long since lost its chocolate-box charm. What had once been cream walls were now stained from the bottom up with red soil splashes, the roof dipped and curved like a stormy sea with two chimneys desperately hanging on, hoping no strong winds would come their way.

The sisters looked at each other, both very obviously thinking that turning around and finding the nearest watering hole would be a better idea. But it was too late. Hilly was there, resplendent in oversized wellington boots, striped trousers and a sweater which might once have been blue but was now streaked red in a similar style to the walls. She marched across the yard, kicking the muddy puddles ahead of her, shooing away two black and white, red-stained dogs and a chicken.

'Come in, come in, kettle's on the hob.'

Laura glared again at Martha, who had bitten her lip to swallow a grin.

'Chop, chop, kettle's boiling.'

They followed like chastised children, picking their way across the muddy yard, stopping abruptly as they reached the doorway. House martins were flying in and out of the broken skylight above the entrance, and there were streaks of their mess across the kitchen floor. The farmhouse table which dominated the room was covered in an assortment of crockery, as though someone had been part way through sorting cupboards, but had given up five years ago.

'Mugs okay?' Hilly said, pulling tea-stained crockery, which might once have been blue, from the sink.

The sisters nodded silently, already looking around for a receptacle in which they could tip their drinks.

The conversation though was an improvement on the hospitality. Hilly, it seemed had known the old lady at various times during her life. 'Originally a contact of mama's,' she gabbled. 'Not entirely sure in what capacity – wartime connection though.' But "short of friends" seemed to be the gist of Hilly's summary. 'Both of us outside of the usual social round.'

'So, you just wanted to get back in touch?' Martha managed eventually to break into Hilly's scattergun style of conversation.

'Well that, and that odious man – something peculiar there.' She slurped at the contents of her mug. 'More coffee?'

Martha assumed she was talking about the nephew – wanted to ask more, but the conversation galloped ahead.

'No – we're fine, honestly – had one just before we left actually,' Laura squeezed in.

'And you then?' Hilly said, pouring more hot water into their mugs, looking between the two of them. 'What's your story?'

Martha hadn't decided how much they should tell Hilly at this stage, but before she could commit to anything Laura had stepped in.

'Well to start with Martha just wanted to know a bit more about her beach hut – my sister has always fancied herself as a bit of an amateur historian …'. Laura rolled her eyes conspiratorially at Hilly. 'But then of course we heard about this nephew – what's he called …?' Laura put on a helpless face, tutting at her supposed poor memory.

'Andrews. It's the Andrews lad you're talking about.' Hilly butted in. 'Never trusted him; met him as a child. Eva's brother's boy, but no love lost there. Hadn't seen hide nor hair of him for years, and then suddenly - spectre at the feast.'

'But isn't he – the lad …' Laura tried to pull the conversation back. '… I thought he was – well - an adult?'

Martha had never seen this ability of her sister's - to take on the persona of the ingenue, the one with supposedly little understanding of what was going on. She sat back and watched as Laura, apparently artlessly, set the hare running, and elicited information from Hilly with little effort.

'Always an irresponsible child in my eyes,' Hilly continued in full flow on what seemed to be her favourite topic. Martha though managed to squeeze in another question which might be more productive.

'So as soon as the property – the beach hut – came up for sale, he just came out of the woodwork?'

'Not just the beach hut – house as well, if you believe what you hear. Rumour is, the solicitor summoned him – Eva's dementia and all that - and the man didn't need asking twice, to step in and start selling off everything in sight …'

'So – he's Eva's – sorry, I don't know her other name …' More artful Laura.

'Bonfield – Eva Bonfield…'

There was a sharp intake of breath from Martha at the hooking of Eva's surname, like a duck from a fairground game. Laura though continued the conversation with barely a beat missed.

'So, he's Mrs Bonfield's only living relative?'

'Well, supposedly. No certainty.' Hilly slammed her mug down on the table, rattling the dishes with her dislike and leaving a wake of coffee to join the other stains.

'What makes you say that?' Even Laura appeared to be taken aback by the apparent animosity.

'Boy I remember, freckles…carroty hair… skinny as a rake. This one's paunch…' she indicated a protruding belly, '… arrives in the room before he does; sandy hair, pasty-faced.' Hilly paused, considering. 'And that one,' she waved a hand over her shoulder as if passing back in time to the child, 'He wouldn't come running for anyone, from what I remember.'

'But if there was money involved …' Laura started to say. And it occurred to Martha that Hilly's description indicated that she had seen the man, and quite recently.

'Well – root of all evil – they do say that.' And Hilly sat back on her chair, as though that was the final word on the matter.

BETWEEN THE LINES

'Well, that's brilliant. We now seem to have more questions than we started with,' Laura launched straight into her thoughts, even before she had reached out a hand to turn the ignition. 'So it would be really helpful if we …'

'Actually …' The only way Martha could squeeze a word in was to talk over the top of her sister. 'It was you who was brilliant …'

'Well, I was just going to say …'

'In less than ten minutes you managed to winkle all sorts of stuff out of Hilly – not least of which is Eva's surname. It would probably have taken me for ever …'

'That's all very well.' Laura was never one to be coy about compliments. 'But what I *was* going to say was that we could actually now do with speaking to this Mr Andrews, because things don't sound as straightforward as they first appeared. And to the old lady as well, if she's not too gaga …'

'Laura!' Martha was horrified at her sister's callousness. 'That's definitely not the word to use.

And any of us could find ourselves going down that awful route, given a few more years …'

'Yes, yes, poor choice – you're quite right. I take it back. But you know what I mean.' She pulled out of the side road rather too sharply and an oncoming farm lorry screamed its horn. 'But you might at least get the true version of events from him … and it would be fascinating to hear what *she* had to say about the letters …'

Martha, who had been holding tightly to the passenger strap, was glad to see that Laura had slowed down a bit, but her thoughts still didn't seem to be entirely on the road. 'Do you think there's something in what she was saying – Hilly – you know, about him not being the same person?'

Martha had been mulling over the same thought. 'Well, I don't think so. For a start, which of us hasn't changed since we were a child? I mean, you look completely different to that chubby great thing in Mum and Dad's photos.' She carried on before the pout on Laura's face could turn into an argument. 'I mean, you look so much better now than you did as a child – so why shouldn't Martin Andrews look worse?'

Laura shrugged in vague agreement. 'I suppose red hair could turn mousy or sandy as the years move on,' she said. 'And as for the paunch – well, you should see Michael without any clothes to hide all his lumps and bumps …'

Martha would rather not have thought of her brother-in-law in that way, or any man at the moment for that matter. She pondered again Hilly's picture of Martin – and wasn't sure that catching up with him was their best course of action, or at least, catching up with him before they had something more concrete to talk about. 'Maybe we should talk to Eva first,' she said, staring out of the window at the disconcerting blur of hedgerows running past on either side of them, like emerald-clad bodyguards.

It was only then, when they were near to home, that the question dangled infuriatingly in front of them both - that the purpose for their visit to Hilly Farrant was still outstanding.

'Hang on a minute … weren't you supposed to set up a meeting, the two of you, arranging to visit Eva together?' Laura sighed loudly. 'For heaven's sake Martha, wasn't that the whole point of us going up to that – that – hillbilly place you've just dragged me to?' Laura continued on one of her rants, peppering her words with "I can't believe's" and "Did you see the state of's".

But Martha had already removed herself from the conversation, thinking that she'd like to put together as complete a picture as she could of Eva and the letters before Hilly too remembered that they had still to arrange the proposed visit. She looked up in surprise when Laura bumped the car onto her driveway and waited for her to jump out.

'You are going to make sure that you ring Hilly - get this meeting set up?' Laura shouted as she executed a perfect three-point turn to manoeuvre her way back onto the main road.

'Actually… I think I'll try the museum first; get a bit of local wartime history, try to find something about "the good old days" that I can get Eva talking about.' She waved as her sister accelerated onto the street, narrowly avoiding a black cat.

She knew she was prevaricating, but Martha acknowledged that her opportunities to talk to the old lady might be few and far between, and she didn't want to let any opportunity slip through her fingers. The idea of the museum though had been a bit of a red herring for Laura's benefit; what Martha really wanted to do was to have another look at the letters – and the photos – and get clear in her own mind where this whole thing was going.

She pulled the letters from their safe space in the kitchen drawer and set them out on the table. Next she took the photos from their yellow paper wallet and lined them up alongside.

There, laid out for all the world to see, was a love affair – a passionate, hasty, immediate, impulsive affair.

But a love affair which had presumably not ended well. Those words - angry bitter disappointed ones – were not standing up in the dark blue ink, but they were surely hidden somewhere between the lines, their presence was most definitely held in the anger which had torn them so finally into shreds.

For a moment Martha felt she should go no further. Looking at the passion and the intimacy which seemed to be behind the letters she felt like a voyeur peering into a poorly curtained bedroom window. It really was none of her business. And after all these years, what did it actually matter? It was something which had been and gone, a love which had been celebrated and then shattered, into all those pieces. If Eva had wanted the world to know, she would have told someone. And she hadn't. So maybe she too should do what had been originally intended, and let the pieces go? Martha visualised herself allowing the pieces to flee from her hand, to float on the afternoon breeze, fluttering over the water, then sinking into the waves. But at the moment she didn't have the courage or the inclination to let go of something which was keeping her own life on track.

In the time Martha had been contemplating the lovers' affair the world outside had turned darker. It wasn't just the evening taking up its place in the world; storm clouds had started to gather, elbowing out the patches of blue sky and standing firm. Although she didn't want to see the summer coming to an end, Martha was fascinated by the drama of the changing sky, the bruised colours, the character of it all; she stood, spectating for an age, allowing her thoughts to wander as she did so.

Whether it was the mindlessness of watching something so completely out of her control, or the passage of time, Martha was suddenly aware of questions fighting for her attention. She slid into a chair at the dining room table and started scribbling, keen to get her thoughts down on paper before they abandoned her. When she had finished, she had several sheets of untidy writing, crossings out and additions, but at least there were things here for her to work on.

In the end, Martha found one of the beautiful notebooks which she kept in the antique chest of drawers. In the past, people had known her liking for them and had bought them as presents, and mostly they were so pretty she had been reluctant to spoil them by actually writing in them, which she knew defeated the object. But today seemed as good a time as any to start using one of them, and hopefully it would be a friendlier touch than heaps of papers, when she came to sit with Eva. Martha had no idea how they were going to deal with the carer who Hilly insisted was keen to keep everybody away, but for the time being she intended to leave that problem for Hilly to sort out. To be honest she had no idea how anyone would argue with the woman – such an imposing figure, with an air of upper-class assurance about her that Martha wouldn't dream of questioning. That, combined with her rapid-fire conversation, presented an intimidating image - enough to make most people squirm on their chairs and happily allow Hilly to dominate events. Martha only hoped that the carer would fall into that "most people" category.

Now that she had her thoughts and her questions ready, Martha was in limbo, with no idea what to do next. She looked around, seeking inspiration. Maybe Laura had been right – maybe she should start doing something about the state of the house. Up until now she hadn't been able to face looking at the belongings which had been hers and Richard's, at things from their shared life.

Her mind wandered, inevitably, back to that day when he hadn't returned. She and Laura had stayed up half the night, most of the time in silence. Laura had suggested television, to take their mind off things, but Martha had known that everything she saw would just underline her predicament. Every ten minutes, she had gone to the window, looked up and down the road, scouring the darkness for any sign of someone who might just be Richard.

The two sisters must have drifted into fitful dozing because the doorbell had startled them into wide-eyed consciousness. Martha had jumped up, tripping on her cardigan which had fallen to the floor. She had kicked it from her foot as she ran to the door. Fumbled with the catch, trying to open up before the lock was fully disengaged.

Michael had stood on the step. He looked at her and it seemed an eternity before he spoke. 'No news, I'm afraid.' And Martha had clutched at the door as Michael walked past. He was too ordinary – everything was too ordinary, in that surreal jumble of an evening.

'What should we do now, do you think?' Laura was saying to Michael, speaking as though Martha wasn't in the room.

'Well, I've tried everywhere I can think.' He sipped his coffee. 'And you've definitely spoken to all the friends?' He asked Laura, not Martha.

'I'm calling the police,' Martha had stood, suddenly decisive. Which in turn had started a train of questions and procedures and more questions.

They had found him, of course, eventually. His employers had confirmed that he'd booked leave from work – several weeks when his absence could go unquestioned. But with access to bank card and phone records, the police had tracked him efficiently enough. And established, in the process, the apex of a whole heap of things that Martha hadn't known about. A separate bank account; ditto a mobile phone – this time one that was apparently switched on and charged, and very much ready for action; much like a Richard that she didn't know.

He had been only fifty miles away, and they had gone there, the police. To check for themselves that he was alive and well, and not coerced or hoodwinked or confined. He was not. And was not wanting to make contact with her either, it seemed.

'He has his reasons – missing people often do.' The sergeant spoke wearily, as if the mess of other peoples' lives was too much for him. 'But he's made it clear that he doesn't want to be "found", and we have no reason to continue our enquiries.'

And Martha had wished that the lost and found of her own life could be so easily decided. How someone could supposedly love you until Friday, and then turn their back on you completely on Saturday, for good and for ever, was beyond her. Her head and her heart had been in pieces, trying to deal with it all – the chasm which had opened up in her life, and which she was now supposed to find the rubble and bricks and stones to fill; to make life whole again. But more than anything, the momentous question was still there, suspended over her head – why?

And so, even now, Martha wasn't sure she was ready to sort out their belongings. What if Richard were to appear at the front door, maybe next week or next month, wanting to know what had happened to his possessions? So, maybe they should stay where they were, for the time being?

But perhaps she could at least clear away some of the remainder of refuse bags which she and Laura had filled when they had tidied up. Martha went through to the front room and looked at what was piled there – far more stuff than any one person really needed, and she hadn't even noticed that any of it had been removed from her day-to-day life. With a sudden boost of enthusiasm, she took the bags which were obviously rubbish and dropped them emphatically into the dustbin, ready to be collected on Monday morning; there were bits and pieces too good for the bin and Martha carried them out to the boot of the car, determined not just to move them from one room to another and back again. She would take them to the charity shop tomorrow. There were several piles of books – something which Martha was always reluctant to part with - but she sorted quickly through the titles, tossing them either on a "keep" or a "to go" pile before she had chance to change her mind. More bags and boxes into the boot, and her temporary enthusiasm had brought a sense of energy. She looked around the cleared room and felt invigorated, lighter. She would do the same in the upstairs rooms, perhaps tomorrow. But her bedroom – their bedroom – might be a much more difficult venture.

ALL THAT WAS NEEDED
EVA

He is trying to fix a bolt, a small brass one, but a bolt nonetheless. The lock on the garden door is easily overcome and Eva is increasingly prone to wander. But even the whine of the drill is not enough to stifle her urge to recount her story, and eventually he puts down his tools and listens.

'I didn't remember much until I woke up in a bed - people staring down at me. And a nurse, telling me what I couldn't do, pulling me upright, punching pillows. It was obvious they didn't have a clue who I was – kept calling me by the wrong name, and I wanted to say "No, that's not me," but they carried on talking as though I was just part of the bedclothes.'

Because you see, I had no voice. There didn't seem to be anything wrong with my face or my throat, but my head just decided it would stop talking. They probably have some grand name for it these days, but back then it was just "shock". So, I couldn't tell them about the crash, or where I'd been going – anything really.'

'At first, they thought I shouldn't be moved. I gathered, from what they were saying, that I'd been taken to the local hospital – you know, that big old building, you know the one I mean…?'

Martin nods, knowing exactly the cottage hospital building she means, now standing forlorn and empty in the high street.

'I don't know how long I stayed there. I wasn't totally with it, some of the time.'

The irony of the situation isn't lost on him – with the same description equally applicable to her current predicament.

'It was a while anyway, and although I was getting better on the outside …' Eva rubs a finger to her cheek, to the almost-invisible scar hinting at her story. 'In here…' she points to her head, 'Well they didn't really know what to do about that…'

'Eventually one of the nurses who had more about her than those doctors, suggested that maybe rest was all that was needed. To be honest I think they wanted the bed – there were more wounded and airmen coming in, and it wasn't the biggest place. Anyway, they scooped me out of bed one morning, made a big fuss of dressing me – goodness knows where the clothes came from, but it was painful I can tell you, all that pushing and pulling. And they stuck me in one of these …' she says, banging her hand against her wheelchair.

'They wheeled me to the front door and I gulped in the fresh air like I'd never breathed it before, making the most of it before they took me back indoors.'

'But I was …' Eva bangs her hand on her lap, trying to bring forth the words. '…definite I wasn't going to stay in that chair, that much I did know, so I was thrilled when they put me in the back of an ambulance. We didn't go far though – just up the road,' she points into the distance. 'Delivered me to the door like a lost parcel, and off they drove.' She looks around for something and he holds out a cup to her. She licks her lips at the sweetness of the elderflower cordial.

'But as they got me out and turned me round, my breath was taken away, I can tell you. I was expecting another hospital, but in front of me was the most wonderful thing I'd ever set eyes on – because they'd taken me to the castle.'

Eva laughs at the disbelief on his face. 'They did that you know – in those days, in the war. They took over big houses and used them for soldiers and airmen who were recovering …'

Martin looks at her, still baffled, but the momentum of the story carries her forward.

'It was wonderful, but the worst possible place to be – in one of these.' Again, she rattles the arm of the wheelchair. 'Steps everywhere; I thought there was no hope of me staying for more than five minutes, but they called two young men who gathered up me and the chair as if we were just a box of groceries, and they charged up the entrance stairs, and put me down in the grand hallway. Stags' heads, shields, all sorts. And then this woman – voice like a film star – glided down the staircase, welcoming me like a long-lost friend. "We'll soon have you out of there," she says, pointing to the chair, and so of course we hit it off straightaway.' She sips at the cordial, hands back the cup.

'They made up a room for me – don't ask me where, but somewhere on the ground floor, and then they got me walking – just a few steps at first, but it wasn't long before I was getting on like a house on fire.' She smiles at her past success. 'Well, I can tell you, being able to move about, that did more for in here …' she points again to her head, '… than any medicine bottle would have done.' Eva takes a breath. 'And with the walking, my voice came back. Strange – one day there was nothing, the next it was back, as if nothing had happened.'

'After that they moved me in with the housekeeper. She had rooms up in the attic, and there was one that they'd used for visiting ladies' maids, way back…'

'Why on earth did they put you up there?' Martin interupts.

'Full of men – the rest of the house. They were using it for officers. The other ranks were outside of course, in tents, on the field. But it wouldn't have been right to put me with the men, would it, so they put me in the only place they could find, I suppose – with the staff.' Eva sniffs, looks around for a tissue. 'Nice little room it was – flowery wallpaper and a fireplace, and a view of the hills …' She blows her nose, gazing into the distance as though still seeing the room for the first time.

'Not that they expected me to do any work of course,' she suddenly continues, 'Although they couldn't help themselves sometimes, wanting cups collecting or the odd bit of dusting. I didn't mind though, it gave me something to do – and it meant I didn't have to keep telling my story over and over. I didn't want to have to think about me, or the wasted plane lying in pieces on the hillside.' Eva blows her nose noisily, and continues.

'And then the woman – lady of the house, I can't remember her name – she suggested walking in the gardens. "Fresh air will do you the world of good," she insisted.

'I was worried to begin with – everywhere you went was either uphill or down, but I wasn't going to give in. The first time I only managed a stroll, but after that I went a bit further each day.'

'One day I went off down the lane that leads to the sea. It was further than I thought though, and I had to stop for a rest. And then I heard this voice coming from the other side of the hedge. 'You look a darned sight better than last time I saw you,' it says. 'Didn't think you was going to make it when we pulled you free.' And the man tells me that it was him and his friend Harry who had spotted my plane. 'We thought you was coming down on our heads at one point…Got my heart fair going,' he says. 'We could see the plane was in a bad way – thought the whole thing might go up in flames, but Harry got us organised, and we got you out.'

I didn't say anything – couldn't – and he says 'Don't remember any of it then? Probably just as well. Well, you look after yourself miss – no rush for you to get back to them planes.' And off he walks, whistling some tune.

But his words got to me, you know, about going back to the Air Transport Auxiliary and flying, and for a moment I was all prepared to go and pack my bags. I was thinking there must be things I should be doing while I waited for my arm to heal. Perhaps I could even do a bit of flying if I took it easy … But as I turned to go, there was someone else walking down the lane towards me.

ANYTHING IN PARTICULAR?

The doorway into the museum was low and the door itself stiff, as if the building and its occupants would rather that people didn't actually enter. But inside, Martha was met by a marvellous assortment of rural ephemera – cider presses and wooden washing tubs, millstones and butter churns.

A woman with a face not much older than Martha's, but with what appeared to be her mother's clothes, was busy at the desk trying to inspire a young family to go and explore the moors. The younger child was fascinated by the map the assistant was holding up, and butted in. 'What happens when we get to the end of this road?' he said, pointing to a dead end at the top of the hill. 'You fall off the end of the world!' she said, winking at the older brother. Eventually she satisfied them and they squeezed past Martha, fighting with the door to get out.

'Sorry for the wait my dear. What can I help you with?'

Martha had been wrapped up in the woman's story, of falling off cliffs and where they might find the ponies and the wilder corners of the moor, and struggled to bring to mind even one of the dozen or so questions she had planned to ask. She smiled feebly, commenting on the weather, until eventually she dragged something from the depths of her mind.

'I was just wondering – do you have any information about this area during the Second World War?'

'Anything in particular?' The woman beamed encouragingly, pulling a shapeless cardigan round her shoulders. 'We've got quite a bit actually.'

'What about the forces. Were there any troops stationed in this area?'

'Oh, there certainly were.' The woman was already moving enthusiastically to one of the displays at the back of the crowded room. 'There's photos here, and various bits written more recently about troop activities along the coast and up on the Hill. The Americans were here in great numbers towards the end of the war, practicing for D Day, I understand.'

Martha's face must have shown that these weren't the kind of stories she was looking for, but the woman was undeterred. 'And then we've got some local diaries as well – you know, people keeping a record of their everyday lives in wartime – a bit like the National Register exercise, but these are local, and we've got quite a few in the archives here.'

Martha hadn't heard of the National Register, had no idea what that might entail, but she nodded encouragingly, hoping there was more to come.

'There's folders of photographs as well,' the woman, who had already scooted to the other end of the room, called out. 'Dated and labelled – well, most of them anyway.' She seemed pleased that at least part of their display was in good order. Martha joined the woman and gazed at the wide range of folders and stacks of paper, and then at the wall display.

'It might take me a while to unearth the diaries,' the woman was saying, moving boxes, creating wafts of dust. 'Did you want to look at them today?'

Martha though was already absorbed. One of the photos on the display board showed a group of men in uniform, standing in the grounds of what she thought was probably the local castle. 'Are these RAF people?' she asked the woman. 'And is this Moyons Castle – where they're standing?'

'Yes to Moyons Castle, and no to the British airmen – they're American. Eleanor Saltrey – the lady of the manor so to speak – opened up the castle as a recuperation hospital during the war, and apparently small groups of American officers were taken there. I bet they thought they were in seventh heaven, being holed up in an old English castle for a few weeks.' The woman looked dewy-eyed at the nostalgia of the story. But Martha had another romance in her head.

'Are there any records anywhere – you know, of the names of the airmen who were here?' Martha pulled her gaze away from the photographs and turned to the woman.

'Not sure about individual names, to be honest. There'll be names of regiments or squadrons, and probably the odd detail attached to a photo, but not lists or anything, not that I've seen anyway. Only on the stuff the American Society sent through … were you looking for someone in particular?'

There were so many new names and lines of information being thrown at Martha – National Registers, American Society - that she was in a daze as to which to pursue. 'Well, sort of,' she said vaguely. 'What about what you were saying about the castle? Would there be any records of those who stayed there?'

'Oh, I don't know about that dear. It's not something we have here, and I suspect that nothing formal was kept at the castle itself. From what I can gather, Mrs Saltrey was a bit of a party animal – she probably looked on the officers as an ongoing band of house guests.' Martha sighed, unintentionally, but enough to raise more positivity from the keen-to-be helpful woman. 'But they do have quite a few volunteers up there these days – you know, showing people round, telling them a bit of the history, and I'm sure I heard the other day that some of them have recently been undertaking a bit more research on the castle. They might have uncovered more details – certainly worth a call anyway, I would have thought.'

Martha nodded as she glanced again at the photos on the board. Plenty of smiling airmen, but no names; nothing which jumped out at her. Perhaps she was driving down an ever-narrowing track with the idea that she might just happen upon the young man from the photo she'd found at the beach hut - an idea which could rapidly find her faced with a locked five-bar gate.

She was about to leave, thank the woman for her help, when another thought occurred to her. 'What about women? Were there any women stationed around here?'

'Well, there were members of the WAAF working at the radio station, up on North Hill.' The woman looked at Martha, as though expecting her to know exactly what she was talking about. 'All a bit "hush-hush" at the time though, so I'm not sure there'd be much in the way of records available…' Her voice faded as she realised that this was another "no-show" of information. 'Tell you what – give me a day or two and I'll pull out those diaries for you.' She pointed to the piles of papers which had fallen from some of the boxes. 'It'll do us good to have a sort-out,' she laughed. 'Call in next time you're passing – or leave me your number and I'll give you a call.'

Martha did just that, taking one last look around as she moved to leave. She was sure that there were answers to some of her questions curled up inside boxes, pressed between leaves of books and albums, but it might take her a month of Sundays to unearth them.

TANGLED STRING

Martha wandered down the high street, considering what to do next. She'd been certain that the museum would give her a baton to run with, but now she felt as if she'd been left at the starting blocks. Two women came out of a shop, and held the door open, assuming that Martha would be going inside. Indecision pulled her in, and she found herself in a small café with gingham tablecloths and ladies stirring gossip with their afternoon tea.

There was one table free, by the window, and Martha slid into the chair facing the street. There was no menu on the table, but an encyclopaedia of choices on a chalk board behind the counter. And an array of glass-domed plates, each containing sponge cake or fruit cake or homemade biscuits. She'd had no intention of eating – had been eating far too much since coming back into the real world, she thought, passing a hand over the slightly rounded belly protruding from her stark hipbones - but the cakes drew her in, and she chose a slice of fruit cake to go with her coffee.

Her thoughts were no more than tangled string; the sort of messy ball you found in the bottom of a drawer, along with wine stoppers and drawing pins and instruction manuals for appliances which had long since moved on to the charity shop. As she put a piece of the spiced fruity cake into her mouth, she tried to find an end of that yarn to pull at, but it seemed that nothing useful would drop into her lap.

Just as she was finishing her drink, Martha became aware of something happening on the other side of the street – somebody waving and gesticulating. Were they pointing at her? She put down the cup and looked again. Yes, someone was beckoning. She paid for her coffee and cake and pulled the door open into the afternoon sunshine, blinding her with its brightness.

It was Hilly – this time in a yellow sou'wester, less mud-spattered than her previous coat but with a definite history.

'Thought that was you – just checking here with Mrs Westerbrook – eyes not what they were.' She carried on her machine-gun chatter, talking to both and neither of them about sheep and a lame horse. Martha couldn't help but look at her watch.

'Yes dear – got to go,' Hilly said, as though it were Martha who had been delaying *her*. The woman turned to leave, then a few paces away called back 'Tuesday – next Tuesday – visiting Eva. Two thirty – see you at the door.' And the yellow splash was off up the street, yelling at a dog which had appeared from nowhere and which now obediently trailed behind her.

'Well, that's told me,' Martha said, watching her go, forgetting that Mrs Westerbrook was still standing with her.

'Take no notice, my dear – just her way that's all. Too late to change Hilly now,' she said, evening up the weight of her two shopping bags, and galvanizing herself into movement.

Martha was left alone on the pavement, thinking that she now needed to add her notes from the museum to her notebook, to see if there was anything else she might be able to talk to the old lady about when they met.

CLEAR A BIT OF SPACE

The front door was ajar. Nevertheless, Martha knocked – a gentle tap, tap, before Hilly could barge in and take over. Martha had visions of her striding in, pushing the door so roughly that it ricocheted against the inside wall. But in actuality, Hilly stood back – stepped off the pavement and into the quiet road as they waited for a response.

Martha tapped again, louder this time, and a voice issued from within. 'Come in – the door should be open …'

They both stood on the threshold, expecting to be challenged by the carer, bustling and shooing and telling them that they shouldn't be there. But there was no-one in the hallway. Martha turned to Hilly who, uncharacteristically silent, just shrugged her shoulders; then as if her decisiveness had suddenly returned, she waved Martha forward, pushing the air along with them.

Eva was sitting in an upright armchair in a crowded room; not untidy Martha noticed, just too full – as if the contents of a much larger house had been squeezed down until every item was gasping for air. The old woman looked up at them, perplexed. They were evidently not who she had been expecting. Each waited for the other to speak.

'Where's my dinner?' Eva eventually piped up. 'Wednesday – Shepherd's Pie – my favourite.'

Silence hung in the room as Eva waited for her answer and Martha scrabbled for words, not wanting to say that it was only Tuesday.

'We're not Meals on Wheels.' Martha took a chance that it was this which had been expected. 'I'm Martha – nice to meet you. And this is Hilly – Miss Farrant. We were just passing …'

Hilly, in the background, snorted at this version of events. But Martha had already decided there was little point in upsetting the woman with more background detail.

'Is it okay if we sit down Mrs Bonfield? – or can we call you Eva?' Martha was conscious that she was rolling too many thoughts together, that as well as the surprise of complete strangers marching into her home, Eva was now being showered with questions.

Eva though, didn't seem to have the same misgivings. She nodded, seemingly unconcerned. 'Move those papers – put them on the table, clear a bit of space,' she told Martha, shuffling in her armchair to get more comfortable.

Martha picked up a pile of newspapers and Hilly belatedly did the same with a stack of magazines. They settled themselves as Eva looked on, an expression of amusement creeping across her face as Hilly found the delicate chair she had chosen creaking beneath her weight.

'We just thought we'd pop in, have a chat,' Martha began again, still not confident where her conversation was headed. 'It's a lovely house. Have you lived here long?' she said, grasping at the first thought that came into her head.

Satisfaction still lingered on Eva's face as she continued to stare at Hilly on the ill-fitting chair. She looked, thought Martha, like a child who'd just wrong-footed an adult.

'Oh years. I've been here years now. She probably remembers better than me,' Eva waved a hand across at Hilly. Martha was taken aback - that the woman had known all along who Hilly was, but had made no attempt to greet her old acquaintance.

'Came here after I finished my job,' Eva was continuing, 'I was a bit of a nomad back then, parents gone, nothing to tie me anywhere in particular, so I thought I'd come back.' She searched around on the table beside her, filled with pens and puzzle books, packets of indigestion remedies and a plate with a half-eaten biscuit.

'Back?' Martha was aware that the query had come out a little too sharply. 'Had you lived here before then?'

'Well – in a manner of speaking.' Eva smiled at her, then frowned as she looked across at Hilly. 'Can she make us some tea?' she said, peering at Martha.

Martha turned, raising an eyebrow at Hilly, who in turn raised both eyebrows in surprise and irritation. 'Oh, I suppose …'

''Don't want her knowing all my business,' Eva said in a stage whisper, a mischievous smile creeping across her face. 'My parents left me a bit of money – they went in the Blitz you know – and I'd just left it in the bank while I was working – test flights for planes and the like. I'd been trying to decide what to do with it, and then, when I had to find somewhere to go, I thought of Moyon's Quay.'

'You used to fly? … Planes?' Martha was incredulous.

'Air Transport Auxiliary,' Eva said, looking as though the fact should be obvious to any sensible person. And then, as if enough was enough, she tilted her head back on the chair and closed her eyes.

Martha wasn't sure if that was it, that she would hear no more about flying or anything else, but then Eva carried on, eyes still closed.

'I had some good times here, in the war … And some bad times as well…' The space beneath her eyelids filled with tears, and a single one ran down the parched pale skin of her cheek. Nothing more was said for a moment. 'But good times – yes.' She opened her eyes and smiled again, a watery thin smile this time.

The door banged against a chair, and a string of curses ruffled the air as Hilly tried to manoeuvre herself and a tray back into the room. Martha jumped up, pulling the door back, clearing a space on a small gateleg table in the corner. After tea was poured and cups handed out, they settled back into chattering small talk, Martha and Hilly balancing drinks on their laps, until the door flew open once more.

'No – no this is not right. Door should not be open. You are not to be here.' The carer was standing in the doorway, hands on hips, shopping bags at her feet. She looked anxious. 'You must go. Now!' she spoke in heavily accented English, moving to one side, pointing to the front door.

Had the situation not been so charged it would have been comical, Martha thought - a scene from a badly produced play, with lines poorly learnt. She could see though that the young woman was stressed, perhaps blaming herself for the unsecured door, keen to get everything back under control. Martha stood, putting her cup down on the table. 'We only popped in for a chat – thought Eva might enjoy the company,' she said, smiling across at the old woman.

'No – it is not …' the carer hesitated, trying to find the right word. 'Not …permit.' She was red in the face, wiping her hands down the sides of her jeans.

'She's worried about Martin … my nephew,' Eva spoke up. 'He likes to be in charge.'

The young woman looked relieved that she was not going to have to battle Eva as well as the two strangers. She nodded in agreement. 'Yes…not today. Maybe other day. But you must call Mr Martin, must ask him.'

It was obvious to Martha that they weren't going to get any further with the conversation, that their time was indeed up. But Hilly was still firmly planted on the delicate chair. She had been watching the exchange of words to and fro, but only now spoke up. 'We're old friends – Eva and I – go way back. Nothing wrong with me visiting is there?' She stared hard at the carer, and then looked to Eva for support. But Eva was looking out of the window next to her chair, no longer taking any part in the proceedings.

'We'll be going then,' said Martha, as though it had been her idea all along. 'We'll call – arrange another visit,' she said. 'If that's alright with you Eva?'

'I'll see you again,' she turned, smiling again at Martha. 'But not her.' And she waved a dismissive hand at Hilly, before once more turning to look out on the garden.

Well – what d'you make of that?' Hilly spoke as soon as they were back outside. The fact that she had effectively been dismissed by Eva, told not to return, seemed to have passed her by.

'I – well – I can't believe that Eva was a pilot. Do you really think that she was?'

'Lots of women did unexpected stuff back then – needs must and all that, when there's a war on. But what did you make of the carer – bit flighty?'

Martha was dumbfounded that Hilly seemed more interested in the young woman than about Eva's revelations. 'Well, I expect she doesn't want to upset the apple-cart,' Martha prevaricated. 'I mean, she probably needs the work …'

'Yes, yes, but *Mr* Andrews seems to have them both exactly where he wants them. And Eva – she seems resigned to the whole damned thing of being told what to do. As if it's pretty much par for the course.'

Martha hadn't really thought about this until now. But Hilly was right. Eva didn't seem upset or angry – just accepting, as if things were turning out much as she'd expected. And for some reason that made Martha angry – that this woman, who was obviously intelligent, who'd had a life, was allowing the world to order her existence without her opinion or say-so. 'Perhaps it's the Alzheimer's,' Martha pondered, looking over at Hilly. 'Perhaps we're only seeing one side of the story?'

Hilly, who had been marching along at a pace which was making Martha breathless, turned to look at her. 'And perhaps we're not,' she snapped.

The abruptness of her comment shook Martha. 'Well, in that case, it's about time we heard the other side. I'm going to contact Martin Andrews.' And before Hilly could say anything more Martha had turned and was marching down the hill towards the town and home.

OTHER PLANS

Martha's bravado had disappeared as quickly as the sunshine. She had just managed to get to her front door before the clouds decided enough was enough, and emptied themselves onto the streets. And despite the words she had been formulating in her head all the way home, she didn't really know how she was going to proceed in any meaningful way with a call to Martin Andrews. Prevarication gave her permission to sleep on the idea, and that in turn gave her permission to put it off until another day. But Martha had other plans to take the place of Mr Andrews.

'Are you having a party?' Laura had come in via the back door and was looking around the kitchen at the mounds of food and wrappings covering every surface.

Martha, busy trying to wrap egg and tomato sandwiches without the filling making an escape, didn't turn as she spoke. 'Oh, I'm glad you're here. I've been trying to ring you.' She swore as yet another piece of the egg got away.

'Here, let me do it.' Laura took the cling film from Martha's hand, expertly wrapping the sandwiches in one flick of her fingers and holding up the package for inspection.

'Great.' Martha squeezed the word out, irritated that her sister could put her to shame so easily, so often; yet determined not to get upset over an egg sandwich. 'I thought we'd take a picnic,' she said, opening an insulated rucksack and beginning to put things in.

'Take a picnic where? No, don't put the sandwiches at the bottom …' Laura took over once more, ordering the packages and the small containers so that they all fitted neatly into their places in the bag. 'Shall I make a flask?'

'No, I thought we'd get a coffee from the café … that is if you want to come?'

'Well, it might help if I knew where we were going ...'

'Sorry.' The plan was so clear in Martha's own head she'd forgotten that Laura hadn't been part of it all along. 'I thought we'd take a trip to the castle. We haven't been there for ages. It will make a nice change – a day out, just the two of us.'

She could see the questions building on her sister's lips, but to Laura's credit she turned the escaping words into a smile. 'That would be lovely – good idea,' and picked out two apples from the fruit bowl to add to the feast.

The car park was busy and they had to leave the car near the wrought-iron gates of the entrance, but it was a glorious morning with a baby-blue sky and the thinnest of clouds, warm enough to walk without a jacket. The two women puffed their way up the steep hill, stopping at the divide in the pathway. 'Castle or gardens first?' Laura asked, but Martha was already veering towards the gate leading to the woodland grounds.

The meandering path leading down through the trees was interspersed with hydrangeas of varying hues. The sisters walked in silence, enjoying the views as the dappled light fell on them. Eventually they reached the small river, emptier now at the end of the summer, but still rolling and burbling its way down to the sea. The two of them stopped to watch two wagtails, swooping and skimming the water, marvelling at the size of the gunneras dipping their heavy umbrella leaves into the river.

They climbed the arching slope of the ancient stone bridge and, without discussion, both sisters stopped at the top to peer over the sides. Martha sighed, tucking her wayward hair behind her ear, looking over at Laura. 'This might have been the place,' she said quietly.

'What place? What do you mean?'

'Their meeting place - our two lovers, from the letters. Maybe Eva would stand here, just pretending to take in the scenery, and then he would come along the path.' Martha looked wistfully around her. 'They would walk and talk … and eventually they would find themselves at the beach hut,' she added, realising that that location needed to come into the picture as well.

'I think you're getting a bit carried away – just because this is called "Lovers' Bridge" doesn't mean it features in any way whatsoever in Eva's story.'

'But we know …' Martha began.

'We know that Eva did some flying during the war, and that somehow she ended up in this part of the world…' Laura began counting things off on her fingers, 'And we know that there were American airmen based here at the castle for recuperation …but that's about all we do know.'

'Well,' Martha was determined not to be out-argued. 'It's not too much to assume that they were *both* in this area, if the letters being found in the beach hut are anything to go by, and therefore …'

At that moment a family with two boisterous children and a crying baby in a pushchair approached the bridge. The sisters crossed to the other side to make space for them, but it was time enough for Laura to have abandoned her long list of everything they didn't know, and for Martha to take on board that her sister was right.

'Let's get a coffee,' Laura said, looking at Martha's despondent face. 'I might even run to some walnut cake – it always used to be very good here.'

They carried on, stopping briefly to watch the mill wheel churning endlessly before continuing to the café under the trees.

'So –was that your plan all along?' Laura asked as she slid a fork through the large wedge of cake. 'To check out where Eva and her "man" might have spent their days? See if some detail might reveal itself?' Martha could see that her sister was as intrigued as she was, despite herself.

'Well, I thought maybe we might see something, or … or, well I don't actually know, but it just felt like this should be another step in the story.' Martha watched bored children darting in and out of the tables. 'It seems a bit stupid, now we're here,' she said, stirring her coffee unnecessarily.

Laura was quiet for a moment, as she too watched the children. 'Actually, I think it was a good idea.'

Martha looked up, surprised.

'No – really. Even if we don't uncover anything about Eva, it's been good to have a day out.' Laura smiled, then, as if thinking she might be getting a little too sentimental, returned to investigative mode. 'But while we're here why don't we ask someone, a member of staff, if they know anything more about the castle being used for troops during the war? Might as well kill two birds.' She pulled a large piece of walnut from the top of the cake and pushed it into her mouth, looking pleased with herself.

As the two women hovered at the bottom of the castle steps allowing time for a large party to enter, they were approached by a grey-haired woman wearing a volunteer badge.

'Good morning, ladies. Might you be interested in a tour we have starting in five minutes, taking in parts of the castle you wouldn't normally see, like the servants' quarters in the attics?'

The sisters didn't need to consult. There was a simultaneous feeling of serendipity between them.

'If you could just wait to the left of these steps, the guide will meet you there.'

They stood enjoying the sunshine until a petite blonde-haired woman with a clipboard bustled to join the waiting group. Her story-telling immediately drew them in as she provided a general history of the castle, then turned, leading them to a black wooden door at the side of the building.

'This was – still is,' she smiled, 'the "tradesmen's entrance". Staff wouldn't have been permitted to use the main entrance,' she said, pointing to the impressive wooden doors. 'Now, we've got a bit of a climb ahead of us, so I hope you're all feeling fit,' she laughed, leading the group to a spiral staircase to begin their ascent.

A sweaty-faced man with slicked back hair insisted on asking too many questions about the structural state of the building, bragging his own knowledge of cracks and subsidence. Martha could see that even the patient guide was getting frustrated, and in the smallest lull in the man's questioning she managed to squeeze in an enquiry of her own.

'I hear that the castle was opened up as a recuperation hospital during the war,' she said. 'Would they have stayed in the main rooms – or would they have been put up here, with the staff?'

The guide looked grateful for her interception. 'Good question. Yes, Mrs Saltrey was keen to do her bit for the war effort and she had a regular stream of young servicemen staying here – mainly Air Force I understand, English and some Americans too.' She flicked through her notes, after a few moments finding a picture. 'This is one of the few photographs that seem to have been taken.' She held the sheet up so that the whole group could take a look, then handed it to Martha.

Martha was disappointed to see a group of men on the lawn outside the castle, smoking and waving at the camera, all looking very like Kenneth More in a film she had watched about Douglas Bader.

'What about women – were there any women here, WAAF or suchlike?' Martha asked, handing back the photograph.

'Well, strange you should ask that,' the guide said, warming to the topic. 'If you'd have asked me a few weeks ago I would have very definitely said "no", but one of my colleagues has just uncovered some diary entries of Mrs Saltrey's which seem to indicate that there *was* a woman here for a short while.' The guide turned and moved the group along, and for a moment Martha thought that was all they would hear on the matter. But she ushered them into a large square room, crowded with tattered lampstands and bedside cabinets and rolls of abandoned carpet. 'This,' the guide said proudly, 'Was almost certainly where that mystery woman would have stayed. It's part of the housekeeper's suite of rooms – she had a very generous set-up here. And the diary seems to indicate that this mystery woman was given a room – this room, we're pretty sure – for the length of her stay.'

Martha was elated yet dejected. At least one woman seemed to have stayed at the castle during the war; but her heart sank at the guide's use of the word "mystery". 'So there's no record of who this woman was?' she asked, conscious that the tedious technical man was manoeuvring his way to the front of the group, ready with his next batch of structural questions. 'No idea of how she came to be here?'

'I'm afraid not.' The guide looked genuinely sorry that she was unable to continue this intriguing story. 'But my colleague is working on it – we're hoping that she might unearth more details.'

And that really was the end. The Subsidence Man pushed forward with his next dull query, and the story was lost.

DON'T SAY YOU'RE SORRY

The rest of the afternoon was spent wandering the grounds, stopping to admire the tropical plants on the south terrace, taking in the magnificent views of the hillsides and across the channel to Wales. The steam train pushed its way along the flat marshland fields below and the two women stopped to watch its progress, looking for all the world like a model train in a toytown setting.

'I need a rest,' Martha said at last, spying a bench under the trees. They both flopped down, legs aching from a day crammed with walking. For a while they sat in silence, taking in the colours and sounds, letting their minds wander across all the words and sights they had come across during their visit.

'I suppose we'd better be making for home soon,' Laura murmured, extending her arms, pushing them down to her toes, stretching out her lower back.

Martha didn't answer. She was lost in thought.

'Penny for them,' Laura said, clicking her fingers in front of Martha's face.

'No – sorry – just letting my mind wander. I was thinking about Hilly actually.' Martha got up, stretching out her back too. 'She's always been a bit sniffy about the beach hut – you know, as if she resents me having it. And she says she's known Eva for a long time, but they don't seem to get on particularly well. So, I think that maybe she knows more about this whole thing than she's letting on. So, I've decided I'm going to challenge her as well, see what it is that she's been holding back on. I don't like being kept in the dark …' Martha started rummaging in the back pack, trying to find another bottle of water.

Laura opened her mouth to speak, stopped.

'What – what is it? Has Hilly told you something? Spoken to you when I wasn't there?'

'No, no it's not about Hilly – or Eva for that matter.' Laura hesitated again, then sat up straight, as if making a decision. 'It's just that, what you've just said about being kept in the dark … well, there's something else I've found out, something you should know ...'

Martha looked up, aware now that her sister was staring at her. 'What are you talking about?'

'Richard. I'm talking about Richard. When I was trying to track down Martin and I found the information so easily, I tried typing in Richard's name as well. But I didn't find anything. It seemed that he, a bit like you, didn't really engage with social media of any sort, and so I put the idea to one side. But then …'

'But then, what? What else have you found?'

'Look Martha … maybe you should sit down.'

Martha had no intention of being treated like an invalid, but she could see that Laura's face was troubled. She sat back down on the bench and looked expectantly at her sister.

'Well, it was Michael actually. You know his fondness for newspapers - he's always picking up abandoned ones on trains or park benches …'

Martha sighed, impatience and a feeling of impending turmoil worrying their way jointly through her veins.

'Anyway, he had to go over Clevedon way the other day, and because it had taken him a couple of hours to get there he stopped at a little roadside café for a sandwich. As ever, there was a local paper abandoned on the chair and he flicked through while he was waiting …'

'Please Laura, just tell me.'

'He saw a photo – a news item about a woman who had been fundraising for the neighbourhood hospice, and had doubled the target she'd set herself.'

'And this is relevant to Richard because…?'

Laura hesitated. 'Because …Oh god Martha, this is really difficult. I'm just going to … Okay. The photo was also of Richard, and two children …'

'Other fundraisers, you mean?'

'No. The caption said that it was the woman … and her *husband* and their two children …'

'I don't understand. Why would they say that? Surely it's just a reporting error …they've got their facts muddled?'

'Well, that's exactly what I thought, when Michael brought the paper home for me to have a look.'

'So, what's the problem? I mean, we know from the police that Richard's alive, and by definition that he has to be living somewhere …and if this paper has just got its wires crossed, well …'

'I rang the paper. Checked with them. They said there was no mistake, and referred me to the woman's fundraising page.' Laura looked around at the flowerbeds, the other visitors enjoying the sunshine, a dog howling at being left tied up; anywhere in fact, but at Martha. She sighed as she continued. 'There were more photos on there – quite a few with Richard in, cheering her on, helping with her training …'

'So maybe he has a double – Richard, I mean? They do say …'

'I found a website,' Laura interrupted. 'Which records births, deaths … and marriages. And they were there – *he* was there. Same name, same date of birth …'

The silence juddered between them, as they contemplated the story which Laura had related.

'And the children?' Martha eventually asked, a tremor in her words.

'They look …' Laura struggled, 'They look incredibly like Richard …'

'How old?'

'Look Martha, I don't think …'

'How old?' Martha's words were cold, as hard as granite. Not to be denied.

'Eleven and seven …'

Martha sat hunched, hands covering her pale face – like a snail squeezed back into its shell, hiding from the world.

'Are you okay?' Laura whispered. 'I probably should have told you earlier … maybe when we were at home … or …'

'It wouldn't have made any difference.' It felt to Martha as if someone had taken a solid branch from the trees above and thrashed it against her skull, then taken another couple of swipes at her chest, leaving her breathless. She swung her feet onto the bench so that she was almost lying down, and covered her face once more with her hands.

'Why?' Her voice was muffled through her fingers.

'What? I'm not sure what …?' Laura tried to shuffle onto the bench as well, close enough to pass a reassuring hand down her sister's arm.

'Why would he do such a thing?' Martha sat herself up, looking her sister in the eye. 'Why? I just don't understand. Are you sure it was …?'

Laura spoke quietly. 'It was definitely him Martha. From the pictures and the names and dates, there's no doubt it was Richard.'

Martha leaned back, looking up at the scudding clouds, trying to hold back her crying. But her efforts were unsuccessful; tears welled, ran along her eyelashes, dripped down her cheeks. A child shrieked, running towards them in pursuit of a ball, and Martha slumped in the seat. She grasped her head in her hands and her sobs escaped silently, drifting down to the grass beneath her feet.

Eventually her anguished tears juddered to a halt. But Martha continued to stare at the ground, not wanting to acknowledge the world around her, or for it to acknowledge her.

'Shall I say more? Or shall I just shut up?' Laura murmured, her arm twitching, a hesitation as to whether it should be around her sister's shoulder; unsure perhaps of Martha's reaction to any display of affection, or the advertising of their story to those around them who continued to relish the day.

Martha sniffed, sweeping the remaining tears from below her eyes, roughly wiping her stained face with her sleeve.

'Look – maybe we should have a walk, let this all sink in a bit …'

'No – tell me,' Martha demanded. 'I want to know everything *you* know – then I'll walk.'

Laura gave out the small pinches of remaining information in fits and bursts, stumbling over the detail.

'So, for all the time we'd been together,' Martha said, processing the facts, 'There's been someone else. And not just any "someone" – a wife, *and* children – who he's been nurturing and cossetting and hiding from everyone. From me?'

Laura nodded, eyes soulful. 'I'm really …'

'Don't you dare say you're sorry – I don't want anyone to be sorry for me. The only one in this whole bloody mess who should be sorry is that bastard of a man who … used me, lied to me. Kept me like an old coat on a hanger, ready to use whenever he felt the need – whenever he had a gap in his life which needed to be filled…' Her face was livid, aflame with anger. 'Why did I not see this … all those hours and days away from home, when he was supposedly on deliveries … How can I have been so stupid, so gullible. Why?' she shouted, slamming her hand down on the arm of the bench, furious tears filling her eyes once more.

'Come on Martha, let's take a walk – it might help …' Laura began packing their things into the rucksack, zipping it, pulling it on to her shoulders.

'I don't want to go back to the river,' Martha said, standing. 'I don't want to be in a place where people loved each other, had any thoughts or feelings or cared for one another. Take me somewhere angry.'

Laura led the way. She strode off at a pace, leading them back to the car, bustling the bags and Martha inside. She pushed her way through the afternoon traffic, and turned down the lane towards the beach. They stopped, got out, sat on the ribbon of grass amongst the sand and pebbles. The sea wasn't rough enough, wasn't raging as it should have been, wasn't pounding or roaring, but it was relentless and strong and that was enough for the time being.

PRETENDING TO HERSELF

Tea wouldn't cut it. Martha had never been much of a one for alcohol – she enjoyed the taste but it seemed to affect her more than most, and she hated the after-effects, the waste of a day recovering. Laura had delivered her back home, but now she foisted the teapot back in the cupboard and searched around for something more substantial, more gutsy, something which would fight with her anger.

And it *was* anger, she realised. She was no longer upset or depressed about Richard and what he had done; instead, there was a rage rushing through her like a river in flood. It surprised her, but as Martha curled up in the armchair with her large glass of whisky, she began to sort through the emotions and her memories, like a box of old papers.

Her friends - when she had had such a thing, before their kindnesses became unbearable and she had shed them like old clothes – had always thought of Richard as "safe"; and that very idea made her laugh now, in a spiteful sort of a way. Safe. Predictable, grey, middle-aged before his time.

Boring. Any of those, all of those. And in scraps of moments that's what Martha herself had thought too. But predictable hadn't been the worst crime in the world, and safe had made life easy – most of the time. At other times she had been desperate to go to a wild all-night party or to abseil, or to zip-wire down a mountainside. None of those would happen with Richard, but neither would violence or cruelty … or so she had thought.

Maybe what he had done had been the subtlest style of cruelty – or the most cowardly, she thought as she wandered through to the kitchen and poured herself another drink. She wouldn't take the bottle back with her, to the living room, that would be too much of a temptation. At least this way she had to make a conscious effort to binge on the contents.

She examined the life they'd had together, looking for the flaws, the gaps, the stitching coming unravelled, and to begin with there seemed to be nothing; no clue that he had been living anything other than a mundane suburban life. But as she picked through the fabric of their life again, she began to see the pulled threads, the torn seams – the times when he'd been away longer than she'd expected on one of his deliveries, the times when he'd been called away at short notice "because another driver was sick", the times when his phone had pinged with a text message at 6 o'clock in the morning. "Just work" he'd always said. "I'll call them later, after breakfast". And she'd accepted it all. Every excuse, every reason, every explanation.

Had she been pretending to herself all along? She walked over to the bookshelf, picking up a photo of the two of them. No, she thought. She genuinely hadn't seen any of the holes in their relationship – she'd just accepted, trusted, as she thought any good wife should.

She let the photo drop to the floor. It remained whole, and she bent to retrieve it, this time slamming it against the wall – once, twice, and then dropping the last of the pieces into the viper's nest of glass which had built up on the carpet.

She marched around the house, picking up every photo, every ornament he had bought her, any item which reminded her of him. When her arms were full, she opened them and allowed the whole lot to cascade down the stairs, accumulating in an angry heap at the bottom. Eventually, she had to clamber over it all to find a black sack, and then stuffed it to bursting. The front door was opened and she flung the whole hefty bag out onto the front lawn. 'Get out' she shouted, as if it were Richard and not a bag of belongings which she'd just thrown out. She slammed the door against the day. Then sat in her armchair and finally cried.

It was two o'clock in the morning when Martha woke, surprised to find herself lying on the sofa. A pulse at the side of her head began to make itself known and Martha glanced despairingly at the empty whisky glass on the coffee table. She could barely summon the will to move, but the thought that she would feel far worse in the morning, pushed her to get up, and she lurched her way into the kitchen, forcing down a half pint of water despite her heaving stomach. She dragged herself upstairs and fell onto the bed fully clothed, allowing the room to spin gently. 'Bloody Richard,' she moaned, hitting out at his side of the bed, until she fell once more into a fitful sleep.

By lunchtime Martha was feeling marginally better, but the thought of doing any of the things she had planned instantly made her headache worse. She took more Paracetamol and forced herself out to the garden while she tried to get her thoughts in order. She was determined not to allow Richard to interfere with her life any more than he had already done, and deliberately hauled her thoughts back to Eva and her emerging story. But Richard's betrayal fought its way to the forefront, and it was only a matter of moments until she was once again churning the whole of her life with him over and over.

The only thing which she could see might change the narrative was to get out of the house and back to her investigations; submerging herself in the lives of others had to be better than this one-sided fight with Richard.

IS THAT CLEAR ENOUGH?

With the fates having seen fit to pull her world, like an old rug, from under her, Martha had not given a second thought over the past days to the assertion she had made to Hilly, that she would contact Martin Andrews. But she woke the following day for some reason with that very matter on her mind. And her anger with Richard had transformed itself into a will, a determination, to manufacture some sort of order and progress into the things which surrounded her – the things which *were* within her control.

'Mr Andrews?' Martha had been dismayed to see her hand shaking as she had picked up the phone. But if anything, the sight made her more determined to sound business-like, efficient, more like her sister if the truth be told. 'Oh, Good Morning. You won't know me, but I …I visited …' Now that she was at this point, despite all her rehearsed conversations in the mirror, Martha stumbled – and that was all that was needed.

'You're her, aren't you? You're that interfering woman who went storming into my aunt's house, upsetting everyone. She hasn't been the same since - you do know that don't you? You bloody do-gooders, who do you think you are – turning up, uninvited, trying to take over – and all the time you're just making things twenty times worse than they already were.' He paused briefly, and Martha tried to step in, to explain.

'Look, I can see that you might be concerned Mr Andrews – I totally understand …'

'You don't understand anything. That's the bloody point. You know nothing about me, about my aunt – and I've no intention of giving you the opportunity either. And after invading my aunt's house, you've got the bloody nerve now to ring me at work and disturb me. I don't know what women like you get off on, but it's not going to be about taking over my life …'

His voice became muffled, and Martha heard him speaking to someone else. 'No – no, all fine, thanks … I'll be with you in a moment …' She remembered what Laura had found out, about him being semi-retired; hadn't really thought until now about him being so much older than her. She felt momentarily guilty about her own position, of being allowed to take an extended leave of absence from her job at the bookshop, after Richard had gone missing.

'I have to go.' He came back to her, calmer but if anything, more quietly angry. 'I don't know how to say this without being … look, just bugger off and leave me and my family alone. Is that clear enough for you?'

The line went dead.

PERFECTLY INTO PERSPECTIVE

The coffee in front of her had gone cold and she got up to make another. Martha had recently taken to making proper coffee, in the Italian percolator, and found the ritual of milling the beans then waiting for the slow plop of the first drops coming through, and then the hiss of the final spits, quite soothing. She warmed a little milk in a jug and took everything on a tray to the back door. The morning sun was still warm, and a stint in the garden would do her good. But just as she turned the key, the phone rang again. Her heart thumped. If it was Martin Andrews calling back, she didn't think she was up to another shouting match. She would have to make things right with him, if she wanted to speak to Eva again, but maybe a little time would calm him down and she could have a more reasonable conversation.

The phone however didn't seem to want to click over to answerphone, and eventually she went to pick it up.

'Oh, you are there. I thought you'd run away from home for a minute.'

Laura. Well, even in sarcastic mode, she would take Laura over Mr Andrews at this moment. It didn't take long for her sister to wheedle out of Martha the reason she was sounding dejected.

'Well, I suppose it was to be expected,' she said, far too reasonably, after Martha had rerun the conversation with Martin Andrews. 'But there was no need for him to get quite so … so arsy over the whole thing.'

Martha almost knocked over the coffee. Her sister so rarely swore or used anything other than the proper way of saying things, that this outburst made her smile. 'And anyway, the man doesn't rule the world. There's nothing to stop you just "happening" to be in that part of town, taking a walk, when you might just happen to bump into Eva, by co-incidence …'

'You are so devious, Laura Wilkinson …but thank you for putting everything so perfectly into perspective...' Martha laughed. 'I almost feel good enough to give up on busybodying, and start on some gardening instead.'

'Give me five minutes – no, make that ten, and I'll come and give you a hand. Just need to sort out a couple of things and I'll be there. Could do with a bit of exercise anyway …Get the coffee on.'

Another dead phone, but this time Martha was still smiling. She knew her sister would do her share of the gardening, but that at the same time she would be planning and plotting and sorting out their next steps. As Martha put the coffee pot back on the stove to keep warm, she contemplated what had happened over the past few weeks. It had crossed her mind, after Martin's dressing down, that perhaps she should put the whole thing to bed, that Eva and her letters and the whole affair would have to remain a mystery – just a fairy story with no "happy ever after" ending. But of course, she hadn't factored Laura and her tenacity into that decision.

'Don't even think about giving up, not now we've got this far,' were Laura's first words as she came through the door, as though there had been no break in their conversation. 'And I'll expect you to report back, as soon as you've found out any more – with or without the approval of the obnoxious Mr Andrews.'

A LOVELY DAY FOR A WALK

A week later, and Martha was at a bit of a loose end. Everything she had started seemed to have put its own brakes on, and left her stagnating, with nothing in her hands to progress. The woman from the museum hadn't yet rung to tell her she'd found the diaries, nothing more was forthcoming from Hilly Farrant, and Martin Andrews had effectively tied her hands with regard to another visit to Eva.

Even Laura had been persuaded by Michael that they should take a few days away. Maybe her involvement with Martha's quest – and her subsequent absence from their kitchen sink – had opened her husband's eyes a little to the woman who Martha felt he took far too much for granted. Anyway, whatever the reason, they had booked a few days in Marazion in Cornwall, and even though it was she who was supposedly the driving force in all of this, Martha felt a little lost now without her sister to pass ideas by.

Her mind drifted around, focussing for a moment on what she might have been doing had she not been on extended leave from work. She loved her job at the bookshop, one of the big chains, and they had been incredibly understanding of her situation when Richard had gone missing. The time they had allowed her to take had been a lifesaver – quite literally, she thought, as she recalled her darker days. But now that she had found something to occupy her, she was beginning to realise that a degree of purpose and structure in life was something which she really needed. At some point she would start making moves to return, to have the conversation with her manager, but perhaps just not yet, she thought; perhaps not until she had got to the bottom of Eva's own story.

And the thought of the old lady brought Laura's words back to her mind – "Maybe you could just happen to be in the area, bump into the woman, just by co-incidence ..." And she was right. Regardless of Mr Andrews' view of her, there was nothing to stop Martha from walking up to the church, or from wandering around the higher town. In fact, the thought of his bloody-mindedness made her all the more certain. Before she could change her mind, Martha grabbed her bag, quickly checking that she had purse and keys, and at the last minute, stopping to shove a notebook and pen in for good measure. She strode off up Eastern Lane, this time trying to pace herself so that she wouldn't be wheezing like a church organ in need of repair once she got to the top. She managed the climb in one go, but was still breathless by the time she had conquered the steepest part, at the top of Church Steps. When she had walked that way before, Martha had noticed a bench in the churchyard, and now she made her way towards it, thinking that she would get her breathing back to some sort of normal pattern before she continued.

Just as before, the area seemed deserted, and as she sat, Martha allowed her thoughts to bubble and blossom, meandering this way and that in the afternoon sun, until she was brought back to the present by the sound of voices. She stood and peered over the church wall; a woman with a basket of multicoloured dahlias was headed her way, no doubt a stalwart of the church flower-arranging committee. But she had stopped in the street, and was talking to none other than Eva Bonfield. Martha grabbed her bag and hurried down the churchyard path. The lychgate opened just as she reached for it.

'Afternoon.' The woman with the basket of flowers spoke as she held the gate for her. 'Lovely day,' she continued as she closed it again. 'Enjoy your walk.'

Martha barely acknowledged the woman's comments, so keen was she to get out into the street and catch up with Eva before she disappeared. 'Thanks,' she called out belatedly as she dashed down the slope to the narrow street and looked around her. Eva's front door was shut, but as Martha turned she saw someone with a walking stick, plodding down the street ahead of her. She quickened her pace and soon drew level.

'Good afternoon, Mrs Bonfield. Lovely day for a walk,' Martha said, mirroring the flower woman's conversation.

The old woman looked up at her, and Martha was surprised to see a stern expression, unsure whether it was a reflection on their previous meeting, or just a reaction to a conversation from an apparent stranger. 'I'm just going down the road – my afternoon walk,' Eva said, continuing at a ponderous pace along the path.

There still seemed to be no glimmer of recognition, no connection to Martha's recent visit. Perhaps, Martha thought, Hilly had been right about the onset of Alzheimer's.

'Do you mind if I walk with you? I'm going the same way… past the post box,' Martha improvised, noticing an envelope in Eva's hand.

The two women walked in silence for a few moments, until Martha summoned the courage to ask a question. 'I hope you don't mind … but can I ask you … did you used to own a beach hut, down there on the sands?' Martha pointed down towards the beach which was laid out before them at the bottom of the hill, like a miniature garden.

Immediately Eva stopped. The colour seemed to have drained a little from her face as she turned to Martha and then back to the scene in front of them. She swayed disconcertingly, as though she might, at any moment, lose balance or consciousness.

'Here, take my arm,' Martha said, quickly holding out a hand. She steered the woman round to the small bench which they had just passed, and positioned the two of them on the seat. 'I'm sorry, I didn't mean to upset you with my question.' She looked across, waiting, hoping, for an explanation.

But the woman said nothing, just shook her head slightly, as though having a conversation with herself.

'Are you okay?' Martha asked. 'Can I get you anything?' Although she had no idea where she would get anything that Eva might indicate she needed.

'No. I'm alright.' The woman took a deep breath. 'Just a bit out of puff that's all. I don't walk as much as I used to.' She looked longingly towards the steep path zig-zagging its way down the sloping hillside to the harbour. 'All these hills …' she sighed. And Martha was unsure if that was a positive or a negative point of view.

'You live nearby though, don't you?' Martha thought it might be easier if she started the conversation from a point of their never having met. 'I could walk you back …?'

'Just – yes, that would be nice, but could you just …' And she held out the envelope to Martha, indicating the post box on the opposite corner.

'No problem,' Martha jumped up. 'I'll run across with it, and then we'll take a slow stroll back.' She took the letter and tried not to make it obvious that she was looking at the details as she crossed the road. But as she approached the box she stopped short. The envelope was addressed to what looked like "Mr Moreth", although the handwriting was unsteady; but more significantly there was no street, no county, no postcode. She was about to turn back, to say jokingly "You seem to have forgotten to write the address", but as she looked across, Eva was waving to someone, or maybe no-one, further down the street, smiling, a look of happiness brightening her face. Martha recalled what she'd been told, about the old woman's memory, and without another thought, slipped the letter into the straw bag sitting on her shoulder.

THE SAME LOVE

The walk back to Church Cottages took some time, with Eva's pace slow to the point of standing still. Martha wondered if the old woman was delaying the inevitable return home for as long as possible, but she was happy to indulge her. She didn't though want to encounter the wrath of Martin Andrews. 'I need to go down here,' she said to Eva, indicating a narrow side street. 'But I'll wait until I can see you're safely home.'

Martha had lingered at the bend in the road, where she could observe the old woman's front door without being seen. She had no wish to upset the carer or get Eva into trouble with the nephew, but neither did she want Eva to go wandering again – not on her watch.

The little street opposite the church remained quiet though, and eventually Martha felt comfortable in making her way down to the beach hut. As she followed the shortcut down the steep path to the sea front, it occurred to Martha how near Eva was to the place which had presumably played a significant part in her life. The wind, as she stepped out onto the esplanade, seemed to have whisked itself into a stiff breeze, and was lifting the sand and throwing it spitefully, and she was glad eventually to be back inside the cocoon of the beach hut.

Martha spent a few moments brushing gritty particles from her skin, but it was not enough of a distraction to stop her pulling the letter from her bag and looking at it again. Without stopping to think too deeply, she took it over to the kitchen counter and flicked on the kettle. To be honest, she thought, she might just as well have slit the envelope open – with such a flimsy address it was never going to reach its destination after all; but Martha knew it would ease her own conscience if she could eventually drop it into a post box and leave the decision with the Post Office about what to do with it. She took a knife from the drawer and held the letter up to the boiling kettle, dropping it twice before she got the angle right and could capture the steam without burning her fingers. The first attempt to ease the knife between the sealed edges just made a mess, but the second go – along with another dose of steam – started to lift the flap. Eventually it was done. Martha reached in and pulled out the contents – just a single sheet of thin paper, covered in the same scrawled handwriting as the envelope, and barely decipherable.

It didn't really matter that she couldn't read every word. The sentiment was obvious. The same sentiment which Martha had seen in the old letters from the beach hut – the same love; the same disappointment; the same longing to be re-united, despite the years and the problems in between.

Feeling uncomfortable, but somehow unable to resist, Martha reached into her bag for her phone and took a photograph of the letter before quickly refolding the paper and returning it to its envelope. Before she could think about it any more, she grabbed her keys and took it along to the post box by the station, sliding it in with a definite push, no second thoughts allowed.

It hadn't really helped, she thought as she stopped to watch the steam train gather momentum before it pushed itself forward, but she was glad she'd done it nevertheless. It left her no further forward though, and she reluctantly made her way back along the high street, dodging in and out of the late summer tourists who were enjoying everything the shops had to offer. She made her way back to the house, trying as she went to decide what she might do over the next few days, but the decision was soon made for her.

TRYING TO FIND SOMETHING

'Hello?'

There was a hesitation, a clearing of the throat at the other end of the phone, but no words.

'Hello – who is this?' Martha was irritated rather than worried. She had enough mysteries to be going on with, without having to second-guess random callers who weren't prepared to make themselves known.

'Sorry. I … my name's Andrews – Martin Andrews.'

It was Martha's turn to be silent.

'You tried to speak to me,' he went on, 'A while ago, about my aunt – and I think I might have been…'. He hesitated, and she wanted to interrupt, to slip "bloody rude" into the gap, but he continued. '…A bit abrupt.'

'Yes. You could say that.' Martha paused. 'What is it you want?' She was determined after her previous experience not to make the conversation easy.

'I … need to speak to you. It's about my aunt, Mrs Bonfield. Things are not going well.' He stopped, but Martha let the silence hang between them. 'She's – well things are difficult at the moment, extremely difficult, and I know that you've … become involved.' He seemed to begrudge the words, the politeness of them. 'Look, I think we really need a conversation about my aunt …'

'So, let me get this right,' Martha butted in. 'When I wanted to speak to *you*, it was a complete brick wall, but now that it suits you, you think you might like to have an in-depth conversation – is that about it?' Martha was surprised at her own assertiveness, but it felt right somehow, to stop the man in his tracks.

'Yes – that's about it.' His words were reluctant, and Martha wondered if he was already considering whether this was a battle worth fighting, that maybe she'd gone a step too far. Eventually though he continued, decision apparently made. 'I accept that I was perhaps rather rude to you before, but …'

It seemed to Martha from the tone of his voice that he wanted desperately to remain on the right foot in all of this.

'… But, I had my reasons. And now it's important, that we discuss …'

Martha waited again, determined not to provide the words for him.

'Look, it really would be helpful if we could have a conversation, and in my book it would be easier if we could meet up, say what needs to be said …'

Various retorts came to Martha's mind in response to the man's bluster. But if she was too aggressive, if she left him hanging for too long, then he might just put the phone down; and she was acutely aware that she had as much to gain from a conversation with Martin Andrews as he might from her.

'Okay,' she said as coolly as she could muster. 'Where do you want to meet?' She spoke just as he was saying 'Where do you suggest?'

'Lucia's, the one just off the High Street.' Martha got in first, suggesting somewhere convenient to them both. She was worried that he might suggest one of the fast-food outlets which had sprung up on the periphery of their respective towns, and was determined that, if she had to be in the man's company, she would at least enjoy the coffee and the surroundings. 'Tomorrow, eleven o'clock suit you?'

Martha's words were definite enough to sound as though they were not up for debate - although in her mind she had decided that Martin Andrews would have little else going on in his life on a Saturday morning.

'See you there.' He put the phone down before she could say more.

'She's becoming difficult – very difficult on some days. But we can manage that … most of the time.' The two of them had met, unnaturally polite in their handshake; but Martin had launched straight into the conversation, even before their coffees had arrived, not a moment's small talk. 'What's really causing the problem is that you've stirred up a hornet's nest … you and that bloody Hilly woman.'

Martha had been expecting, if not reconciliation, then at least polite discussion. She opened her mouth to counter his criticisms, but Martin held up his hand. She stared, irritated at being shut down before she had even spoken, and he sighed, dropped his head. 'Apologies,' he muttered, 'But this is all getting out of hand, and … well, I just need to say what I have to say …'

Martha took a sip of her coffee, nodded. 'Okay, I'll listen.'

'Well, it's just that …'

For someone who needed to get his thoughts out, the man bumbled and faltered an awful lot, Martha thought.

'Since you came to see Eva … well, she hasn't been the same. She's always wanting to tell stories, going back over the past, right back to when she was a young woman.' He picked up his cup but didn't drink. 'But now it seems she just wants to re-live one particular bit of her life – and I sit and listen but I have no idea where the whole thing is going. But I can't stop her.' At last he drinks, gulp after gulp, rewarding himself for getting the words out. 'And then,' he throws in, as though he's just remembered something else, 'She keeps wanting to go out – as if she's trying to find something…' His words faded as he stared into the empty cup.

'Well, I can see that must be difficult …'

'I keep thinking about it, and it must be something to do with what you talked to her about

– it has to be … something started all this off, and it's a bit of a co-incidence that it all got worse around the time you visited … and what I really don't understand is why you were there in the first place …'

Martha was unsure – about what to say, but also whether Martin realised about her bumping into Eva in the street, and the episode with the letter. It might well be that Hilly dropping into Eva's life, and her own questions about the beach hut had triggered memories, but she hadn't really got as far as having any in-depth conversations with the woman. Nevertheless, she didn't want to say anything which could lead Martin to the conclusion it would all stop if only she disappeared off the scene again.

'Look – I realise that I had no right to just … start poking my nose in. But the truth is that I …' Now that she was at the point of revealing the story, Martha was hesitant; but she guessed that Martin wasn't the sort of person who was going to be fobbed off.

'I bought the beach hut – you know about that?'

He raised a sceptical eyebrow, nodded.

'Well, I bought it because … well mainly because I found some letters in there.'

Now it was Martin's turn to open his mouth, and Martha's to hold up a hand. 'I know, I know, I had no right to be in there, and even less right to start poking about and taking stuff …but it was just scraps of paper, and I was intrigued …'

'They belong to my aunt.' He was indignant now. 'You should return them …'

'They're *scraps* of paper –literally. They'd mean nothing,' But even as she said the words Martha knew that wasn't true.

They sat in silence, Martha finishing her coffee, Martin looking at anyone but her, face red, as though he were barely holding in everything he wanted to throw at her.

'Look – I just want to help,' Martha said eventually.

'No – what you want is just to get your own way – to do the things that suit you and b…b.. blow everyone else …'

'I just thought, that if I met with Eva, if I spoke to her …'

'The trouble with you is, you haven't thought at all,' Martin jumped in. And for a moment Martha conceded he was probably right. As much as she wanted to, she was struggling to find anything to say which might justify her actions.

He looked at her as if he was daring her to find any words which would not just make the situation worse.

'…Well, maybe we could help each other out.' Martha's words faded as she heard the futility of them. She waited for Martin to start again, but he just shook his head disbelievingly. 'Look, all I'm saying is …that poor carer seems to be struggling to manage everything, and even I can see that Eva … well, she can obviously be a bit difficult when the mood takes her. If I were to take her out now and again, the carer would be able to get on with other things, and Eva would get out and about – as she so obviously wants to, and you would have some peace of mind that she wasn't getting lost…' Martha's argument fizzled to a stop.

Martin started tidying the coffee things in front of him, putting the milk jug inside his cup, adding the spoon. He took his jacket from the back of the chair and slipped his arms in.

'Look,' Martha started again, wanting to resolve things at least to some degree before the man left. 'I can't deny that my original plan in all of this was to get Eva talking about the beach hut and how she came to own it, and … well, just to tell me the story of the letters ….and I'd still like to do that ….' She could see the objections about to emerge from Martin's mouth, and so she continued with what was obviously going to be her last chance. 'But mainly … I can see the poor woman is unhappy. I know, before you say it, I know why you're doing what you're doing – for her own safety – but in her mind, she is still the able woman she was forty, fifty years ago. If I could just give her some sense of the freedom she used to enjoy, well then it would make Nadya – it is Nadya, isn't it? – well it would make her life easier, and yours as well.'

Martin stopped in his tracks, chewing his lip, mulling over her words, presumably trying to fathom whether she had some other agenda that he just wasn't seeing, not wanting to be taken for a complete fool. But Martha was sure that any further words on her part might be over-egging the pudding, or over-gilding the lily, or whatever such expression she was sure Laura would be familiar with.

'We'll try it.' He said firmly, thumping the back of the chair. 'But – anything that goes wrong I will lay the blame firmly at your feet,' he paused, seeming to debate the words he wanted. 'And you will *never* come to my aunt's house again, or have anything further to do with her.' He looked down at the table, as though there ought to be paperwork there that he should get her to sign. But there was nothing except Martha's goodwill. 'Do I make myself clear?'

Martha felt like a ten-year-old being given detention. But she nodded, assured, agreeing that she would give her upmost attention to Eva's safety and wellbeing. He stood, still unsure, buttoning his jacket. 'I'll know how it's gone, after your first visit - outing,' he corrected. 'It'll be obvious from Eva.' And with that he left, and Martha remained, looking at his empty chair. She hoped the story was worth the responsibility she had just loaded onto her own shoulders.

HAD IT BEEN THAT EASY?

It was more nerve-wracking than a job interview. Martha had changed her mind constantly – ridiculously, she knew – about what to wear, where to go, how long to be gone … the list went on.

Finally, she got herself to Church Cottages, parked outside with hazard lights flashing. Nadya must have been looking out of the window for her, or have been prompted to monitor her arrival by the old lady. Either way, the front door opened before she had a chance to knock. Eva was in the narrow hallway, coat on, ready to make her exit, presumably before anyone changed their mind.

There was much shuffling and re-arranging and getting everything in place before they were ready for Martha to drive away. She slipped into her seat and let out the breath she hadn't realised she was holding. Prompted by the stories told by the woman at the museum, Martha had decided to take them up on the hill behind the town, where the road went to the very end of the promontory and the views were spectacular. She started to explain this to Eva, but the old woman seemed hardly to notice her words;

she was too busy turning this way and that, watching the all-too-familiar sights around her front door melt away and turn into the trees and ever-climbing slopes of North Hill. The road was initially narrow and the need for them to stop, to allow cars to pass, caused the old woman to sigh. But eventually they were on the more substantial roadway which climbed and wound its way up and up. Eva looked out at the aerial view of the town which fell away to their left, then, as soon as that had disappeared, focussed straight ahead, in the direction of travel. They slowed for the cattlegrids and then, as the trees thinned, there it all was – an ever-widening panorama, sea to one side, a rollercoaster of hills and fields to the other. As she concentrated on where she was going, Martha heard Eva sigh again, but this time it was not a groan of irritation or impatience; it was the satisfied appreciation of a place of beauty, a landscape which could calm the most turbulent of minds.

Martha had been about to start on the small talk, the pleasantries appropriate for a semi-stranger in the car. But she could see, even from a quick glance, that Eva was content just to take in everything that surrounded her. She left her to her enjoyment and carried on driving, past the swaths of gorse which still blanketed the hillside, the dying heathers, the path diverting off to the beacon. If Eva had been more mobile Martha would have considered a walk along that path, where the views from the top swept up from north, south, east and west. But there was no possibility of that, and so she continued along the unmarked road right to the end, realising that she was at the point she had heard described by the museum assistant, where children might think they had come to the end of the world.

The world did not end here, but in Martha's view, it might begin. She helped Eva out of the car – something which she seemed to manage a lot more easily than getting in – and ensured she was well wrapped up, for even though there was still a strong sun the breeze on top of the promontory was robust. She took the older woman's arm, linked in hers, and they walked just a handful of steps. The bay below them curved round in a perfect arc, and even from that distance they could see a couple of boats bobbing on the small tide and the waves to-ing and fro-ing in their never-ending dance.

'Have you been here before?' Martha asked, more to start the conversation than with any real wish to know something specific. To her surprise Eva pointed across to the hill on the opposite side to the bay. 'That's where it happened,' she said, standing silently, as someone might do when a funeral cortege went past. Where I came down, when my plane …' Eva banged her fists together, the impact she was describing plain for anyone to see.

Martha looked at the old woman in disbelief. 'Hang on, wait. You told me before that you'd piloted planes, but you never said anything about …' She hesitated to use the word "crashing", concerned that it might push Eva too far. But Eva was continuing, with or without her.

'And him too. That was where he …' And although that particular thread had snagged and broken, Martha gasped. A name, *the* name – of the other letter-writer, was hanging so tantalisingly just beyond her reach.

Eva turned, the unfinished sentence forgotten, and Martha took her arm again, guiding them towards a small bench which had been thoughtfully placed to take in the best of the views from all sides. She had thought to bring a flask and poured a cup of tea for the old lady and one for herself. Eva didn't look particularly taken with the thought, but smiled brightly at the sight of the small tub of biscuits which Martha also produced. She munched away happily on a fig roll, staring out at the constant yet ever-changing view, and it seemed to Martha that it was a "now or never" moment.

'How did you come to meet … your … young man?' she asked, her voice as matter-of-fact as she could manage, while her heart galloped in pursuit of the man's name.

Immediately the old woman smiled, licking a crumb from her lips, and clasped her hands across her stomach - in storytelling mode it seemed to Martha.

'He just called out to me, as I was walking down the road.' Eva's face had lit up. "Lovely day for a walk". And then he said, "I'd have thought you'd still be taking it easy." I was flummoxed – I had no idea who he was or how he knew anything about me. "You're the talk of the town," he said, laughing – at the look on my face I suppose. "Well, the talk of the castle at least." The way he said "castle" gave him away – he was an American - and then I noticed the air force shirt, although he had the sleeves rolled up and it was open at the neck.

'You're there too?' I asked him.

"Two weeks so far." As he caught up with me, he held out a hand, introduced himself with a smile – such a lovely smile. "Were you headed this way?" he said, pointing down the lane towards the sea. 'Mind if I join you?' And he held out his arm for me to take. And that's how it all started. We spent the whole afternoon chatting as if we were old friends, sitting on a washed-up tree trunk at the edge of the beach, just watching the waves going in and out. After a while I plucked up the courage to ask what had happened to him.'

'He didn't really want to talk about it. It was only later I found out that he was the only one left, and why he was so … you know … about what had happened.' Eva waved a hand around, and Martha wondered whether it was the word she was trying to summon, or the story itself. Either way, nothing appeared. Martha was left, abandoned mid-story, with no idea how to rescue the situation. 'It must have been hard for him,' she said eventually, hoping a general expression of empathy might be enough to encourage Eva to pick up the story from where she had dropped it. But still nothing. Eva's eyes welled with tears but she bit her lip, seemingly determined not to allow her emotions to overwhelm her … or simply keeping the man's story tucked inside herself for a while longer.

'And what about you though? What happened to you?' Martha decided that the story of the young man had, for now, reached a definite dead end, that a change of direction might be enough to jolt the older woman onto another track of her tale.

'How did your … accident… happen?'

'Eva shrugged, as though she had no idea. 'Fog, sea mist …' she said. 'And a hill where it shouldn't be … same as him.' She peered out over the bay, seemingly mesmerised by a small boat which was chugging its way towards Mariners Weir.

The thought that the young man had also been a pilot brought a symmetry to their stories, and, from Eva's brief words, Martha had to assume that he too had crashed.

'So, if you were flying, you must have been in the Forces – during the war?' Martha tried, coming at the question from a different angle.

But Eva seemed not to have heard her words, or was very determinedly not acknowledging them.

Martha opened her mouth to ask something else, another from the trunk-load of questions which were weighing on her; but she could see, as she turned to the old woman, that she was shivering. That the warming tea had gone cold. She should have brought a travel blanket, Martha thought, should have anticipated the weather. She was desperate to hear more of Eva's story, now that they had got this far, but Martha had to concede that there was no way the frail woman should be sitting there for a moment longer. She helped her to her feet and walked her back to the car before returning to collect her bag of flask and cups and biscuits. She turned the car's heating to full blast, then poured more tea, allowing it to steam the windows as they both tried to get warm. Martin Andrew's voice was clanging in Martha's head, and the thought of Eva getting a chill or being in any way unwell after this outing filled her with horror. As soon as the poor woman seemed to have recovered a little, Martha put everything away and turned the car round, ready for their return to town. She began a burble of chitchat, wanting to jolly Eva along, wanting to prepare the ground for future outings. 'We'll go somewhere a bit less blowy, next time,' she joked, 'Go and find a little café somewhere and have tea and cake …'

But Eva seemed to have grasped a different thread of conversation. 'He never answers my letters you know,' was all she replied.

'Who do you mean? The man you met …?' Martha left an opening for the name to be slotted in. But nothing more was forthcoming.

MORE TO IT THAN THAT

Martha snatched a glance at Eva as she drove. Despite what the older woman had told her, she was smiling once again, and Martha wondered if she was toying with her, knowing perfectly well how obtuse she was being and enjoying her small moment of control.

'What *was* the name of that woman?' Eva sighed heavily, strapped into the passenger seat, smacking her hand against her lap, as though that might fire her memory. 'You know - that friend of Mrs Saltrey? I used to see them sometimes, walking in the garden, arm in arm, whispering and laughing, and sometimes she would come down the staircase in an evening gown – so elegant – letting the officers gawp at her with their mouths open.'

All of Martha's concentration was channelled on getting back down the narrow lanes without hitting a wall or another car. She had no idea who this woman might be that Eva was talking about, or where the story was going, but she might never get this chance again. 'Was she your friend?' Martha tried, but Eva just shook her head.

'"I can't bear it." That's what she said to me.' Eva looked over at Martha, as though trying to chivvy her into joining in the story. 'I can hear her saying it now. Olivia, that was it. A husky voice she had – deep, but still, you know …'

Martha assumed the word Eva was searching for was "sexy", still trying to picture this unknown woman, trying to get a grasp of where she might fit into the whole thing, but it evidently didn't matter what she thought, because Eva was already moving on.

'I was in the gardens, just watching the river gushing along while I waited for him.'

'And who was it you were waiting for…?' Martha started to ask, taken aback by the similarity of the old woman's words to her own imaginings, but Eva was in full flow and there was no holding back the flood.

'"Here – take this." Just like that she said it, and she was holding out her hand to me.' Eva held out a clenched hand in the way you might offer a hidden surprise to a child. 'I didn't know what she was giving me, and I must have looked confused, because she started to explain. "I've seen you here a few times now," she said to me, "And I can't bear the idea of the two of you not being able to meet *properly*." She … you know …' Eva underlined the final word in the air, depicting the woman's emphasis. 'But to be honest I still didn't cotton on to what she was saying. Then she started explaining that I would need to go down to the beach. "Bit of a walk I'm afraid," she said, "but not impossible".

I was none the wiser – I had no idea what she was talking about, but she just smiled, and walked away. When I opened my hand, what she'd dropped into it was a little silver key.'

Martha had been trying to drive as slowly as she could, to allow time for Eva to get to the nub of the story. But they were back at Church Cottages and Nadya was on the doorstep and Eva was tugging at the seatbelt.

The story was gone, with Martha having no opportunity to flip back a page to check on the missing details. 'Bugger,' she said, banging her hand on the steering wheel. Her action triggered the horn, and Nadya opened the door again, thinking that something was wrong. Martha had to wave and smile and pull away from the kerb to demonstrate that all was well.

'Bugger, bugger, bugger,' she shouted to herself as she carried on down the road back into town. She had been so tantalisingly close to finding out, if not about the flying and the crashes, then at the very least the young man's name; had come close to the story of how Eva came to have the beach hut … but not quite close enough.

SOMETHING WHICH MIGHT
PROVE USEFUL

'I've got something here you might be interested in ... I don't know though, it's not specifically about troops in the area. It's difficult - when I don't really know what you're looking for ...' It was Valerie on the phone, the woman from the museum, and Martha gladly put down the pile of ironing she had been working her way through.

'Well, anything you've got might be of help,' Martha said, keen not to let any potential opportunity pass her by. After all, the information she had collated so far seemed to be sending her round in spirals of frustration at the moment. 'What is it that you've found?'

'Well, I've been going through the diaries – you remember me telling you that local people kept a record of their lives throughout the war – and I found one about an incident I'd completely forgotten about. I'm grateful to you actually; I would never have started reading through all these records without your enquiry, and I'm really enjoying what I've found ...' Valerie carried on, her words meandering round the houses, causing Martha's mind to drift. She was picturing the woman for some reason ensconced by her fire in a tiny cottage sitting room, swathed in cardigans, sipping weak tea as she fingered her way through dozens of dusty records.

'So, what do you think?'

Martha realised that she hadn't been properly listening to what the woman was saying. 'Well – it definitely sounds as if it's worth a look,' she said, having no idea what she was signing up to. 'Shall I pop into the museum and pick the diary up?'

'Oh, I don't think I could let you take it away, not the original anyway …' Valerie paused, and it occurred to Martha for some unfathomable reason that the woman might be lonely, that this might be her way of getting a bit of company, of getting Martha to spend some time with her at the museum. But just as this thought was going through her head, Valerie began again. 'I could photocopy it though – if that would be of any help…?'

Martha reprimanded herself. This woman was going out of her way to be helpful, and all she was doing was looking at her as a bit of a "hanger-on". 'That would be wonderful,' she said enthusiastically, 'When should I pop in for it?'

She could tell by Valerie's response that she was pleased to have a fellow researcher to share information with, and Martha felt guilty all over again, realising how lucky she was to have Laura around to fill the gaps in her own life whenever she needed. They discussed days off and times and within a few minutes all was arranged.

It was only after she had put down the phone that the photo she had seen on the display board on her previous visit to the museum came back into Martha's head. Although she hadn't really thought about it, she realised she must have been carrying it in the back of her mind, and Valerie's call had presumably brought it to the forefront. She wondered whether, subconsciously, she had seen something which might prove useful, either to rule it in or rule it out of her investigation. Patience, never Martha's strong point, pushed her to go, sooner rather than later, for a second look; but she didn't feel she could bother Valerie again so soon, after all the time the woman had already given to her quest. She leaned back in her chair, eyes closed for a few moments, weighing eagerness against politeness. And then Valerie's words about her days off came back to Martha, and she realised she could call in to the museum earlier than they had arranged, and take a quick look at the picture without Valerie being offended – or even aware of her presence.

ANOTHER QUICK LOOK

And so, on Wednesday, Martha parked up in the small car park adjacent to the museum, and made her way to the ancient building.

Instead of the woman she had met previously, there was a man was at the desk; his dark-rimmed glasses and his fingerless gloves giving an image of someone much older than Martha suspected he probably was. Was it being surrounded by all these archaic objects which made museum people seem like antique artifacts themselves? Did they absorb some of the age-old air which surrounded them, mummifying themselves into an older version of their real selves? She greeted him cheerfully, explaining that she just wanted another look at a photograph she had seen here on her previous visit. 'Is it okay if I just go and have a quick look?' Martha said, already turning to walk the length of the museum to the spot where the picture had previously been.

'We've been having a bit of a sort out, actually.'

Martha stopped abruptly to find that the man had followed and was standing immediately behind her.

'It was just here.' She pointed to the area where the display board had been. 'If you could just tell me where you've moved it to, it won't take a minute for me to check … I'll be out of your hair in no time...' She rattled the words out, unable to stop herself.

'No rush,' he said, stepping back, perhaps sensing her unease at his proximity. 'I was just going to say that you might need to look over here …' He pointed to a table which hadn't been there at her last visit. 'Valerie, my colleague, has been trying to catalogue things so that we can find them a bit more easily – pick out things to update our displays and so on. We should probably have done it ages ago, but you know how it is – you sort of get used to your background, it becomes part of the everyday, and you don't even notice the mess …'

Martha thought of her own house, of the chaos which Laura had helped her sort out, and nodded in agreement. 'I know just what you mean. I've …', stopping herself before she burdened this complete stranger with her troubles. 'It was of some airmen – the picture I saw before – Americans, I think. I just wanted to have another quick look, to see if I might recognise anyone …'

She realised that she was gushing, that she had said as much to this man in just a few minutes than she had to Valerie during both their conversations. But he was that sort of person – the type who seemed to be able to entice words out of you which you'd had no intention of releasing, but in such a gentle way that you hardly noticed what you were doing.

'It's probably in that folder.' He pointed to a large blue lever arch file. 'Blue for Air Force – I think that's Valerie's system,' he smiled, bringing her in on the joke. 'We're getting them all into folders first, and then we can decide what goes back out on display.' He spoke as though he might have done things differently - not unkindly, but in the indulgent way you might have for a favourite aunt or grandmother.

Martha reached for the folder and slowly turned the pages. It was indeed filled with numerous photos of air crew, some British, some American – or perhaps even Canadian; she wasn't knowledgeable enough to distinguish between the uniforms.

And then, there it was. The one that had caught her eye before. She glanced round at the man. 'Is it okay if I take it over to the light?' she said, indicating the folder. 'Just to get a better look?'

He swept his arm towards the window, stood back so that she had clear passage.

Martha held up the photo, but there was no-one even close to the dark mediterranean features of the young man in the beach hut photos. And no matter how much she tilted it this way and that, he refused to appear.

THREADS OF THE STORY
EVA

She looks up at him, not sure if he is with her or ahead of her, in the story she is telling – about the beach hut and the key and the friend of Eleanor Saltrey.

'Olivia, that was it.' It has taken all her efforts, and Eva is pleased with herself that she has remembered the woman's name – even though she has a feeling she may have told this story before. 'She'd just finished talking to me, was waving as she walked away, and then I saw him coming towards us. She stopped to have a chat with him.'

Martin knows that interrupting will not go down well with his aunt, but he has no idea who or what she is talking about. 'I'm a bit lost here,' he ventures. 'Who is this man you're talking about?'

But Eva carries on, wanting only for the story to be told.

'It was seeing *him* that made the penny drop, about what that woman had said to me. In those days I was a bit – what's the word – had no idea – green, but when I thought about what she was suggesting, it made me a bit scared to be honest.'

Martin tries several times to put a question to her, to get the smallest idea of what she is telling him about, but Eva is looking anywhere but at him, accepting no eye contact, all her concentration going into remembering.

'I'm trying to tell you,' she snaps. 'At first I had no idea what the key was for. And then, when I did, I realised that it was going to be up to me to decide what would happen next – or if I was going to allow anything to happen at all. You know – with this young man. I remember closing my eyes, thinking of the what-ifs. But back then, in the war, people were doing all sorts of things they wouldn't have dreamt of doing in peacetime …'

None of what she is saying is making the slightest sense to him, and Martin is beginning to think that Eva's condition is deteriorating, that she is just rambling about anything and nothing. But the look on her face is the most determined he has seen so far, adamant that she is going to carry on with this story of hers. So, for the time being, he has to let her continue without interruption.

'When he arrived, I couldn't say anything. I was – you know …' Eva rubs her cheeks, indicating the blush of embarrassment. 'He asked me what was wrong, was I unwell, I do remember that. I couldn't bring myself to say the words, so I just took his hand and led him down the path away from the river. "Where are we going?" he kept asking, but I just put a finger to my lips,' Eva mimes the action, 'And we walked down to the crossroads.'

'He started laughing, like it was a game.' Eva looks into the past, smiling to herself as she sees his face again. 'He looks so lovely when he laughs.' She pauses her story while she watches her younger self.

Martin recalls, uncharacteristically, a phrase he has read somewhere about stepping on the dreams of others, and holds back on another interruption.

'He must have asked me a hundred times where we were going, but I didn't say a word until we got to the beach. Olivia must have told me – I don't remember - but somehow I knew where we needed to go, and I waved the little key at him.' Eva holds up a hand, shaking an invisible key. 'And then, I couldn't get it to work. I was turning it this way and that, thinking that it must all be a joke, but I couldn't imagine Olivia playing a trick like that – she wasn't the sort.' She watches the scene playing in her mind's eye, turning her finger and thumb to loosen the imagined lock. 'He took it from me in the end, held the little padlock in his hand and managed to work it free.'

Eva watches in her mind's eye the best part of the story. Perhaps she won't tell this bit ... she can see that he is uncomfortable, doesn't really want to hear what he thinks might be coming next. So she will simply unfold it for herself. And surely he has already put two and two together? That's why he can't sit still. So there is no need to … what's the expression? Something about a lily, she concedes, as she turns to the window and restarts the story, but just for herself this time.

Sunlight is pushing its way through two small chinks in the wooden wall. The rays of light hit her eyes, piercing her consciousness. She looks around, unsure for a moment where she is. A gust of salty breeze outside causes the wooden walls to quiver and moan, and the moaning in turn refreshes her memories of the evening before. She inclines her head and sees the reality of what has, until that moment, been a sweet dream. He is snoring gently beside her, buzzing like a contented bee. The blankets are tangled in and out of his limbs, and his bare shoulder is cold to her touch. She shivers, not at the coolness of the air, but at the realisation that they are still here - have been here all night, when he should have been lined up with the other officers, and she should have been tucked up in the housekeeper's spare room.

She shakes his shoulder, once, twice. He rolls away from her, and she has to clamber nearer to find his ear. 'My love,' she murmurs, although why she is whispering when there is nothing but the sea to hear, she doesn't know. His eyes blink and open, close, then open. He smiles at her, brushes a strand of hair from her face.

'It's morning, it's…' she looks around for a clock or a watch. But the sunlight has woken his thoughts as well, and he silently begins gathering belongings - jacket, trousers, shoes. He looks into her worried eyes.

'It'll be fine,' he says, kissing her forehead. 'Give me a ten-minute start. I've been out for an early morning walk on the beach, went a bit further than I intended…that'll be my story, okay?'

He kisses her again and she is left to conjure her own story. She gathers her things, tidies the room as best she can, and locks the door. No-one is about – just a fisherman down at the shoreline, and he seems too busy with his catch to worry about a young slip of a thing getting away. She walks briskly at first, marching out, trying to make up the time which has been lost. But then she realises, as the world is coming awake, that it is too late. That the housekeeper will long since have been up and breakfasted, will be issuing orders to the parlourmaid who has now become the maid of all things. Her absence will already be etched on their minds and her quickening steps will do nothing to erase those marks.

She diverts and walks into the village, calling at the newsagent to buy a morning paper, giving herself the slimmest of alibis for being out. The wonders of the previous evening have already been smothered in a rough blanket of guilt, and she decides to leave them there until she can enjoy them again in the comfort of her room – if she is still permitted a room, that is.

She wanders along the main street until there is no village left to distract her, and then turns through the side gates and up the steep hill. The castle is, as ever, its imposing self, glaring down at her, and, she is sure, nudging all its occupants to run to the window, to look out on this brazen woman who failed to return home last night. But there is no-one around, not even the garden boy, and she sidles round to the staff entrance and cranks open the heavy black door, hoping that Cook will be too busy to see her, and that she can corkscrew her way up the spiral staircase, into the attics and take refuge in her room until she can be sure of what she is going to say.

'Mrs Saltrey was asking after you at dinner last night,' the Housekeeper, stands on her landing, darning in hand, looking directly at Eva.

'Oh,' is the best Eva can offer.

'I told her you were unwell.' The statement is brazen, challenging Eva to argue, to defend – or to concede.

'You *were* unwell, weren't you?' It is a statement - no hint of it being a question. 'I don't like to be telling lies.'

She can't work out the housekeeper's strategy. Does she know where Eva was – has she guessed, or is she covering her own lie, her own assumption?

'I wasn't feeling my usual self,' Eva manages, a lie disguised in an almost-truth. 'I thought it best to stay in bed.'

'Hmm.' The housekeeper looks over the top of her glasses. 'Well, you look fine now – a bit pale, but fine. So maybe you could help with some mending – at the very least it will take your mind off things, and it will …'

"Pay me back for lying for you" is what Eva can see the woman wants to say. This may be the beginning of a long line of tasks to "pay her back", but Eva is willing to go along with the charade, if it means the two of them can be together.

Martin waits, allowing her to gather up the threads of the story again, but it seems, by the length of her pause, as if this particular strand has encountered a knot, and for the moment there is no untangling it. 'I'll make some tea,' he suggests, his fallback position when he has little idea what should come next. But she doesn't seem to hear him. There is a teardrop on the papery skin of her cheek and he thinks about reaching out and brushing it away, knowing that any other person might do just that. But Martin doesn't feel, despite everything, that he knows her sufficiently well. He slips into the kitchen and fills the kettle, sets cups and saucers onto a tray. At least he knows now that she always prefers a proper cup and saucer.

'Where did I get to?' she asks as he puts the flowery china cup down beside her. 'I don't remember where I was up to …?'

He shifts uneasily in his chair, unsure whether he should remind her of the situation she had begun to describe, or just allow her to pick at whatever thread comes to her in that moment.

'Tell me,' Eva implores, looking him in the eye.

'You were laughing – you and whoever it was you were with, trying to open up the beach hut I presume. But you haven't told me who this man was, or what was going on?' His irritation comes to the fore, having to dip into the story only where she allows him to.

But she's finished that bit of the story, done and dusted. She won't go there with him again. Suddenly another thought comes into her head. 'He didn't like me,' she starts, struggling to put her cup back into the saucer.

Who? Who didn't like you?' he demands, but she continues as if he hasn't spoken.

'Not since I'd said "no" – you know – to going to his room.' Eva doesn't look at Martin, can sense him taking in her frail body and trying to transpose it into that of a young desirable woman. 'So he was just looking for … something … something he could report me for, or either of us, I suppose. He would've hated him too if he knew that someone else had had what *he* couldn't get …'

Martin fidgets, reaches out for the sugar bowl, adds another spoonful to his already sweet tea. It is too much to be forced to look into the intimate world of your elders, and he would much rather he didn't have to go there. 'Don't forget your tea,' he tries, to swerve her from her route, but she shakes her head vigorously against his distraction.

'You could tell he was itching to find a reason. Maybe he thought we were both fit enough to report back for duty. And I was really, but I didn't know whether I had the courage to climb back into the cockpit. I wanted to, I really did, but I also wanted, more than anything, for us to be together, for the short while we might have still have.'

Martin can't look at her, has taken to staring out of the window at the lowering sun, and the plants seeming to change colour as they move out of the spotlight.

'Anyway, we agreed – to keep the beach hut just between the two of us, and not to talk about the likes of that awful man. We just took our chances while we could.'

Her face is such a mixture of emotions, the threads of her story becoming ever more tangled as she tries to recall all that has happened.

'Let me call Nadya,' he says. 'You look really tired. She can help you to bed, and I'll be back another day … you can tell me more then.'

She looks at him as they wait for the carer to come and help her up. He doesn't know the half of it, Eva thinks.

ROMANTIC ENOUGH
EVA

Tea is over – sausages and some fancy onion thing which Eva hasn't eaten. She is slumped in her armchair with no sign of Martin, and she can't remember what he'd said, the last time, about coming again and when that might be. She tips her head back on the cushion, closes her eyes and allows her thoughts to drift; and the story which has been so much on her mind is opened again, at the right page.

We met, again and again, at the beach hut, but each time now being careful to take heed of the time, to set an alarm which Joe has borrowed from one of the other men. To return to the Castle under its night cloak, to be in the right chair and the right room by daybreak.

'Perhaps we could write to each other?' Eva says one afternoon, pulling a blanket over her naked arms. They had been bemoaning their lack of time, that everything was as fragile and ephemeral as a day lily. Joe lay still, tipping his head to and fro, as if he were shaking a snow globe to get the full picture.

'What – you mean, even though we might see each other, we should write letters?'

'Well, we're not going to get away with this indefinitely. At some point someone is going to see us and spill the beans. We've been lucky so far, but …' Eva lets the words float in the chill of the air. 'And anyway, it's quite romantic, don't you think?' She muses on the idea, recalling a scene from an almost-forgotten film in her head. 'You know – either of us could come here on our own, when the other isn't able to, leave our letter – maybe hidden somewhere for the other to find,' she laughs, realising she might be getting slightly carried away with the notion.

'Don't you think our meeting here is romantic enough?' Joe laughs. But he can see that she likes the idea for its own sake, not just as a way of being together when they can't actually meet. 'Okay then,' he sits up, pulls another blanket round both their shoulders. 'But you have to go first.'

She had hoped he might take the lead. Having suggested it, she is unsure the form the letters should take, how explicit she would be expected to be. And by his comment she can see that Joe is probably thinking exactly the same. But if the only way to make it work is for her to go first, then that is what she will do. And perhaps, just perhaps, she might be able to broach the subject in writing which has never been allowed to step into the room with them – of what their future together might be.

They pull clothes from between the covers, and clumsily start to dress, each busy in their own tasks, not looking at the other until they are ready to leave. Their ritual is always the same – Joe will leave first, and Eva will watch the hand move round the mother-of-pearl face of her small watch, leaving after ten slow minutes have passed, taking a circuitous route back to the same destination. They never acknowledge each other within the castle grounds.

EXACTLY WHAT YOU NEED

'Oh, hello?' The voice was unsure, and so was Martha. 'Hello,' it started again. 'Is that Ms Townsend? Martha Townsend?'

'Yes.' Martha aimed for non-committal, uncomfortable that the caller hadn't revealed themselves.

'Oh, sorry to bother you. My name's Simon Morton – I'm calling from the museum …'

A picture of the man who had pointed her in the direction of the photos came immediately into her head. 'Oh yes, sorry, we met, the other day …'

The caller had presumably not put the fact of their meeting together with her name. She seemed to have confused him, so that he presumably decided eventually to stick to the bald facts for the moment. 'It's just that there's a note in the museum diary – that my colleague, Valerie, was due to meet with you today?' He had made it into a question rather than a statement.

'Yes, that's right,' Martha said, at the same time as he was continuing with his explanation. 'Well, unfortunately Valerie has gone down with a cold, well, more like flu really, I think…'

Martha's heart sank. Yet another barrier along the road to her finding out even the smallest bit of possible information. But Simon hadn't finished. 'So anyway, I was just calling to say that I'm happy to keep the appointment instead, if that would help …'

She arrived at the car park far too early. The museum was still shuttered and closed to business, and she sat, not really listening to a debate on Radio 4, allowing the words to wash over her as she thought about other things.

And there were so many other things to think about. Had Laura not dropped the bombshell about Richard, Martha would be sitting here now itching to know what Valerie or Simon had unearthed about servicemen and local wartime events.

But her thoughts fluctuated between Eva, Richard, herself and Martin Andrews, and the complications of all their lives, and their intertwining; then something caught her eye, and she looked up to see the door of the museum being pulled back. The person she assumed was Simon Morton stood on the threshold, and she was tempted to duck down so that he didn't think she had no other life than that of the long-gone. But he was looking down the street, waving at a white-haired woman supported by a shopping trolley, making slow progress to the mini-supermarket. The woman tentatively straightened herself and waved back, a smile transforming her face. Martha found herself smiling too, realising that not the entire world was made up of complications and selfish individuals; some people could still enjoy the simplicities of life.

She waited a few moments more then made her way across to the museum. Simon was in the entrance, sorting leaflets, putting stray ones back into their allotted spots.

'Oh, hello there. You're very prompt.' He smiled, and Martha wondered if he remembered her after all.

'Yes, it didn't take me quite as long to get here as I anticipated – you know, you usually get stuck behind a tractor or a bus or some such …'

He didn't seem to see the lie written across her cheeks, just turned and found a home for the last leaflet. 'Children love re-arranging them,' he said turning back and smiling again. 'Shall we go and have a look at what Valerie has unearthed?'

She followed him, thinking of nothing to say until they reached the back of the gloomy room. On the table were any number of folders and papers, neatly laid out. 'I got in a bit early. Thought it'd be easier if I got everything into some sort of order for you, rather than just a big heap …'

'That's great – I really do appreciate it.' She looked again at the neat piles. 'Umm, where would be a good place to start? Is there any particular order…?'

He rested a hand on a red folder. 'These are the wartime diaries – I think that's what Valerie was going to show you? And these,' he pointed to a box file, 'Are more photos which might be useful. But without knowing exactly what you need …?'

Martha was ready to sit down at the table and tell him the whole story. 'Well, I …'

A voice called from the door. 'Coo-ee. Anyone home?'

'Oh, that'll be Miss Farrant – come to collect some documents we ordered for her, from the museum in town. Give me a minute, will you? Take a look, see if anything is what you're looking for …'

Martha pulled out a chair, plastic and scratched. She was keen to look at the diaries – they might be a great help, but she was even keener to listen in on Simon's other conversation. It seemed more than a co-incidence that Hilly should be here, just at the time she was, and it reminded her of her unresolved assurance to Laura of unearthing more information from Hilly. She flipped open the folder, attempting to read while she listened, but she couldn't hear properly – just Hilly's loud exclamations, and then Simon saying "I'd love to help, but I'm in the process of assisting someone else just now. Would you be able to come back … yes, tomorrow's fine..."

Hilly went, and Martha re-concentrated her efforts on the paperwork in front of her, trying to find at least one thing she could comment on, to show that she had been taking an interest in those, rather than eavesdropping. In fact though, as soon as she started reading the diary there was no need to feign interest; seeing the war years from the perspective of people who had actually been there - not fighting, but dealing with the everyday – was truly fascinating. And then she saw it. The reason presumably why Valerie had marked the page with a Post-it note. A reference to a plane and a woman and an accident. She flicked back the page and re-read the whole paragraph, making sure she had missed nothing.

'Sorry about that,' Simon said, looking back over his shoulder. 'People look on us as a library and a records office and goodness knows what else, as well as a museum. Anyway, how's it going?' He looked over her shoulder. 'Oh yes, Valerie mentioned that story – don't know why we haven't made more of it before – it's the sort of thing that would appeal to visitors and locals alike …'

He carried on, enthusing about what a great display it might make, but Martha was still absorbing the possible significance of it. Two men – local farmers – had been out inspecting their land, when they had heard the whine of a failing engine, then an "almighty crash" as they put it. They made their way "fast as we could" to the place where they'd seen the plane go down. They'd run as best they could across the hummocky fields and "was bowled over to see a plane balanced at a precarious angle, on the tip of one of the wings".

'This did actually happen? It's not just a local legend that someone's retelling?'

'Oh no, no, these are all original records, written at the time the events happened,' Simon said, picking up the papers Martha had been reading.

'Such a good story … I'm surprised we don't hear more about it. In fact, Valerie said that once she started reading it, she remembered her mother telling her about it, when she was growing up.' He slid into the spare chair at the table. 'It must have been quite something – seeing a plane coming down, right in front of you – and then to find the pilot was a woman. I mean, it would still be a bit unusual now, but back then … And I've definitely heard about the two men before – local heroes, obviously, at the time. And of course other planes came down around this part of the world during the war too – even a German one.' He looked over at her. 'There's a monument that was put up to commemorate an American plane, down on the marsh, you've probably seen it …'

Martha looked up at the mention of Americans. That would fit in with the US airmen at the Castle. 'No, I don't think I've heard about that …' her words faded as she tried unsuccessfully to organise so many competing thoughts. 'Whereabouts would that be?' she asked, convinced that, despite all her beach walking, she'd never come across anything of the kind.

'Well, it's not actually on the beach now – it's back on the path that runs behind the marsh – part of the Coastal Path actually. I think they moved it there so that more people would see it. Anyway, all the airmen from the plane – it was a Liberator - are listed on the monument …'

Martha reeled a little, overwhelmed by the barrage of information which might, or might not, be contributing to her gathering story.

'I could take you there if you like – if you think it might be of use, that is …' He hesitated. 'Or maybe you've got too much on your plate at the moment …?'

'No – well, yes, I have, but it would be really useful – to see the memorial and all the names.'

They sat in silence, neither knowing what to say next.

'Just going back to this woman for a minute – the one who crashed in the field,' Martha tried to put her tangled thoughts into words. 'Is there anything more on her? I know there's a lot here, but …'

'I could copy some pages for you,' he said, echoing Valerie's previous words. 'We've got a copier out the back. Then you could look through at your leisure.' He stood, then paused in his tracks. 'Not that you're not welcome to stay, of course, and look at all of this for as long as you want … or come back. We can put it all in a box for you, leave it on the shelf so it's all together whenever you come in …'

Martha smiled.

'I'm rambling, aren't I?' he said, laughing. 'How about Friday? – you know, to go and see the memorial?'

'Friday would be great – and perhaps that might give you time to photocopy the diary by then?' He held a thumb up as he turned at the sound of more visitors arriving at the door. Just as he was walking away Martha called out, 'Oh, by the way, is it okay if I take some pictures on my phone, of these photos …' she indicated the file on the table. There was a whole squadron of images lined up for her inspection and it had occurred to her that having digital versions of them would allow her a much-enlarged view.

'Help yourself. I'd better get on with some work, otherwise Valerie will be telling me off when she gets back.' He smiled again. 'See you on Friday – ten okay?'

Ten was brilliant, Martha thought, but not quite as brilliant as the scribbles she'd just spotted on the back of one of the photos in the clear-plastic folders.

A SHORT MAN WITH CREWCUT HAIR

Martha left the museum with the feeling that she had bagged a haul of treasure, with details from the diary and the photos. She knew there were things to do back at the house – yet more bags of unwanted belongings which needed moving on to new homes, clutter and rubbish which needed no more of a journey than to the bin or the tip. But the pictures were calling to Martha, asking for her attention, and she was only too willing to give it.

To avoid the dilemma, she decided to bypass the house and go straight to the beach hut. True, she would have no large computer screen there to help her examination of the images, but she could enlarge the photos on her phone, zoom in on faces almost as easily there. And it wasn't in the least difficult to persuade herself that a breath of sea air while she did so would bring a glow to her pale cheeks.

Ted was outside when she arrived, gathering up the remains of the decorating equipment he and Carl had been using. The man was always keen for a chat, and they laughed at the sight of dogs chasing seagulls, and children chasing dogs, on the wide stretch of low-tide sand.

Smalltalk with Ted concluded, coffee made, Martha pulled a chair onto the small veranda and positioned it out of the light so that she could see her phone screen more clearly. The sun was nowhere near as strong as it had been in what now seemed far-off days when she had first found the beach hut, but it was still bright and concentrating enough warmth to her little spot to make sitting outside enjoyable.

She found herself having to flick backwards and forwards between the images of the fronts and the backs of the photos, trying to make sure she matched the corresponding ones together. The photo she had seen when she first went to the museum simply had "Chas and Co – Moyons Castle" written on the back. Which was infuriating, because that was the one that had a clearer view of the faces of the servicemen. She moved on to another – a more blurred picture, but this one had far more information. Neatly written on the back was a list of names, presumably in the same order as the men arranged on the front –

Buzz Philips, Vernon Casey, Al Nugent, Chas Brookner, Sy Norman, Laurie Symonds…

And there, not one but two faces which caught her attention. The first, on the end of the row, was listed as Joe Moretti. Martha returned to the corresponding photo and zoomed in on his face. Surely this had to be the same man who was in the beach photos she had found here, in the cupboard?

She went inside and pulled out the bag where the pictures still nested, and held her phone up alongside the black and white print. He had the same Mediterranean-looking features - very handsome, thought Martha, as she compared him with the rest of the raggle-taggle bunch in the group picture. Tall, lanky, short, plump, crooked-toothed. None of the rest of them fitted the bill. And the "J" … of course there was that. The "J" of the name on her letters, must surely fit with Mr Joe Moretti?

Martha was sure the letter-writer and the man in both photos was one and the same. She was convinced – but she had been known to jump to conclusions, she smiled. She would take all the pictures round to Laura, get her to give them the once-over. Unlike her, Laura wasn't given to flights of fancy – far from it – and she would give a definite and considered opinion. Martha put the printed photos in her bag, and began to click at her phone to shut down the images. But as she did so, the other face which had been bugging her came back to mind, and she re-opened the image with the list of names.

It was him, the one standing slightly to one side of the group – the one now identified as Vernon Casey. A short man with crewcut hair. She had definitely seen those eyes before, that skin pulled too tightly across the muscles of his face; but any resemblance had to be pure co-incidence. Didn't it?

NO-ONE WOULD BLAME YOU

'So, what should I do now – about Richard?' Martha felt that, despite the sea views all around her, she was sitting in a hall of mirrored doors with not a single key in her pocket. She and Laura had decided to walk along the coast path to Anchor Bay, and the autumn sun was surprisingly warm.

Laura glanced across at her. 'I guess it's more about what you want to do than what you should do ... I'm not sure there's any *should* in a situation like this.'

'Yes, but – should he know that I know? Should he know that we've found him – found him out, with all his guilty secrets? Should I tell the police ...' She stopped abruptly, the thought suddenly hitting her like a stray tennis ball. 'I mean, isn't it bigamy? Is that the right word? And that means that I might not actually be married…depending on which of us was first ... or not any more anyway.' Martha looked unsure whether this was good news to her or bad. 'I don't know what to think,' she finally confessed.

'You lost him months ago.' Laura stood with her, shoulder to shoulder in all ways. 'It was like a bereavement – you lost him, and you mourned him, and you were angry and upset.' She paused. 'You've done all that – there's nothing wrong with allowing yourself to move on. But if you felt you needed to lay it on the line to him, to make him squirm for the way he's treated you – well no-one would blame you for that Martha.'

'I want to show him up for the bastard he is,' Martha snapped as they carried on walking. 'I want the whole world to know what their neighbour, their friend – their *husband* – is capable of …' She wiped a hand across her tearstained face again, avoiding eye contact with the cyclist who had dismounted and was pushing his bike towards them. 'But I don't know if I've got the energy, or even whether I want to put that much effort into him any more. I hate the man for what he's done – but is he worth my time? I'm not sure that little worm is worth more than just stamping on …'

'How would you feel if you were her?' They had stopped again, allowing a harassed woman with three dogs to pass.

'Her? Who – the wife? You mean would I want to know?' Martha hesitated. 'To tell you the truth, I've no idea at this moment, I really haven't.' She paused again, thinking things through. 'But those poor children … would you want to know that your father was such a little shit?' She glanced across at Laura. 'How old are they again?'

Laura ignored the question, kicking a small pebble from the pathway. 'Look, I don't think you should do anything – make any decisions – just yet. Give yourself a chance. It's a massive shock … I'm not sure *I've* got my head round it all yet, let alone you …'

'You're probably right – you usually are.' Martha managed a watery smile. 'But I can tell you now, he's not getting away scot-free, whatever else I decide …'

The two sisters gave each other an uncharacteristic hug. They pushed on, with the small collection of holiday shops now in view, watching as two dogs chased each other, smiling at a child who was trying to hula-hoop while jumping insignificant waves. Their steps sped up a little as they neared the ice cream kiosk. 'Blackberry and clotted cream,' Martha requested, relishing for once the advantage of having a "big sister" to organise things.

TRUE OF US ALL

'Olivia Laurenson – mother's name. Local beauty – socialite – different as chalk and cheese, the two of us. No-one would pair us together as mother and daughter,' Hilly laughed. But it was a laugh so full of resentment and bitterness that it carried the cargo of a dozen more stories in its wake.

Despite everything else which had erupted in her life over the past weeks – or perhaps because of it - Martha hadn't forgotten what she'd said about contacting Hilly, to challenge her about the beach hut and Eva. She'd set out, driving recklessly down the country lanes towards Hilly's farm, and then, after a near-collision with a four-by-four on a blind bend, had stopped in the driveway of a house, given herself a serious talking-to as her hands shook on the steering wheel. She'd driven home, so slowly she was barely moving at times, yet still ignoring the hoots from the frustrated driver behind her.

She'd reached for the coffee, but then abandoned it in favour of some camomile tea, thinking that that might settle the turmoil which was churning inside her. She knew it wasn't all about Hilly – that the bohemian woman was a symptom not a cause. But it was an urge to be doing something, anything, which was not about Richard. After forcing down the whole cup of herbal tea, Martha had picked up the phone and invited Hilly to come to her.

Martha realised her mouth was hanging open at Hilly's revelation and picked up her cup to disguise her surprise. She had meticulously laid out cups and side plates and teaspoons while she waited for the woman to arrive, but everything was in danger of jumping from the coffee table as Martha jerked forward in an attempt to absorb this woman's words the better. Because the name which Hilly had just mentioned was the name which Eva had struggled so hard to recall. Olivia - the name of the woman who had provided her with the key to the beach hut …

Understandably, the question of why Hilly and her mother had different surnames was one of the first to emerge from the heap of questions buzzing in Martha's head. She had heard no mention of Hilly ever having married, and although she disliked herself for thinking it, she had assumed that Hilly had never been the marrying kind. With just a small hint however, the woman launched into a stuttering explanation, and it transpired that it was Olivia who had remarried, while Hilly had retained her father's name.

'Look – another thing – I hope you don't mind me asking …' Martha veered suddenly down a different pathway. She realised she was faltering but she found Hilly's unpredictability and abruptness disconcerting.

'Speak up – hearing's not what it was – won't bite you know!'

'Well, what I was going to say - what I really don't understand – is that if the beach hut belonged to your mother – Olivia – then why didn't she leave it to you when she died? It would seem the most logical thing; you were her only child after all.' The whole thing was coming out in a torrent of words, but now she'd started Martha couldn't stop herself. 'And, if you don't mind me saying, your mother was a bit – well it was a bit hurtful for her to leave it to a complete stranger, wasn't it?'

Hilly was quiet. And Martha had never known Hilly quiet before, without a view or an opinion on anything. 'I'm sorry,' she blurted. 'I've offended you …'

'No – quite, absolutely – couldn't have put it better myself.' Hilly sipped her tea surprisingly delicately, for a woman of her size. 'Fact is – don't know. Reason I wanted to talk to Eva – shed some light and so on.' She took more tea, and Martha's heart suddenly melted for the woman. Bold, brash, unphased by almost everything, but undermined by a simple question of family.

'But she left you the farm, the house – everything else?' Martha asked, more to fill the desperate silence than because she wanted that particular information.

'Yes, house, land, livestock – whole kit and caboodle…' But Hilly still looked dumbstruck, and the question of the beach hut hung on the end of the sentence, unspoken. 'Not that a beach hut is of any practical use …' she added, seemingly persuading herself as much as Martha. 'Just frivolous, personal.'

Martha could see now the distress that the possibly insignificant gesture had caused. Good old Hilly, headstrong, unendingly practical. Give her the farm and the business and the rambling house – she'd make good with all of that. The romantic, impractical, pretty beach hut – not her style – give that to someone else. She wondered if Hilly had ever been pretty, had ever liked dancing.

'Eva told me …' Martha wondered whether what she was about to say would make Hilly feel better or worse. 'She told me that your mother said she couldn't bear to see Eva and her young man – so much in love – unable to fulfil their relationship …'

Hilly just nodded, as if that made perfect sense to the girl who'd always been the wallflower at the summer ball, the embarrassment to a glamorous mother.

'I'm sure your mother didn't mean …' but Martha wasn't actually sure about anything in her world at that moment. She paused again, trying to get her thoughts in order. 'Can I ask – do you mind …?'

Hilly looked across at her, with a face that could as easily have cried as barked an order. Martha hastily continued. 'I just wondered why … you've never asked Eva about all this before?'

Hilly suddenly looked old – greyer, wearier than Martha had seen her before. 'Sometimes, we don't want to hear what has to be said …'

Martha wanted to reach out, to take hold of Hilly's hand, say something reassuring. But this, she guessed, was exactly what Hilly didn't want. 'I suppose that's true of us all occasionally,' she said, thinking about Richard and the times she had turned away from hearing what others had wanted to tell her.

They both sat looking into their teacups, until Hilly sprang up, almost knocking the china teapot flying. 'Well, this won't get the baby a new bonnet,' she said cheerily, as though the past ten minutes of conversation had never happened. 'Sheep to deal with, dog to feed …' and with that she was gone from the house.

Martha was left contemplating the words they had exchanged. She was sure that, despite Hilly's ongoing disappointment, there was no big mystery about the beach hut legacy – that her mother had, at worst, misread Hilly's desires, but it was good to have sorted out one little conundrum at least. Martha half-smiled at the various pictures of Hilly which she had in her head. The tangled hair, the mud-stained clothes; who would have thought that the eccentric woman cared about anything? But it just went to show – assumptions were a dangerous thing. And if Hilly for once in her life was showing a soft side, if she felt better about getting to the bottom of the story with someone else sitting at her side, then Martha was happy to be that person.

VERY THERAPUTIC

Martha swerved into the layby just outside the village. She was early again for her rendezvous at the museum, and she convinced herself that the surplus time could be put to good use by scribbling down notes about what she hoped to find out. But the truth was that she could feel a squirming in her stomach that she hadn't felt since she was a teenager – that if she was honest, she didn't remember feeling in those early days when she had first met Richard. She sighed, reminding herself that that was all gone and she needed to put it all – the good and the bad of it - from her mind.

But her daydreaming had eaten into the early minutes, and now Martha realised, as she looked at her watch, that she was in danger of being late.

She hurried along the road to the car park and pulled at an angle into a space, darting back to collect her phone which was still sitting on the passenger seat, and then returning once more to check if she had actually locked the doors. Her face was flushed as she rushed across the tarmac to meet him.

'I got you a ticket,' Simon said, waving the flimsy white square at her, smiling at her flustered face. 'Just in case,' he said.

In case of what? Martha wasn't sure if she was pleased at his consideration or annoyed that he so obviously thought her scatty, but she took the ticket graciously and walked back to put it on the dashboard. The whole awful saga with Richard had made her suspect everyone's motives, everyone's honesty, she realised.

'What a beautiful morning.' Simon was gazing up at the blue sky with its perfect puffball clouds. 'I've got my car here, but as it's so lovely, shall we walk down to the beach?'

Martha had assumed that this was what they would be doing anyway, had put on sensible shoes. 'Yes, that would be good. Too nice to be indoors – well, in a car …' She was rambling, desperate to make some sort of conversation. 'So – are you from this area?' she asked, as they began their walk. 'You seem to know it well?'

'Comes with the job, I guess – knowing where the history fits into the landscape,' he said, turning down Anchor Lane, where an ancient hand-painted sign pointed to the sea. 'I'm not from round here originally – you can probably tell from my accent – but I've lived here for several years now, and I really love it.'

They walked in silence for a while, Martha dawdling as she looked around at the jumble of ancient houses leaning in on each other, their pastel shades reminding her of the beach huts.

'What about you?' Simon paused, allowing Martha to catch up. 'Have you always lived round here?'

'Well – Moyon's Quay – I've lived there for … ' she quickly calculated in her head. 'About six years now I think, so almost a local.'

'But you've never been here – to the memorial?'

'To be honest, I wasn't much of a walker when we first came here. Richard …' she paused, words caught in her throat. '…My ex – he loved walking, and at first he tried to persuade me to join him, but I couldn't keep up with the treks he wanted to do, so I tended not to walk at all, well not any distance anyway.' They both stopped, looking at three horses contentedly munching in the adjoining field. 'It's only over the past few months that I've started walking, just to …' She didn't want to explain, to go into the whole painful episode.

'It can be very therapeutic, walking,' Simon spoke to the trees and the greenery, not looking at her. 'I found the same when … when things weren't going too well for me.' He stopped again, pointing out a buzzard which was circling overhead. 'I just started walking, and found I couldn't stop,' he laughed. 'If I'd have kept going, I could have been in The Outer Hebrides by now.'

They turned down a lane off a lane, each time the pathway getting narrower, until they couldn't avoid being caught by the overflowing brambles of the hedgerow. Simon stopped, plucking a dark ripe berry from a branch. He popped it in his mouth, then picked one for Martha, both rolling the luscious berry juice round their mouths. 'We should have brought a bowl,' Martha said, stopping to take more berries, holding out a handful to him.

They spent five minutes gorging themselves on the sweet sharp fruit, then, rubbing the purple stains from their hands, they continued.

'There it is – just across the bridge,' Simon said, pointing to a rustic wooden structure, more like a ladder, which crossed a small stream. 'As I mentioned before, the monument used to be in the middle of the marsh, where the plane actually came down.' He waved towards the flat expanse of land which sat between them and the sea. 'But they wanted to put it somewhere where more people would see it, so they moved it next to the coastal footpath.'

'Who are "they"?' Martha asked, stumbling a little as she followed Simon down the uneven grass-lined path.

'Sorry – The British Legion. It was them who created the original monument to commemorate the crew of the Liberator. It crashed in bad weather when its wing caught the edge of the hill over there, and brought them down on the marsh.' They both held up hands to shield their eyes, looking at the solid cragginess of Berenden Hill. It looked beautiful caught in the morning sun, patches of late gorse and dying heather colouring the spaces between the harsh greyness of the rocks.

'It looks so benign this morning,' Martha said, scanning the height and the length of the hill. 'But I've seen the moors when a mist rolls in, and you can switch from June to December in the space of a minute.'

'Yes – I think that's exactly what happened to the Liberator. One minute they were flying in a clear sky, using the coastline as their route-finder, and the next they were flying blind, entirely blanketed by sea mist.' He scanned the horizon, as if the story might replay itself and a phantom plane appear before them. They walked the last few yards to the memorial and stood in front of it in respectful silence. Birds were singing, but away in the distance, and a quiet had descended on the spot.

Martha couldn't help but think too of what Eva had told her - that she too had crashed. It seemed an uncanny mirroring of two stories and it crossed her mind for a moment that Eva might be confused, might be overlapping someone else's story with her own. But she was here, with facts displayed in front of her, and she needed to focus on what Simon was showing her.

She crouched down, peering at the small granite cross. At its centre was a distorted piece of metal, bearing the crudely stamped names of the airmen.

'It was made from part of the fuselage,' Simon said, as Martha leaned nearer, trying to get a better look. 'Somehow that little piece of battered metal seems so much more powerful than any words.'

And he was right, she thought. Despite the newer plaque at the side, more formal, more readable, the sad buckled piece of machinery called out so much more of their story - the inventory of the lost men. And the one incredible survivor.

Martha knelt to read the list of names; then read them again, lingering over that last singular soul. Captain Joseph Moretti. Present and correct yet again perhaps - the Joe of the photos, the "J" she had found on the torn letters? Was this the love of Eva's life – and if so, might she be able to find him at last, through those who had erected the memorial?

Martha sat back on the rough ground, flattening the long stalks of grass beneath her legs. Her breath was quicker, anxious, as though she had unexpectedly been faced with a glimmer of the past walking in front of her. Joe might be sitting here with her now; the question was, could she bring him back for Eva, before it was all too late?

There was an unnerving stillness, broken only by the anguished cries of the curlew.

NO HIDING ANYTHING

'You look a bit pale – are you okay?'

'Yes – yes, I'm fine. Just a bit overwhelmed, that's all.' Martha pulled herself straight. 'Just give me a minute.'

Simon rummaged in his backpack, pulled out a water bottle and thrust it at her.

Martha smiled at his consideration, unscrewing the top, taking a sip.

'We could walk back to the café, if you like,' he said. 'Get a proper drink – maybe something to eat?' He looked awkward, unsure.

'A cup of tea would go down well. I'll be with you in a moment.'

He crouched beside her, gazing out across the marsh. 'He was lucky I guess – the one who survived. Bit of a miracle really, when you consider the others …'

Martha's head was in a turmoil. She might – just might – have the answer to the riddle she had been trying to solve for weeks, but she couldn't just walk away now that she had her potential prize. And anyway, what was she going to do with the information now that she had it? She sipped more water, giving herself time to think. A few more hours wasn't going to make a difference, not after all this time, was it? And she owed Simon at least some tea and cake; it might have taken a lot longer to get to this point without his help.

'Okay – I'm good now,' she said, pulling herself to her feet.

Simon took her arm as they made their way across the tussocky marsh grass and slowly back to the stony path.

The Pippin café with its green gingham tablecloths was doing a fine trade, but there was a table in the corner. Martha wasn't sure she could stomach anything to eat – her guts were doing somersaults – but she chose a small Italian cannolo from a glass jar on the counter, while Simon opted for toasted teacake. They chatted about nothing while they waited for their order to arrive, but once they had tea poured and teacake oozing with melting butter, Simon asked what had obviously been on his mind.

'I know it's none of my business, but can I just confess to being an inveterate nosey-parker …'

Martha laughed, catching a crumb in her throat, coughing until her eyes watered. 'It's so good to chat to someone who's so down to earth – no agenda,' she smiled. 'I'm sorry I haven't given you the whole story …'

'Well, any of the story really,' Simon threw in, laughing himself now.

Customers at the other tables turned to look at the two of them, chuckling like children. Martha looked round, taking a breath to calm herself. 'When we've finished, perhaps we could go for a drive and I'll tell you the whole thing, beginning to end.'

They talked of the mundane, of the weather and places they'd visited while they finished their cakes and tea, eventually walking out into the autumn sunshine.

Martha drove in silence, as though the afternoon crowd at the café might still be eavesdropping on what she had to say. It wasn't until they had reached the moors, up above the village, and could pull in to a clearing looking out over the cliffs and across to Wales that she silenced the engine and turned to Simon.

'This is all a bit cloak and dagger, isn't it?' he said, laughing once more, and Martha thought what an easy natural laugh he had.

'Shall we walk for a bit?' Martha asked. 'I always find it easier to talk when I'm walking.'

They set off across the moorland path, the sea on their right, the fading banks of heather on their left. A wild pony swished its tail as it fed under a ragged tree and they stopped for a moment to watch.

'I found some letters,' Martha said suddenly, worried that if she didn't make a start soon, she would never tell her story.

'Old letters?' Simon asked, 'Letters from the people you've been trying to track down?'

'There's no hiding anything from you, is there?' she smiled. 'Yes – two lovers, Eva and I think Joe. They sent each other letters during the war, and I found them – except that they were in pieces. I put them back together, well almost, but ever since I've been trying to find out the story behind them …' Martha paused, unsure. 'It all sounds a bit stupid now, but I needed something – to distract me I suppose, and this came along at just the right moment.'

'So, you put on your Miss Marple hat and went in search of the strangers – and what did you find out?'

Slowly at first, Martha began to tell the story. When she had finished, she stopped walking and turned to Simon.

'Well, that's some story.' Simon paused, taking it all in. 'But you're not quite there, I'm assuming? What you saw today – on the memorial – that puts another piece into the puzzle?'

'If I'm right – and I think I probably am – then I've found the man I'm assuming to be Joe, well on paper at least. And the obvious next step is to try to track him down. I'm guessing he returned to the United States when his stint in England finished, but I don't even know that for sure. And then there's the question of whether he's still alive of course …' That thought had just come to her, as she was talking; that she might have come this far, done all this work, and there might still be no Joe.

'Well, I suppose you won't know until you try?' Simon said, his hand brushing Martha's as they turned back the way they had come. 'I have to say that you walk an awful long way when you get talking, don't you?' he said, smiling broadly at her as they sauntered, more slowly now, along the track towards the car.

As they pulled back into the car park at the side of the museum, the clouds, which had been gathering in an angry crowd overhead for some time, decided to release their burden. The rain came down so heavily that they could barely hear themselves speak over its beating on the car roof.

'There's no way you can get out in this lot,' Martha said, putting on the windscreen wipers once more, attempting to see what was happening. 'Shall I try and get a bit nearer to the door?' she asked, indicating the museum.

'No, it's fine – I don't need to go back into work,' he said, turning to look at the building as well. 'I don't actually live there, you know.' He raised an eyebrow, teasing her gently.

'Oh, I thought you could only survive amongst the dust and the archives, tucked up in the corner covered in papers while you sleep…' Martha grinned. They both laughed, envisaging this picture of Simon.

'I think we'd better head for home before someone starts banging on the car, thinking we're up to no good,' Simon said, indicating the rapidly steaming windows.

SOMETIMES IT HELPS TO TALK

'I was …' The words seemed to teeter on the edge, like a reluctant acrobat. 'I was – ashamed.'

As she had previously promised, Martha had taken Eva out again, this time to the tearoom near to the watermill. She had thought that the sight of the nearby castle might itself inspire the older woman to tell more of her story. Eva though barely seemed to recognise where they were – was in fact more interested in which cakes might be on offer, and whether the tea would be in a pot. Interested, that is, until Martha diverted to the subject of Eva's flying career.

'But what did you have to be ashamed about?' Martha slipped to the edge of her chair, reaching out a comforting arm to this woman she barely knew. 'You'd done a huge service to your country and to your fellow pilots. I know that no-one really appreciated all of that for years, but you and all those other women beavered away relentlessly to make sure the Air Force could do what it needed to do … so what on earth was there to be ashamed of in any of that?'

Eva looked up from the tissue she had shredded in her lap. 'I did love the job, so it wasn't hard for me to go out every day up into the skies, to leave behind all the rationing and the … the … what's the word? … oh, women's lives were so dull back then.'

'Well, I don't see anything wrong with wanting to do something interesting,' Martha said, knowing she herself would have chosen to avoid the drudgery, had she been a young woman at that time. 'And I don't think anyone would hold that against you, particularly today, when women are trying to …' Martha hesitated, now finding it was her turn to try to unearth the word she was looking for, but Eva stopped her thoughts in their tracks.

'But they would hold it against me that I didn't stay with my child …'

The woman's quiet unhesitating words hit Martha hard. While her lips tried to form questions, her voice had hidden itself in the back of her throat. It took several attempts before she could transfer her thoughts into comprehensible sound. 'Well that's … I didn't know … I didn't think ….'

'Nobody does,' Eva sighed. 'In those days, it had to be one or the other – either you had a family or you had a job and stayed unmarried …' She lapsed into thought and the two women sat in their own silences for a while. 'Not like now … you can have it all.'

Martha felt a weight of guilt come to rest on her shoulders. She didn't think she had it all – didn't want to have it all, but felt guilty that perhaps she hadn't taken full advantage of the possibilities which modern life had held up in front of her. Eva's dry cough brought her back to reality, as though the old woman were prompting her to put forward the obvious questions.

'So – the child,' Martha asked, trying still to form her thoughts as the words spilled from her. 'What happened to her – him … do you know what …?'

'It was a boy. He was taken for adoption.' The old woman paused again, seeming to fight some inner turmoil, deciding which words should – ought – to come out. She looked directly at Martha, looked away again. 'Well, that's not really true – I sent him away. Didn't even want to see him…'

Martha knew she was treading a delicate path; yet she also had the feeling that Eva *wanted* her to pull the words from the wreckage of her memories, to hold them up to the light. 'You don't have to …' she began, 'But sometimes it helps to talk …'

Eva was motionless in her chair, head bowed. 'A baby is special,' she began, 'I didn't see that at the time. I didn't like this baby, and I didn't want to look at him …' Her words were coming in waves, a few small ripples, then every now and then, a surging breaker. 'I made sure he was all right, that he was going to be looked after … the least I could do …' She looked at Martha from the corner of her eye then turned to the wall. 'But then, I just walked away. I thought about how my life might be, and I chose the way which suited *me* best – selfish some might say.'

Martha was stunned. There was so much here to take in, so much that she wanted to ask. She needed to say the right things, not shallow, not offensive … but, in the end, she simply laid her words on the table. 'I don't wish to pry, but can I ask …your friend, at the castle; was he … the child's father?' It was this scrap of the story which made no sense to Martha.

A silence hung in the air like sea mist.

'If he had been,' Eva eventually whispered. 'If my wonderful Joe had been the baby's father, I would have done anything to keep that boy by my side, no matter how hard it might have been.' She paused. 'But he wasn't.'

Martha could only think of the shreds of letters. Had that been the reason the love affair had ended so suddenly? Had Eva simply given herself to another? But that didn't make sense either. She looked across at the old woman leaning back in her chair, pale with the effort of dragging her past into the present, eyes closed to further conversation.

Martha collected their belongings and helped Eva on their leisurely stroll to the car, commenting on the gardens of the ancient thatched cottages which they passed. Their journey back to the house was quiet for the most part, and Martha put the radio on, softly, just to ease the lack of words between them. "Daniel" was playing, a song Eva might possibly be unfamiliar with; but to Martha it seemed somehow appropriate – about flying and waving goodbye. And she was close now, to closing all the gaps in Eva's remarkable story; but just not quite close enough.

There was a bustling and banging as Martha tried to help Eva through the front door and back into the house. Nadya, hot and flustered with vacuum cleaner in hand, came from the kitchen to greet them.

'Ah, Mrs …'

'Martha – please call me Martha.' Eva was already making her way in a daze to her favourite chair in the living room, and they both followed her in. 'I think I've worn her out, getting her to tell me some of her stories,' Martha laughed nervously, expecting a reprimand from the carer.

'She will be fine, but maybe no more for today?'

Martha nodded, glad to have gained an exit permit so easily. There was so much flying about in her head that she really needed to allow it all to settle before she could even begin to make sense of it.

ONE SMALL SIMPLE ACT

EVA

The sun is streaming through the window, tucking a calm warmth around Eva like a quilt. She dozes, allowing the pictures in her mind's eye to play out in unravelling spools.

There is a rapping on the beach hut door. Of course, my heart leaps – it's Joe – and I get up from the chair, waiting for the door to open, waiting for his smiling face to warm my whole being. But there's nothing. And then I wonder - why would he be thumping the door like that? We have a knock, just the two of us, a gentle tap, then tap, tap, just to say "it's me", that no-one else is going to intrude. So this is an outsider, someone not in the know.

    I creep to the door, put my ear to the wood and listen. Someone stamping, snorting, impatient breaths. I wait for them to move on, to make space for Joe to arrive with arms held out to me. But they don't leave; they're still pacing, and the hefty knock comes again. They're not going to go. So I call out, quietly, so that fate can take a hand; if they don't hear me I can ignore them… if they reply, I will have to deal with it.

Of course, they hear. They've been tuned in, waiting for the voice which will be their key.

"Sergeant Casey, Ma'am."

I think he is going to give his serial number, tell me it's the United States Air Force – that's the sort of voice it is. I wait.

"I have a message Ma'am. Can you open the door?"

As quickly as my heart had leapt at the expectation of Joe, it sinks to the floor. Something has happened to him – he's been injured, he's picked up an infection…

Reluctantly I tug at the door. The man standing there is crisp-pressed, muscled, hair short and oiled.

"Perhaps I could …?" he says, pointing to the inside of the beach hut.

I open the door fully, standing aside. He is altogether too big for our little space; I feel closed in.

'I'm sorry Ma'am …' But he doesn't look sorry. He looks pleased, glad to be the bearer of bad news.

'Captain asked me to report to you Ma'am. Moretti's group has had to leave, short notice – instructions from on high.'

'Where? Where has he gone?'

'Not at liberty to say Ma'am – but they're not likely to be returning this way.' There's a smirk, a definite snigger, and I want to slap his face.

"Ma'am," he starts again.

'Stop calling me Ma'am,' I shout at him, shooing him towards the door.

But he's having none of it. He grabs my wrists, holds them to his chest.

"You need to calm down …' He stops himself from saying "Ma'am" again. "Just calm down," he insists, and he guides me – forces me – towards the chair.

I push against him, but he's stronger, and my – what is it? – anyway, it's draining from me as I think about what he's just told me.

'Why didn't he say? He must have known…'

"Like I said … Miss … last-minute order."

He stares, something obviously going through his mind. 'You're in shock,' he says, 'You need a drink,' he drawls, as he pulls a hip flask from his pocket. 'Here, take a swig – do you good.'

I don't want it, but I'm struggling to breathe and suddenly I'm shivering. He pushes the flask into my face and I take it from him, have a sip. The whisky burns as it goes down, but I take another swig, then thrust the bottle back at him as I start to cry.

He stands awkwardly. Then pulls me from the chair, yanks me towards him, squeezes my face and pushes hard with his lips. Somehow he links his leg around mine and collapses me to the bed.

And then I'm raging, angry, and I manage to scrabble away from him. But he's not giving in. He drags me back from the door and throws me down, unbuckling his belt as he goes. I kick and scream, don't care now who knows I'm here; reach out and scratch his face, his neck, but it seems just to spur him on. His weight pins me down and I'm helpless. All I can do is turn my face to the wall as he pushes and forces and grunts.

I lay there for an eternity, curled up like a baby, long after he has thrown something at me and slammed the door behind him. I pull a blanket over my head, shutting it all out. Maybe it was the whisky, but even though the scene kept replaying in my head, I must have fallen asleep eventually. I don't remember any more anyway – not until the squawking of the gulls drags me back into the real world. And then I can't stop myself remembering.

I have no idea of the time, can't bring myself to move to look at my watch; the air and the hut and my body – everything feels grey and bleak and pointless. And I feel dirty, desperate for a bath to scrub every trace of that despicable man from me. But tangled with my loathing is the purpose for his intrusion in the first place – the fact that Joe has left - and that in turn sparks anger. Such anger I have never known; it bubbles up like a volcano, spitting and overflowing … anger with myself, for ever allowing that animal into the hut, for not stopping him doing what he did. I know, deep down, that there was no way I could have fought off his bulk, prevented him from pinning me down – but it's still my fault, still down to me to have done something to stop him.

And I am so so angry with Joe. For not being here, for not sending the man packing, for marching off so suddenly without a word or a goodbye. The anger surges in me and I fling the chair across the room, hoping it will crack into a dozen pieces. But even that I can't do successfully. It just stops, leaning against the wall of the hut, but its movement reveals something. An envelope on the floor close to where I lay. I reach out, then recoil, realising that this must be what Casey had thrown at me as his parting gesture.

Joe's writing – bold and neat - is on the front of it. I pull it open, anger overwhelmed, if only for a moment, by the urge to bring him back, and I begin to read…

My wonderful darling Eva

This letter is the hardest I've ever had to write. My hand is shaking, and I don't want to write a word of it, but I have to.

I don't know how to tell you, so I will just plunge in. I have been ordered to return to the United States. A few of the boys and I are being shipped back to the airbase tonight – and there is no question of me getting out of it. Believe me, I have tried.

Our time together was so special. Maybe we had some feeling of invincibility, having both survived our planes going down, and somehow we thought our precious time would never end. But now the gods have ripped us apart again, and I only wish I could turn back the clock.

I am so so sorry my wonderful Eva. Words cannot tell you how much my heart is breaking. There is nothing in this world I would rather do than be with you. I cannot imagine a day without you - a day without your wonderful face and your laughter and every wonderful part of you.

This is more painful than anything I have ever had to endure, and I would give anything for another night with you. Look up at the stars tonight Eva, and think that I will be looking at them too. I will look at them every night until we can be together again, and I will never stop thinking of you.

You are my life, and it is nothing without you.

With all my love, forever

Joe

It breaks my heart. The words are making things worse and I can't bear to read any more. The anger stirs in me once more, and I want to scream at Joe for leaving me behind. I pick up the letter again, tear it in half, and then into smaller and smaller pieces, but even then I have spiteful energy left. There is also my own letter for Joe, the one I had written while I was waiting for him yesterday. I glance at the sentiment I had so happily scrawled, the words which now seem so futile, redundant.

My dearest Joe

I spend my time, all day and every day, just thinking of you. I've never felt this way before. It is wonderful, glorious, and so perfect that I can only think that someone somewhere meant for this to happen, that fate, or the gods, or whatever you want to call it, aligned to bring us together. And it all started on that day I got that letter.

Have you ever thought about things in that way – that without one small simple act or incident, the rest of your life would have gone down a different path? If I hadn't had that letter – the one inviting me for the interview, if I hadn't gone and joined the ATA, if I hadn't been given that plane on that morning on that route, I would have been somewhere else, and wouldn't have been caught up in the blankets of sea mist, wouldn't have clipped the hills, wouldn't have crashed into that field, wouldn't have been taken to the castle to recuperate ... and wouldn't have met you. And the same could be said in your case.

We were so obviously meant to be together, and that is the way we should stay – not just today, or tomorrow, but for the rest of our lives.

I love you Joe Moretti, and you will be in my heart, no matter what, for the rest of our lives.

Your ever faithful
Eva

And I rip that too, flinging all the pieces as hard as I can. I have no idea where they end up - I just want to destroy anything that remains of the two of us.

And then, on the table, I see the photos, the ones which we had taken of each other, sitting amongst the trees at the top of the beach. We look so happy, it might as well be another couple in another world. Something of the steam has gone out of me – or perhaps I just can't bring myself to rip through our faces. Anyway, I don't destroy them; I just shove them into the cupboard, out of my sight.

Somehow I find my way back from the hut, somehow I manage to drag myself up those stone steps to the castle. I have no idea whether I've seen anyone or spoken; my body is a sack of rubbish, weighty but worthless. I barely remember getting back to my room. I must have thrown myself on the bed and allowed the greyness of the summer's night to throw its blanket over me, because in the morning I am still there, face down in my clothes. My first thought is of Joe. And then slowly the reality of what has happened overwhelms me once again, the tide of my misery washes over me in ever-increasing waves, and I am as helpless as a drowning child.

I hear, in that echoing underwater way, a voice. And then someone is sitting me up. Mrs Armitage, the housekeeper, I suppose, but I can't even raise my head to see, much less respond to the stream of … no not questions, she doesn't ask anything – but of commentary. The state of the day, the weather, the lady of the house, the mess and confusion left by the abandoning officers. Which of course brings me back to Joe. And the fact that he isn't here, will never more be here. And that other obnoxious evil heartless man. I hold my body close, not wanting to reveal its abuse, but it seems that the housekeeper has by some means absorbed what has happened to me.

'A bath,' she says, 'That will make you feel better.'

A bath during the daytime is unheard of in the day-to-day of the Castle. I can see the fact isn't lost on Mrs Armitage either, as she bustles and cajoles me towards the bathroom, with a towel she has mustered along the way. She runs the clanking taps – more than the permitted wartime six inches of water - until the steam rises in the deep tub, handing me an unused bar of Pears soap – another unheard-of – and pulls the door to, telling me to join her in her rooms when I have finished.

I languish there, allowing the initial heat to overwhelm my thoughts. I stay until the water has cooled and covered my skin in goosepimples, and my teeth are talking to themselves. The towel – large and soft - holds me, and I think of mother, rigorously rubbing my childhood skin as she clamped me between her arms, applying the same vigour to my hair until it stood like dandelion seeds around my head. The comfort of that scene brings forth tears, and once started I can't stop. Mrs Armitage reappears, efficiently handing me clean clothes, chivvying me into shoes, until I am back into the respectable world of the clean and dressed.

'Come along.' And although I feel like a child, I am content to follow her to her rooms, allowing her to take charge of the situation.

She tips water from the steaming kettle, and I wait while she stirs and pours and hands me a delicate cup and a plate of warmly buttered toast. She sits with socks awaiting darning on her lap, saying little, but the gaps in her words are as good as questions and slowly I begin to retell the previous evening's events.

For someone who appears as prim as her buttoned-up shirts, she is surprisingly matter-of-fact. She nods, accepting of a difficulty which needs to be dealt with, like a broken vegetable dish or a rip in a favourite evening gown.

'Stay here,' she says, as though I have a dozen choices about what I will do with my day. But I am grateful for having someone else to think on my behalf.

She doesn't say, when she comes back, where she had been, but I assume that she has probably discussed my situation with Mrs Saltrey. I wince at the idea of my intimate details being conferred over in the morning room, but decisions already appear to have been made.

'Your parents.' It is a question from Mrs Armitage rather than a statement.

'No – I can't … they're gone …'

'Well, other family …' This time it is a statement.

'I'll go back – to the Air Transport Auxiliary.' In the face of unacceptable choices my boldness has returned. In a moment of absolute clarity, it seems to me that if I return to a life before Joe, then I might begin to deal with his absence. What I have given no thought to, but is written clear on Mrs Armitage's face if only I had the wherewithal to notice, is the potential outcome of my encounter with Sargeant Casey.

AN UNWELCOME PARCEL
EVA

Words and pictures are swirling in Eva's head like leaves in a whirlpool in a river, submerging her as she desperately tries to reach for the safety of better times. This part of the story - which has bubbled to the top, revived by the questions of the woman who takes her out - is the one she has never wished to revisit; but it is the one that needs to be faced - the one that she will have to relate one more painful time.

She writhes in her chair as the agonising memories find their place, far more excruciating than anything she had experienced after the crash. At the time she had prayed to a god she had little belief in, prayed that she would black out, escape from the here and now, just as had happened when the plane had collided with the hillside.

But it was as if those women – supposed women of god, in their black habits - had relished seeing her in pain, as some sort of punishment for what they considered her immorality. She had found an old ring, slipped it on her finger, but it seemed to mean nothing. The sisters needed no sixth sense to know that they were dealing with an unmarried woman; and in their eyes, that gave them the right to inflict or allow as much pain as humanly possible.

People say that nature makes a woman forget, otherwise no-one would have a second child, but Eva hasn't forgotten any of it. And the pain was made doubly worse, arising as it did out of something she had never wanted. Even now she can see the raised eyebrows, hear the tuts of maternal disapproval; but really, why would anybody want a child that someone had forced upon them? And just the thought of the child brings an image of that bristling barbaric lout of a man - heavy, small-eyed, soulless, not an ounce of care or thought for anyone but himself. Her screams had been as much about the force of his assault as they were about the pains of childbirth.

They thrust the resulting child at her, the Sisters of Mercy, triumphantly, as if to say "Go on – take a good look at what you've done. Are you pleased with yourself now?" And she would have been, if it had been Joe's child, if it had been a creation born of love and caring. But in their short time together, they had always been so careful – Joe had seen to that. And so, as desperately as she wanted it to be different, all her senses told her that the baby wasn't Joe's. She had screwed up her eyes, and pushed it back at them; she couldn't even bear to look.

They made her look of course, and that just underlined what she had convinced herself was the truth. The child had none of Joe's mediterranean looks, no brown eyes or curling dark hair, just an insipid paleness and a fluff of fairish tufts on its head. It was like one final triumphant sneer from that despicable man, and they had had to force the infant into her arms ... "He needs feeding *Mrs* Andrews, he needs a clean nappy..." They emphasised that "*Mrs*" every single time, the deception she'd presented to them so easily pierced and deflated in their heartless eyes.

And what was to become of the child? Adoption was tossed backwards and forwards in every conversation. He was an unwelcome parcel; Eva didn't want him, but at the same time she couldn't bear the idea of any child being advertised or "auctioned off" to some pinched and lifeless couple.

And then David had come to visit. In his big-brother way he held her hand while he chatted about this and that, everyday nonsense, keeping entirely away from the subject of the baby. And then he turned, dragging his gaze away from the door at the end of the ward, and spoke quietly. "Dolly would love a baby." That was it; simple plain honesty in the end. And it was the obvious answer which had been hovering over them all for days. David's wife Dolly had been unable to conceive, despite the long and many months of trying; and Eva now had a child she didn't want. It was the obvious solution, and they were welcome to it.

Eva can recall nothing of the subsequent procedures, the arrangements. Just that one day, the thrusting of a child into her face at regular intervals stopped. Her milk kept coming, and she kept mopping it, but she no longer had to face the offspring of coercion and intimidation.

Eva supresses a sob, strangely emanating from that sense of deep loss which she can feel, even now. Even though it was something she had never wanted, it had then departed. And it had left a gap in her life – a gap which she increasingly needed to fill with something. She can still hear David, excited, happy, inviting her to stay with them, after she was discharged from the maternity home. There couldn't of course have been anything worse, to be back with the child, but in reality she'd had nowhere else to go. And so she had gone, standing by as her brother and his wife registered the child's birth as their own. But she stayed with them only for the few days it took for her to contact the Transport Auxiliary and to get a response. She thinks, fleetingly, of all the letters she has sent since which have received no reply. But as soon as that one thin letter arrived on David's doorstep, and she found it was the response she had hoped for, her bags were packed and she was on the train – back to the ATA and her beloved flying.

Beneath her closed eyelids, Eva is aware of the creaking of the floorboards, telling tales of someone in the room with her. Someone who is knocking into the furniture, filling the room with animosity. She realises at that moment that the words of the story she has been watching in her mind's eye may actually have been being playing on her lips; that perhaps Martin has heard the opening and closing of this chapter of her story. And although these are the lines which she has wanted him to know from the beginning, it seems that the story has not landed well.

SOME SORT OF GUILT
EVA

'Enough. Just stop! I don't want to hear this – not a single word. I don't want to hear any more of your ridiculous lonely-old-woman stories. You just keep putting them out there so that you can keep me coming back here week after week, but it's all lies….' Martin stops and she thinks he has run out of steam; but he is obviously just winding himself up like a clock, for another jarring outburst.

Eva wants to tell him - that her story has got ahead of itself and that he has jumped a few chapters and reached the end while she's still struggling to turn the pages. But she sees he has guessed what she's been trying to tell him for the past weeks and days. She wonders why she has bothered with all those stories, when he has so easily seen through them; when he has looked already into another world and found things he'd rather not know.

He hasn't gone though, not yet anyway. If it had been her, Eva thinks, if their roles had been reversed, she might have placed her hands over her ears, or slammed the woodwork hard enough that pieces would fall out. That would have been her.

But for now he is standing at the window, staring past the choked rosebushes and those gaudy flowers that probably neither of them remember the name of. And there are tears on his cheeks. And that is the thing that breaks her. After all those years of not being at his side, not bathing a cut knee or kissing a broken heart, now he is a grown man standing beside her, crying unashamedly, and inside her a taught wire, which has for all these years held her world together, is no longer able to hold on, and simply snaps.

And at the same time, something in the man himself snaps too.

'For god's sake woman. You're just putting all this total nonsense out there so that you can hang some sort of guilt on me and keep me where you want me. Do you think I don't realise that?' Martin turns, picks up his coat. 'But I don't need any of it, so don't bother going any further – just shut up.' His face is stretched fit to burst, spittle issuing from his lips, straying down his chin. She opens her mouth to placate him, but it just makes matters worse. 'Shut up. For God's sake woman, just SHUT UP!'

The lounge door and then the front door slam, with so much vigour that Eva is surprised not to hear glass shattering. And then Nadya appears, wanting to know what on earth is happening. And Eva can only answer with more tears.

GOING HOME
EVA

The emptiness of the room grows like the bindweed on the garden fence, choking everything it finds, until she's really struggling to breathe. Nadya has previously opened the window but there is no air coming through; the reassuring cup of tea she has brought has gone untouched. Eva clutches at her wretched stick, leaning on it so hard she thinks it might snap, but she manages to heave herself to standing. She pushes her way past the heavy furniture and all the belongings, none of which she wants or needs. There's not enough room, or she's too clumsy, and the folds of her dress drag some bits and bobs to the floor – china and glass. She doesn't mind that the pieces are broken, only that they will bring Nadya back to check on her. But no-one comes, and she tries to gather her thoughts; what is it that she must do next?

She has to go out, she knows that much, and she gets as far as the front door. Everything has become a bit too much, and she finds herself gasping for air, feeling like she's almost drowning. But it's cooler there, on that side of the house, and a few minutes is all she needs – because she knows she has to go, that there is something that she needs to do. And then it comes to her – Martin. She needs to find Martin.

There is no sign of him, anywhere out in the street. He must have long since disappeared amongst the jumble of cottages and down this lane or that one; who knows which route he has chosen. But Eva thinks she has a good idea. She shuffles her way down the path, turning down the road that she has wanted to walk down many times before, but from which she has always been distracted or discouraged. She stops for a while to watch a man atop a ladder, reaching out to trim the unruly hedge which has climbed to twice his height; he nods good afternoon, taking no real notice of her, and she's pleased to see that there is no intention from him of turning her back to the house. She has to stop after every few steps, the whole thing getting more difficult as the path begins to wind its way uphill.

She sees the postman but this time it's not George. This one just smiles and says something about the weather; no trying to return her like a lost letter to where she's just come from. She has to collect herself though, as soon as he is gone, get her breath, just enough to get her to the top of the little hill … probably only half a dozen steps, but they're the hardest steps. She is sure there used to be a seat here, you know, like those ones in the park, but there is no sign of it now. In the quiet of her stillness she can heard the birds, calling to each other. She's not sure if it's a robin or a blackbird, scans the trees to see …

'Mrs B.' Someone is calling her. 'Mrs B, can you wait …'

It might be the woman with the hair, and she turns to greet her. But instead it is the help – Nina or Norma or whoever she is. Eva expels a long despairing breath. She will be going home.

'I need to find him … Martin. He's gone,' she tells the carer.

'Mr Andrews will be fine. He will not be lost. He will find his own way home.' She smiles at Eva, takes her arm, turns her back the way she has come. All that effort, and now she is going home.

'I want to find Martin – he doesn't understand…' Eva tries to explain, but her breath is taken with all the walking.

'Don't worry, Mrs B. I will ring him, when we get home. Everything is alright.'

And that is it. Eva is home before she knows it. There is of course no Martin – he hasn't returned, and she will not be able to explain the story properly to him. And then a stubborn thought overcomes her. If he doesn't want to hear – about her and his father - then she will keep the story to herself. 'He will never know,' she says out loud, as she hears Nadya talking to him on the phone.

RATTLED

'Martha – it's Martin…'

She'd been in the process of trying to collate all the information which she would need to take to the solicitor – the one who was going to help her sort out the mess which was Richard. It had taken all Martha's resolve to make herself sit at the table and concentrate on something which batted her emotions between angry, agitated, upset and back to angry, like a pinball machine. But she had promised Laura – and herself - and she really couldn't prevaricate any longer.

'Hi Martin. Is everything all right?' The thought suddenly occurred to her that there might be a problem with Eva.

He sighed. 'Yes and no.' There was a silence on the end of the phone, and then 'I don't know … I could really do with some help …'

'Okay, I'm all ears,' Martha began, but she could tell that a phone call wasn't really going to cut it. 'Or did you want to meet up? Would that be better?'

She heard him breathe out, a long low breath, almost a whistle. 'I was hoping that's what you'd say. That would be really great. Could you manage lunch … today?'

Martha looked at the jumble of paperwork scattered across the dining room table; she could really have done with getting it sorted, once and for all, but there was something about Martin's voice which was anxious, worried. Not like him at all. 'Okay, give me half an hour – well, three quarters. I'll see you at the café.'

She left all the paperwork in place so that it would be easier to pick up where she had left off. She changed her top, put a bare skim of makeup on her face and found her keys. She didn't want to underplay Martin's problem, but she had to admit that she was intrigued to find out what it was that had so obviously rattled him.

He'd suggested a café on the outskirts of Moyons Quay, and had already ordered coffees by the time Martha arrived. He must have been already in town, or nearby at least when he phoned, she thought, but he looked shaken, dishevelled. 'Are you okay?' She slid into the seat opposite him. 'You look …' she struggled for the least offensive word. 'A bit stunned...' she settled on.

'You could say.' Martin looked around the room, avoiding eye contact. 'I visited Eva yesterday.' There was a long pause which Martha itched to fill, but she knew she should give the man his own time to say what he needed to. 'Look, I just need to say this … can't dress it up … she told me that she's not my aunt.'

Martha looked straight at him. It seemed a minor point, in the scheme of things, for so much drama. She opened her mouth to say so, but he continued before she could speak.

'She's not my aunt, apparently, but my mother .'

Martha's jaw dropped, but no words came forth. She had been expecting almost anything. But not that. So many questions competing for answers that she struggled to pull just one from the melee. 'Well, why – how – why didn't she bring you up then? What about your parents – where do they fit in …?' The questions were pouring out of her like a leaking bucket.

'It seems I was just handed over – from my mother to her brother. And before you ask – no I don't know who my father – my real father – is.'

The waitress arrived with their coffees and the menus they'd requested, but both sat in silence, not even looking at what she had put on the table in front of them.

'Well…' She expelled a long breath. 'That's certainly stopped me in my tracks.' Martha picked up the menu then immediately put it down again. 'Hell, Martin, I don't know what to say.' The waitress reappeared, wanting to know their choices. They both made a cursory scan of the options, ordered a panini, with little regard for the filling.

'Do you remember her – Eva - when you were a child?' Martha ventured, when the woman had left them again.

'She used to visit, maybe once or twice a year. She brought me presents, usually a book, and she'd thrust a ten-shilling note into my hand as she was leaving. She never spoke much to me, but I was aware that her eyes were always on me. I never thought much about it at the time – adults always seem odd when you're a child – but perhaps now I can see why. But I don't understand why she didn't visit more, if she was that interested …that "involved".'

The waitress returned, putting napkins and cutlery in front of them.

'She was always smartly dressed, I do remember that. Dad would constantly be going on about how brave Auntie Eva was, what amazing things she'd done during the war. But, I don't know, maybe because she wasn't in uniform, or because she was a woman, I didn't really take a lot of notice. The war already seemed a long way away, even when I was seven or eight. I certainly never asked any questions. I suppose I was more interested in playing, but she would never get down on the floor with me, playing with my Dinky cars, like you'd see relatives doing today.' Martin stopped, his mind very obviously elsewhere.

'What about your birth certificate?' Martha asked, her mind flitting to a different track. 'Wouldn't it have been obvious from that that you were adopted?'

'It wasn't an issue. My parents dug out the certificate when I first applied for a passport, and they were there, listed as my mother and father. Why would you ever question what you see in a formal document like that?'

Martha thought about this for a moment; thought about the story which Eva had relayed to her about the birth of her child, and handing it over to someone else. 'I suppose,' she said, thinking aloud, 'That the whole thing was completely unofficial, and that Eva hadn't had chance to register you anyway. Amongst all the turmoil of the war I bet loads of things like that went unnoticed. And once your father – uncle - took over, he and his wife just registered you as if you were always theirs. Which effectively you were, of course.' Martha paused, thinking of so many things. 'And they never even hinted …?'

'Nothing.' Martin paused again, but just as Martha was about to fill the gap he continued. 'D'you know, it's bizarre, but the first thing I wanted to do after she'd told me, was to go and visit my parents' grave.' He took a sip of his coffee. 'I don't know why, but Eva's news … it was as though I somehow needed to share it with them. Ridiculous, obviously …' his words returned to matter-of-fact as he replaced the cup precisely in its saucer.

'I don't think it is,' Martha mirrored his actions, taking coffee, replacing her cup. 'They were your mainstay, for the whole of your younger life. It's not really surprising that you'd turn to them when you're troubled.'

Martin sat forward on his seat, keen, it seemed, to argue the point. 'But they knew – they kept the secret; more than Eva did really, when you think I was with them every day. And they never as much as gave a hint …'

Martha swept her unruly hair away from her face. 'They did it with the best of intentions – all three of them, I'm sure.'

Martin sank back, unconvinced, it seemed to Martha. They were quiet for a moment, and then Martin began again, as though, now he had started, there was so much he wanted to say.

'I spent last night looking through old photos. Plenty of mum and dad, of course, but I struggled to find many of Eva. In the end I found three, none of them particularly good. I even got the magnifying glass out, and …'

'And?'

'And I don't know how I hadn't seen it before. There was a much stronger resemblance to her than to mum or dad, but I suppose all I'd seen before was an ageing aunt …'

The paninis arrived, and Martha ordered more coffee. A double brandy might have been more appropriate, but the café had no licence.

Martha picked up her plate, put it down. 'But why? Why tell you after all this time … I don't understand. And, without wishing to sound rude, why are you telling *me* all this?'

She could see that Martin was struggling with precisely the same question himself. But he didn't come across as the sort of person with dozens of friends – particularly not close friends.

'I wanted to see what you've found out …' He swigged from his cold coffee cup, replaced it very deliberately on the table as though he might otherwise drop it. 'I thought that you might be able to throw some more light on things …'

'But hasn't she told you the whole story – Eva? Surely if she's got as far as dropping this bombshell, there'd be little problem with her carrying on with the rest of it?'

'I walked out.'

Martha raised an eyebrow, mouth full of smart remarks; but Martin's head was bowed, he was fiddling with a spoon, and she held back.

'I know. It sounds pathetic, childish,' he looked up at her. 'But I didn't want to hear any more. It was all too much – realising that you've been lied to for the whole of your life. And the truth is I couldn't take it.'

Martin looked at the food as though there was no way he would be able to swallow let alone digest. 'And now, well, I can't ask her, can I?' He glanced across to the window, unable to look Martha in the eye.

'Couldn't you eat humble pie? Take her flowers, chocolate – say you're sorry?' She took a bite from her panini. 'I mean, it's such a big thing, you really do need to know …'

Martin let out a long sigh. 'D'you know, standing at the graveside, I had a ridiculous thought – that maybe my father was my father after all. That it was just my mother who had been playing the game.' He looked over at Martha. 'But that would be an even worse can of worms, wouldn't it?'

'I don't think that's likely, Martin.' Martha said, with no idea why. 'I really think you need to go back to Eva, ask her, before this whole thing drives you insane.'

'She's elected not to speak to me.' He broke off a small piece of bread, but only played with it. 'According to Nadya, she doesn't mind me going to the house, sorting things out, but she won't talk to me about anything more. So, I just thought that, maybe you might be able to at least fill in some gaps, and if not, well … I don't know. But I'm not sure I can deal with never knowing the whole story.'

Martha sat, picking at her sandwich, stretching out the melted cheese. 'God, Martin.' She paused again, looking over at him. 'I don't know what to say.'

He made a pathetic attempt at a smile, at a "welcome to my world" sort of shrug, but Martha just sat, shaking her head.

Eventually Martin broke the silence. 'So, is there? Anything you think you can throw any light on?'

Martha put down the food which had been sitting uneaten in her fingers for the past few minutes. 'Well, there's plenty of bits and pieces I can tell you, things that Laura and I have routed out, stuff about Eva's previous life and how she came to be here,' she paused, looking down. 'But the one thing I can't tell you at the moment, is who your father might be …'

NOT GETTING ANY OF THIS

They had finished the paninis, couldn't face another coffee. 'Shall we walk somewhere?' Martha suggested.

Martin looked perturbed, then simply confused.

'Nothing sinister – it's just easier to talk sometimes, when you're walking,' Martha suggested, picking up her bag.

They wandered down to the water, and as they strolled along the bank Martha began to relate what she had found out about Eva. 'She was active in the war - the Air Transport Auxiliary – you knew that?'

Martin looked shamefaced. 'She tried to tell me, but her stories were going all round the houses – or so I thought, so I was only half-listening. But now I think back, she was obviously setting the scene to tell me all this other stuff – or trying at least.'

'But Eva flying planes – don't you think that's amazing, when you look at her now? Amazing that women did anything like it in those days …' Martha paused, thinking that for some women, their position in the world hadn't changed that much over the years. 'Anyway, we're not entirely sure what happened – but it seems she turned up at the castle – Moyons Castle – along with numerous injured airmen who were sent there for R and R.'

Martin was nodding, as if at least some of what Eva had told him had, despite his best efforts, stayed in his mind, and was beginning to slide into some sort of picture. 'She told me – about the castle. I'll fill you in on that later … but you carry on with what you were saying, otherwise the whole thing will just get in a godawful muddle.'

Martha could see that he had braced himself, perhaps had some idea of what was to come, and wanted to get the unpalatable medicine swallowed as quickly as possible.

'Well, those letters I found – at the beach hut,' Martha kicked a stray pebble along the path as they walked. 'They were between Eva and someone else, someone she was obviously fond of …' She paused, contemplating the thought that this "someone" she had been so interested in might, at one stage, have been a contender as Martin's father … that what for her was an intriguing mystery, might for him, have been part of his life history.

'Could I see them – the letters?' he said quietly.

'Of course. I told you that they were in shreds when I found them? But I've managed to put most of the pieces together. They're at least partly readable now.'

'So who was he – this other person?' Martin had stopped at a gap in the trees, was looking out to sea at two small boats drifting on the water. 'I'm assuming it was a "he"?'

'Well, that was the problem,' Martha stood alongside him, taking in the same view. 'All I could see at the end of his letter was a "J" ...'

Martin swore. 'Well, that's the end of that then,' he said, his hope for a name, for a father, dashed before it had even begun. He started out along the path again, leaving Martha still looking out to sea.

'Not entirely,' she said, catching him up.

'It's okay, you don't have to sugar-coat anything. I realise it's my own stupid fault that I didn't have the balls to wait and hear the end of the story ... it's just that, it's really bloody hard, realising that your whole life, and everyone in it, has been a lie ...' He strode on, causing an on-coming cyclist to swerve across the track to avoid him.

'Martin,' Martha called, out of breath now at trying to keep up with his long strides. 'Martin, just stop ...' Her words were loud, firm. The face of the toddler, coming towards her on a trike, crumpled, as she assumed she was on the receiving end of Martha's harsh words. She waved a hand in apology to the parent, and rushed to catch Martin up. 'Martin, for god's sake. Stop acting like a spoilt child.'

He looked ready to allow a river of abuse to burst its banks at her.

'I get it,' she grabbed his arm. 'I understand what it's like for someone to take your life and shake it upside down like a rubbish bag.' She couldn't help but think of Richard and the way his lie of a life had made her feel. 'But there is more that I can tell you … if you'll just stand still long enough.'

He held up a hand in apology, and Martha continued. 'I went to the local museum. I wanted to see if they had anything about the Forces being in this area during the war – you know, someone that Eva might have met when she was recuperating at the castle.' He turned to look at her directly, and, as they approached a bench, indicated that they might sit.

'And?' He kicked at the weeds which had encroached on the paving slabs beneath their feet, then glanced back at her. 'What did you find?'

'Well, they had quite a few photos of airmen – mainly American – and after a bit of digging I found one with names scrawled on the back. And there was one "J" – a Joseph Moretti …'

Martin turned sharply. 'So, that might be him …?'

'He …' Martha hesitated, trying to find the right words. 'I don't think so Martin,' she said gently, looking at his sandy features. 'He has – had – dark hair, dark features …Mediterranean looking …'

'But there might be others, you don't know that's him. Just because his name begins with a "J"…that's a big leap.' He stared, challenging her.

'True. But I found some other photos,' Martha said gently, 'At the beach hut. The same face, the same man. This Joe Moretti was almost certainly Eva's … friend, lover …but not your father, unless the laws of genetics went completely off track at that point …'

So actually, what you're saying is, there is no further information? I'm no further forward than I was two days ago …?'

'Actually, there is someone else,' she butted in. The other face in the photo came to her, the one which she had recognised, but hadn't completely acknowledged why. 'Another of the airmen, who … well, has more of your colouring, features …'

'But not a "J"?'

'No, sadly not…' Martha took a moment, hesitating whether to put forward her theory about the man in the photo and the story which Eva had told her. But the decision was taken for her.

'Oh, for god's sake … I'm not getting any of this.' Martin stood, face shouting out his frustration. 'You tell me Eva's lover – and therefore possibly my father - had a name beginning with "J", but that the most likely candidate name-wise is not the right man. And then there's this other person you've hit upon, who, according to you, fits the bill appearance-wise, but is not the person Eva was writing to …' He turned to go. 'Well, I can tell you I've had enough of this charade. It might all be a bit of fun to you, some "whodunnit" game that you and your sister can play detectives on when you've nothing better to do …' He wiped spittle from his lips. 'But to me …Oh, forget it.' And he strode off, leaving no opening for Martha to follow.

She remained on the bench, head tipped back, wondering how she had got herself into this predicament, and how she would get herself out of it, without Martin's wrath pouring down on her yet again.

'Why is it me who has the bad news to tell?' she asked herself, at the same time knowing that this might be an inevitable outcome to poking your nose into other peoples' lives. She thought too about the question which Martin *hadn't* asked her – who the other man in the photo might be – and also of his possible link to the story, the awful story of the attack, which Eva had recently told her; and when and where she might reveal this even more unpalatable news to Martin. But before she could draw any conclusion, Martha's phone rang.

HOW COME I'VE NEVER HEARD OF THAT

'So – what have you been up to while I've been away?' It had been Laura who had called, wanting to visit, obviously desperate to be updated. She chattered like a sparrow as she unpacked her bag, placing her gifts of expensive coffee beans and a luxury box of Cornish Fairings on the table, ignoring the pot of coffee which Martha was in the process of re-heating. 'Thought you might at least have sent a text, let me know how things were progressing …'

She carried on in the same vein for what felt like five minutes, leaving no gap between words for Martha to jump in and explain. 'So,' she said eventually, 'I'm assuming from your "radio silence" that you've been too busy finding things out to be able to send messages? You must have some really interesting news waiting for me…'

Martha had expected to listen to at least half an hour of detail about Laura's trip to Cornwall, but it seemed that that held far less interest to her sister than the story they were trying to pursue. Martha took a breath; she had every intention of telling

Laura about the photos at the museum, about her trip to the war memorial, and all the possible leads in identifying "Eva's man". She did not however, have any intention of telling her sister about Simon. The questions would be unending, the assumptions, the words of advice ... she really wasn't ready for any of it, and despite a little butterfly of hope fluttering in her chest, there might not even be anything to be advised about. No, she would hold fire on following that particular strand of the story – for the time being at least.

'Well, I had quite a successful trip to the museum,' she said eventually, putting Laura's coffee beans in the cupboard, but opening the box of Fairings, and breaking off a little piece. 'Although they've got so much stuff there that it might take a while to plough through it all ...' Martha began to choke on a small crumb of the biscuit which had found its way into her throat, and there was no further information while Laura thumped her on the back, and she had eventually to wave her away so that she could grab a glass of water.

'See, that's what you get for stealing bits before you offer anything to your guests,' Laura's words were abrupt, but she continued to pat Martha's back before refilling her water glass, and pushing her into a seat. 'Now, what's all this about the museum? What did you find there? You look like you've got news – and good news at that.'

Martha swallowed more water, giving herself time to consider what she might say that didn't involve Simon. 'Well, as I say, they have loads of stuff – but I saw some photos of American airmen which could well be what we're looking for.' She thought that if she included Laura in the search – that she referred to "we" - then her sister would be suitably satisfied that this was still a joint venture. 'They also had some diaries – not war diaries, but stuff written by local people about their wartime experiences at home.'

'Oh, like the National Register,' Laura interjected, and Martha could only smile. Why was it no surprise that her sister would know all about something which she herself had never heard of?

She took another gulp of water. 'Yes – exactly that sort of thing. And there was one diary in particular which told the story of some men rescuing a woman from a crashed plane …' Martha allowed the words to fall lightly on the table, but Laura wasn't fooled.

'A plane crash – what, round here? How come I've never heard about that before?' She barely took breath. 'And who was this woman, was she someone famous …?' Her own words presumably took a few moments to reach Laura's consciousness. 'Hang on … do you think? … Do you mean … is this woman our Eva, is that what you're trying to tell me in such a roundabout way?'

Martha smiled once more at her sister. The woman had tied herself up in all manner of knots, and was then blaming Martha for the resulting muddle. But she had got to the crux of the story quicker than Martha herself, nevertheless.

'Well, it's not absolutely definite – not yet anyway, but I think, and...' Martha paused, holding her tongue to stop it revealing Simon's name. '...And people at the museum think, that it's quite possible the two women might be one and the same. The dates seem to tie together, and Eva talked, albeit pretty vaguely, about her plane coming down... And of course, we're working on the basis that she was sent to the Castle to convalesce around that time, implying she'd sustained some injuries. So, it all seems to point in that direction ...'

'So, we must go and see her – Eva – and get her to confirm or otherwise. Or perhaps that nephew of hers could condescend to provide the tiniest bit of information about the family history?' Laura started rummaging in her bag, muttering about notebooks and pens.

'I don't think we're going to get anywhere on that front,' Martha said firmly. 'In fact – and I know I should have told you this before – Martin Andrews has been in touch with me.' She could see that Laura was about to interrupt with a sackful of questions and quickly continued. 'But actually, things are the other way round - he wanted to know from *us* what we'd found out about Eva. It transpires that he has plenty of questions of his own about his family history.'

'Well, why doesn't he just go and ask the woman himself? He's better placed than any of us ...'

'It seems that Eva has told him quite a lot – about her past life and how she came to be in this part of the world – but now she's no longer talking to him.

Apparently, she's completely clammed up and is refusing to say anything more.'

'But why? If she was so keen to tell him in the first place, and now her lips are sealed, then something must have happened.' Laura raised an eyebrow at Martha, implying that it was clear to her what that "something" might be, but Martha made no response. 'Well,' Laura went on, talking as if Martha were a particularly obtuse child, 'It's pretty obvious to me. Mr Congeniality has either been rude to the old woman, or not particularly listened to a word she was telling him … or, or …' Even the usually voluble Laura had run short of steam and ideas.

Martha never ceased to marvel at how her sister could get to the nub of a situation with only the thinnest of information. She hadn't even hinted at the details which Eva had related to Martin, let alone the fact that he had shouted at the old woman and walked out on her. And yet Laura had instantly conjured the whys and wherefores from thin air.

The two sisters sat in silence, contemplating where all this was going – where they were going with it.

'So,' Laura eventually started, taking Martha's silence for acquiescence. 'What's the plan? Where do we go from here?'

There was so much which Martha needed to get clear in her own head. She felt she needed one of those boards which TV detectives seemed to be forever scribbling on and squinting at – where she could write up all the facts which she currently had swimming around in her head, and then start joining the arrows between the parts which linked together. In fact, she thought, that wasn't a bad idea. She could tape together some sheets of paper and tack the whole thing to the wall, begin writing all over…

'Hello …?' Laura was waving a hand in front of her sister's face, impatient to move things forward. 'Is there any chance I might get an answer this side of Christmas?'

'Sorry – I was just thinking. There's just so much going round in my brain at the moment.' Martha stood, beginning to clear the cups from the table. 'How about if I try to see Eva again – perhaps take her out somewhere even better for tea and try to get her talking? If I can butter her up a bit, she might start to tell me the things she's holding back from Martin?'

That idea, and an extra Fairing, seemed to placate Laura. It seemed to have passed her by – for the moment at least – that Martha hadn't given the details of what Eva had told Martin that had upset him to the point of desertion.

READY FOR BATTLE

As soon as Laura had left, Martha readied herself for a walk; she needed some fresh air, but wasn't up for a long hike. Instead, she sauntered along the streets with her head a ragbag of the news and thoughts and theories which the two of them had discussed; then her phone rang.

'Ms Townsend? Julia Frost here – Lawrence & George Solicitors. We have an appointment on Thursday.' No niceties, just straight down to business. She could be another Hilly, Martha thought, if she ditched the smart navy suit and the immaculate make-up she was no doubt wearing. 'Something's cropped up, and it would be helpful if we could meet earlier …'

Martha wondered if the "something" was anything to do with her, whether Richard had decided to be difficult and put obstacles in the way of her sorting her life out.

'Would tomorrow, 9.30 am be suitable?'

Martha thought about the pile of paperwork on her dining room table, still not properly sorted, but the aptly named Ms Frost made it clear that although she had posed a question, it was in fact, not up for discussion.

Erm, yes – I suppose I could make …'

'Wonderful, I'll see you then.' And the call was ended before Martha could enquire about Richard, or whether there was anything she should be aware of.

Martha would have loved to have taken Laura with her. But it appeared that her sister had plans of her own for the day. 'For goodness sake Martha – she's not going to eat you. You're a grown woman, you can stand up for yourself. And besides, she *is* actually on your side …'

A point that Martha needed to remember. As she got herself ready, it actually brought a smile to her face – the image of Richard having to stand in front of the dreaded Ms Frost and explain himself. That would be worth seeing, and she hoped it would come to that point, because she knew it would go a very small way to evening up the balance of affairs … and she knew on whose side she would rather be.

In the smartest outfit she had worn for some considerable time, Martha arrived at the solicitors with ten minutes to spare. The new deadline had forced her to put Martin's plight to one side and to sit back down at her dining room table until nearly midnight to sort and gather the relevant paperwork – or what she hoped would be relevant anyway, and now she felt ready for battle.

At precisely 9.30, Ms Frost appeared and summoned her to a room on the other side of the double-fronted solicitors' building. It was an imposing old house, and the room they sat in had presumably had a previous life as a sitting room or dining room, still boasting a Victorian fireplace and cornices. Despite the formality of its current arrangements, it had a generous, benevolent feel to it, something which put Martha slightly more at ease.

'Mr Townsend,' the solicitor announced, looking predictably over black rimmed glasses. 'Has, you will be pleased to hear, come to his senses.'

Martha had no idea what that might mean, but Ms Frost was evidently about to leave her in no doubt.

'He has admitted – for the sake of the record, although we had already established the fact – that he had been having a dalliance with the said woman for some considerable time, and had in fact entered into a marriage with her before he married you.'

Despite her having previously come to the conclusion herself, the words – official now - hit Martha like a heavyweight punch. They stripped any communication from her mouth, any thoughts from her head, and the blood from her chest. 'Would you like a glass of water?' Martha must have looked at least as bad as she felt, and she was convinced that if she didn't lie down immediately, she would faint to the floor. But the thought of making a fool of herself in respect of that heartless bastard of a man brought her upright. She managed, by directing the most evil of thoughts at him in her mind's eye, and by taking deep breaths until her water arrived, to keep herself on a par with the fiery Ms Frost.

'So what does that mean exactly – for me?'

'Basically, it means that your marriage is null and void – that you were never legally married to Mr Townsend. I have reported the alleged matter of bigamy to the police, and will leave it with them to decide on what further action might be taken. In the meantime, we have more practical matters to attend to. I understand that your current property was bought in equal shares by yourself and Mr Townsend?'

No time for sentiment. Which Martha thought was for the best. And she sent a silent message of thanks to the grandparents who, together with her parents' legacy, had left sufficient funds for her to be able to pay her own way. Just concentrate on the facts, she told herself. 'That's right.' And she went to her folder of papers, so glad now that she had spent those late hours the previous evening going through them. She handed over the purchase documentation.

'Hhmm. I see.' Ms Frost looked at what she had been given, consulted her own notes. 'Well, it may take a bit of unravelling, but I'm sure we can sort this out pretty quickly. Presumably you would like Mr Townsend to sign over his half of the property to you?'

Another statement disguised as a question. Martha sat open-mouthed. She'd already set herself off on a chain of nightmares about having to sell the house and put belongings into storage and… and …

'Is that not what you wish to happen?' Ms Frost looked over her glasses, disconcerted that Martha might think any other course of action might be even passingly possible.

'Well, yes, but I just thought that …'

'Think of Mr Townsend as just a professional transaction – a passing stranger with whom you entered into a business agreement. We are now in the process of winding up that business, and I, as your legal representative, wish to obtain the best possible outcome for you.'

Some pep talk, Martha thought. When it came to assertiveness and action, this woman could leave Laura and Hilly combined, at the starting blocks. She was reeling – but she also wanted to hear Ms Frost add something along the lines of "if the said Mr Townsend is imprudent enough to get himself into such a ridiculous position, then he deserves everything we can throw at him …"

Ms Frost, if not enunciating the actual words, had them written all over her face – a face which, on anyone else, would have been described as smug. Instead, she took the remainder of the paperwork from Martha with assurances that she would be back in touch very soon. Martha would not have been surprised to find herself ushered back to the front office with an efficient clap of the woman's hands. But, as she made her way down the steps of the building, she felt the urge to kick up her heels and skip down the middle of the road. Instead, she pulled out her phone, knowing that there was only one person who she should contact.

LET ME TELL THE STORY

Laura had been there at the beginning, the middle and now the end of proceedings, and had supported Martha through all of it. It was only right then, that she should be updated on the latest news, but perhaps not over the phone.

Martha called her sister, suggesting that they take a walk – up to Selworthy Beacon. 'I could do with the fresh air,' and that they could call in at Periwinkle Cottage for a rewarding cup of tea afterwards. She had waited until they had clambered through the gorse and dying heather, reaching the summit before telling her of the solicitor's words.

'Well, she's absolutely right,' was Laura's immediate response. She had no need to preserve a professional front like Ms Frost, and she didn't hesitate to make her feelings known. 'That stupid ignorant man deserves everything he gets. And I hope he doesn't think he's in a position to put up any sort of argument to what she's suggesting.'

Martha pointed out that she didn't think there was any question of "suggestion" on Ms Frost's part. What the solicitor had decided would become fact, no doubt, no room for discussion. For a fleeting moment she felt slightly guilty – that everything Richard had put into the house would be lost to him. As she looked out along the meandering Somerset coastline, hand to her face to shield her eyes from the unexpected sun, she wondered if he had any share of his current home; whether, if that relationship went to the wall, he would have any assets to fall back on. But Laura seemed already to be reading her mind.

'Don't even think about feeling bad about it, Martha Townsend. He's sown, and so shall he reap,' she said, following Martha's gaze out over the channel. Laura was not normally one for quoting religious texts, but the words did seem to fit the situation perfectly. 'Now, let's leave the wonderful woman to do what she needs to do, and get down to that tearoom. Then you can tell me all the latest about Eva and her oh-so-wonderful nephew.'

But it seemed that Laura was unable to hold back for the time it would take them to descend the hill. 'I mean, it's obvious that something has gone on,' she said, skipping nimbly over the uneven path alongside the stream. 'That there's something you're holding back on telling me…'

Although Martha longed to share the information she had been made party to by Martin, she was unsure what she should actually do. What would she want, if she were in Martin's shoes, she thought, as they clambered down the stony descent. Would she have wanted her story shared with all and sundry? On the other hand, it was fairly obvious that it would only be a matter of time before Laura wheedled the information out of her. And only a matter of time perhaps before it became more public knowledge too, Martha guessed. 'Yes, you're right,' she admitted quietly, 'Things have moved on a bit.'

As Laura stopped, a triumphant "I knew it" look on her face, they heard a rustling in the quiet of the woods. The two sisters looked up simultaneously, and there amongst the trees were two Exmoor ponies. They watched wordlessly as the two creatures made their way to the water which had gathered in a natural pool, to take a drink.

While her sister's gaze was directed elsewhere, Martha began to tell the story. 'Do you remember that I told you Martin had called me again - said that he needed to talk to me?' She expected some flippant comment from Laura, but none was forthcoming. 'Well, we did meet up and he told me that …' Now that she was faced with the same announcement, Martha could see why Martin himself had struggled to find the right words. And her hesitation gave space for her doubts to creep back in. It had obviously taken a lot for Martin to confide in her, and, having done so, would he expect her to share his very personal information with others? Martha could see that Laura was about to chivvy her along, to tell her to stop stringing things out. 'Hang on a minute, just let me tell the story …' She decided that a part-admission was the only way round the problem; there had to be something now to satisfy Laura's curiosity.

'Well, he told me that his parents aren't his parents, and that Eva isn't his aunt …'

'What!' Laura's exclamation was loud enough to make the ponies take flight. They pushed their way through the trees and foliage on the opposite side of the stream and were immediately gone from view.

Martha could see that her sister's reaction was much the same as her own had been. So many questions jumping to be chosen that she couldn't bring any one of them to the front of the queue. She pre-empted the most obvious one, trying to keep things vague. 'But he doesn't actually know the whole story though.'

'Why not? Didn't he ask? Isn't that the most … the first thing you would …' Laura began a rapid descent of the pathway, as if the questions had produced in her an overwhelming energy that needed to be dispelled. And then stopped again, as more thoughts bundled into her head. Martha picked her way down the path more carefully, unsure that she would be able to hold back on the details if Laura challenged her head-on.

'Well, surely Eva would have told him who his parents actually are – were - having dropped the bombshell on him,' Laura continued. 'Whether he wanted to know or not?'

'I think she probably would have done … if Martin hadn't walked out. Don't you remember me saying that Eva was refusing to talk to him? And you saying that he must have behaved badly? Well, you were right it seems. And because of what he said and how he left things with her, he feels that he can't go back.' Martha felt a little surge of relief, that the conversation had switched from the facts of the matter to something which would likely sidetrack her sister. And it did.

'Why does that not surprise me? That man seems to have even less moral fibre than …' Laura stopped herself.

But Martha knew the words which had been about to spring from her sister's mouth. 'Than Richard?' she filled in, expelling a long low breath.

'I'm sorry, I shouldn't have …'

'No, you're right – about Richard anyway. I'm not so sure about Martin though. I actually feel a bit sorry for him …'

'Oh, good grief Martha – after everything he's said and done. You really are a lost cause.' They had got to the bottom of the woodland track in record time, despite – or because of – their conversation. Martha opened the five-bar gate and let Laura through, and they turned down the narrow flower-bordered path which led to the thatched tearoom. 'Anyway, why did he call *you*? I can't imagine Martin Andrews wanting to air his dirty linen in public?'

'He wanted to know what we had found out – whether we would be able to throw any possible light on his parentage, now that he's burnt his bridges with Eva …'

'And can we … can you … deduce anything, from all the stuff you've unearthed?'

'Well, there is one possibility …but it's a really difficult idea to contemplate.' Martha paused, thinking about the story she was holding to herself. 'And I don't know if I am ready to share it with anyone yet – and especially Martin.'

ONE MORE THING

'Have you thought any more about trying to find Joe?' Simon and Martha had taken to calling each other most days, and their conversation inevitably turned to Eva and her story. Martha's response had been woolly, moth-eaten.

'You'll never know 'til you try,' Simon had advised, throwing in a suggestion that the British Legion might be a good place to start. 'After all, they're the ones who erected the memorial, so they're probably as good as anyone,' he concluded. 'And if they can't help, I'm sure they'll be able to give you details of organisations who might.'

It was enough of a push. The following day Martha collated a list of "facts so far", found a number to call and plunged in. She had surprised herself with her efficiency, her business-like approach. And in return the British Legion had proved extremely helpful. They had searched their database for appropriate American veterans' organisations who might be best placed to help her, had given all the contact details she might need, had even given a reference number for the memorial at the marsh. Their proficiency had spurred her on, and before she could lapse into any pool of doubt, she typed out an email to one of the veterans' groups, explaining the circumstances and her request, and pressed the send button.

She had been delighted when she had seen a reply ping back within 24 hours; opened up the email while she was still eating her breakfast toast. Only to be submersed in disappointment.

Of course they wouldn't give her an address for Joe, or his relatives – she was a complete stranger asking for the private details of another, apparently random, stranger. Why hadn't she expected that response, or at least anticipated it? "Of course you will understand," the email read, "that we are unable to give out personal details …". Yes, she did understand, would not have wanted her own details given out in such a circumstance, but that didn't stop the wave of disappointment washing over her.

Having pushed herself to this point, Martha was eager to see her plan come to fruition. She would be the first to admit that she wasn't strong on patience; she certainly didn't appreciate unnecessary hurdles being placed in her way. And that was how she was looking at this bit of – albeit essential – bureaucracy. With a sigh she read the email again, forcing herself not to skim the words this time, already formulating a pleading response in her mind. But this second, more thorough, reading revealed that the veterans group were in fact offering to "forward on any correspondence you might care to send". Martha thought this over as she made more tea, sneaked a biscuit from the barrel she had pushed onto the top shelf of the cupboard to stop herself picking, and gave herself a good talking-to. Why she had got it into her head that this third party might open the very personal letter she was about to write, she had no idea. And to be honest, even if they did, they almost certainly wouldn't be interested in the story she was about to tell, would they? And did it even matter if they were? After all, she had poked her nose into a story that wasn't her own …

'Richard Townsend, you have a lot to answer for,' Martha shouted at the kitchen wall, thinking once again how that man's selfish behaviour had brought out in her an inclination to be suspicious of everyone and their motives. 'Just get on with the letter,' she demanded of herself, realising as she checked the date from the wall calendar that time might not be on her side – not if she had any hope of re-uniting the nonagenarian couple.

Simon was busy at the worktop which separated the kitchen from the rest of his open-plan flat.
'I've managed to contact them,' she said.
He looked up from the peppers he was slicing, an inquisitive look on his face. 'Who? – the British Legion?'
'Yes. It took me a while though,' Martha said, getting up from the comfortable armchair and pouring more wine in Simon's glass. 'But

eventually they gave me the name of a society in America who would probably be able to help.'

'So – have you written?' Simon scraped the chopped peppers into the roasting tray then took a swig from the glass of red sitting beside him on the worktop.

'Well, obviously they said that they couldn't give out any addresses, but they did agree that they would pass on a letter if I sent it to them.' Martha too took a swig from her own glass, picking up a stray piece of vegetable and absentmindedly putting it into her mouth.

'Oy, that's for the casserole!' Simon tapped her hand playfully, smiling at her.

'Chef's perks – well sous-chef, anyway,' she laughed, pinching another piece from the chopping board.

'So, don't keep me in suspense – have you sent off a letter?'

'Not exactly,' she said, her mind going back to her letter-writing attempts.

Twenty pieces of paper had sat snowballed on the table. It had taken every bit of that effort for Martha to realise she had no idea what to say – either about the delicate situation or to someone she had never met; someone who might or might not be alive, and who might not even want to be contacted. She couldn't even decide on "Dear Joe" or "Dear Mr Moretti", although she could hear Laura's voice already nagging her, like the English teacher she was. "If it's someone you've never met then it should always be formal – no question."

She was probably right, but for the creator of such beautiful love letters – well, it seemed far too official. For a fleeting moment Martha had thought about asking Simon, thinking that he could look at it from the male perspective. But what if he were to say that if he were Joe he would rather the whole thing was left in the past … then where would she be?

'I have come up with a final – well nearly final – version,' she told him. 'But I'm still not sure I've got it right …'

'Do you want me to have a look? Simon leaned across, taking her fingers in his. 'Not that I'm saying I'll be any better than you of course, but sometimes two heads and all that …'

'Give me another glass of wine and I'll be happy to,' Martha tipped her head to one side, smiling diffidently. 'I've got it here – in my bag – just in case you offered …'

The two of them sat side by side, and together read through the letter Martha had typed out.

Dear Mr Moretti

I realise that you will be surprised to receive this letter as you don't know me. However, I have been in contact with an old friend of yours who has been extremely keen to get in touch with you. Over the past weeks and months, my friend – Eva

Andrews - has been telling us some of her life story and it seems that ...

Once the words had started running, they eventually took up the sprint for themselves and brought Eva's story perfectly to the page, without Martha having to give too much thought to it. She had thought briefly that perhaps she should be writing the letter with Eva at her side; but the element of surprise -when she was able to produce Joe from thin air – was too enticing.

'I think ...' Simon hesitated as he finished reading, '...I think it's great. Says all it needs to say without getting over-sentimental. Just one thing though...'

Martha sat up, alarmed.

'Don't worry, nothing serious. I just think that maybe it would be better – more friendly – if you hand-wrote it...'

'Well, if that's the only criticism you've got, I'll take that as a nine out of ten,' Martha chinked her glass with his. 'And you're absolutely right,' she said, as they stretched out on the sofa. 'If I was going to receive a letter like that, I'd like to think that it was more than just a bit of business correspondence.' She took a large sip from her glass. 'I'll sit down tomorrow and write it all out....'

They sat in silence, simply enjoying each other's company while their dinner burbled to itself on the stove.

'There is one more thing,' Martha said, after they had finished eating, as she soaked up the last of the rich tomatoey sauce on her plate with a scrap of bread. She glanced over at Simon from the corner of her eye.

'Oh God, this sounds serious.' He was smiling, but he couldn't hide the concern which was wrinkling his eyes.

'Oh, it's not that bad,' Martha said, moving her plate away before she dropped any more sauce on the table. 'It's just that, well, when I started out on this story, my sister Laura – well she helped quite a lot; helped *me* quite a lot as well, actually, when I was in the depths of despair …' Martha had told Simon, gradually, about Richard and his disappearing act, and being found by Laura.

'You haven't shared the rest of the story with her yet?'

'Well, yes and no. We've talked about quite a lot of it, but then I promised her a meal and a "big reveal"; I think she was feeling a bit left out.

'You want me to meet her …?'

'Well, that is one of the missing pieces – *you* are one of the missing pieces,' Martha said, leaning over to touch his hand. 'Would you mind?'

'I'd be delighted.' Simon paused, thinking about what had just been said – and not said. 'She's not a man-hater, a real dragon, is she? Is that why you've been keeping us miles apart?'

'Well, no to the former, sometimes to the latter,' Martha laughed loudly. 'Not a dragon exactly, but

Laura can be more – forthright, shall I say - than is good for the rest of the world sometimes…'

'Forthright I can manage,' Simon said, beginning to clear away their plates. 'Valerie at the museum can be "extremely frank" when she chooses, I can tell you …'

The thought made Martha recall her visit to the museum. 'Talking of that,' she said, 'When I was there – you know, looking at the photos - you had to go and talk to someone – Hilly Farrant.'

'Yes, I remember.'

'Could I be very nosey? Can I ask what she was trying to find out about?' Martha explained the background to her question, their attempt at seeing Eva and the obvious animosity on Eva's part.

Simon was silent for a moment. 'Let me think about that one. I'm not sure if it counts as "data protection", but I don't want to incur Valerie's wrath unnecessarily.'

Martha had, in her head, allowed two weeks for the letter to arrive in the United States. 'And then perhaps another week for them to deal with it at the Veterans' Group' – she had no idea how busy such an organisation might be. Then another week for it to be forwarded on and to reach its destination. And then … and then what? How would *she* feel if a story like this came pushing its way onto *her* doormat? It wouldn't presumably be just a case of reading the letter and dashing off a quick reply. It might even be an embarrassment, another life that he – Joe - might have put into a locked box in his memory, which was suddenly being opened in front of his eyes, and of those around him. Martha immediately thought of Richard and the impact his "other life" had had on her when Laura had unwrapped it for her. It had shaken her confidence in her own thoughts and actions, clattering everything down like a pile of balancing stones. She should never have sent the letter, she conceded. And what if the man had a wife, children, to whom he'd had no intention of telling his past? Those other children, the ones Laura had glimpsed on the internet - Richard's children, she reluctantly acknowledged - what would they think if *she* suddenly turned up in front of *them*? And Eva's wasn't even her story to tell. Martha wandered around the house, picking things up, putting them down, throwing things irately into the bin, things she didn't even know she wanted to be rid of. 'What the hell did I think I was doing?' she shouted to the mirror. But somewhere inside Martha's head, there was still a longing to see a small envelope arrive on her mat, with a United States stamp in the corner.

The thoughts were still tangling around in her head when Simon drew up outside the next morning. They had arranged a walk and a picnic over on the Quantock Hills, well away from the areas which wove themselves in and out of Eva's story. Although the weather wasn't at its best, it was still dry and a day out in different surroundings was probably what Martha needed. Her mood though must have been written on her face.

'Still nothing?' Simon opened up the boot of the car for Martha to store her jacket and bag and the picnic box. Martha shook her head, not wishing to start on any words which might re-accumulate into the rant she had had with herself the previous day.

'Well, I suppose there are all sorts of things which might have held the process up,' he said, pulling on his seatbelt, waiting for her to do the same. He enumerated the very same list that Martha had already gone through herself – delays in the postal service, both on this side of the Atlantic and the other, delays at the Veterans Group … 'And of course we have to accept that he might not want to get involved, or …' Simon spoke tentatively, but Martha was with him, ahead of him.

'Or that the poor man is no longer with us, or in no fit state to respond …' The thought brought a sadness to Martha, caused her to think about Eva, and the memory which dived in and out of the old woman's life like a slithering fish. 'Why did I ever think this was a good idea?'

NOT LOST
EVA

A sigh – a very gentle sigh, but in the quietness of the empty wood it sounds like a rush of wind.

But she isn't lost.

'I'm not lost,' Eva whispers, holding her shrivelled hands one inside the other. 'Daddy says you're never lost if you can see the sea.'

And she *can* see the sea. A thin blue strip, like her satin hair ribbon, beyond the trees.

She isn't lost.

She's been here many times. They always came up here when they were on their holidays. The first time, when she was seven and Daddy had wanted to find the ruined chapel. He'd read about it in one of the volumes he was always poring over, and she'd followed in his footsteps – always with some story on the go. But he liked fact – mechanical books, biographies, guide books – and that's where he'd found the details of the chapel, and the reason why they'd come searching.

And once they'd found the place they returned, again and again. It was always quiet, apart from the buzzing of the bees on the bramble blossoms – no-one else seemed to know about it, and you could spend a whole day here and not see another soul. Like today. Today she has walked along the tracks and not even a dog-walker has passed, exchanging the time of day. She's taken all the right paths – she knows she has - but the chapel isn't here.

As Eva scans the trees for the blackbird which is singing fit to burst she notices a pool of water – what was that word? – anyway, something she's never seen here before. The stone bath is decorated with dark green moss, crawling in patterns that might have been there years, but she can't say; it wasn't here last time she came.

But she *isn't* lost.

She is tempted to scoop a fistful of water from the pool. She is thirsty and no-one seems to have remembered the picnic this time. It is always David who carries the picnic, in his rucksack, and Mummy has more things in her basket – apples or biscuits or sometimes chocolate.

Eva feels in her pocket for a sweet – a sherbet lemon – but there is only a lipstick. She pulls off the top – the vivid scarlet looks like a wax crayon. It is soft and moist in the heat and a smear streaks her finger. She places it carefully down on the path – it's not hers, not her colour at all; a nice coral pink, that's what she always chooses.

A rustle in the trees. It must be David with the rucksack, and she walks to meet him. She doesn't remember this path either, too many stinging nettles and the brambles are scratching her legs. The rustle comes again, amongst the greenery on the slope which towers over her head. David's playing Hide and Seek! She'll find him, she's always been good at Hide and Seek.

And she isn't lost.

The light is fading. She is sure she can hear the church clock, chiming three – or is it four? She passed the church to get here, so maybe if she works her way back towards the ringing bells she'll find the others.

The church. She knows she always walks past the church to find the letterbox, to post her letters to Joe. He must get her letter – it's important that he knows. She checks her pocket; there is no letter. No letter but there is a biscuit - a Ginger Cream, her favourite.

She bites into it, and the crunch is loud in her head, grinding out all other thoughts until it's finished. It's good; ginger's her favourite, but she'd like another – and a cup of tea. Perhaps if she walks down *that* path, the steep one through the trees, she'll come to the promenade? Of course she will, and there will be the harbour and the teashop and she can have a drink and she knows her way home from there, of course she does.

And she isn't lost anyway.

What looks like a huge bumble bee in its yellow jersey is flying towards her. Its buzzing is irritating, and Eva tries to bat it away. But her arm is lifeless.

'Go home bee, go home – I've nothing for you,' she tries to say, but the words are stuck in the dryness of her mouth.

'Over here. Over here!'

Those aren't the words she wants to say. Someone else has said that. Someone else is here – but it doesn't sound like Daddy or David.

They keep talking, asking if she can hear. Well of course she can hear – her ears are fine, it's just her mouth which isn't working. She forces open her eyes, hoping that will stem the flow of questions, but it just brings more.

More voices – too many – all talking at once. One of them bats away the bee as well, but it's coming closer. 'We'll all get stung,' she tries to warn them. But they don't understand what she is saying.

She tries to move away from the thing – it's as huge as a hornet – but they hold her still, wrapping her in foil.

'I'm not a chicken,' she wants to tell them, 'I'm just cold.' Her teeth are chattering, chewing up her words before they can get out.

She can still hear the bee, but she can't see it. Someone is lifting her, but it's not Daddy, trying to put her on his shoulders.

'They've tied me down; they're carrying me away so that I can't win the Hide and Seek game. And they're pushing me inside the bee. I want to go home, but it's swallowing me.'

'Check her blood pressure again… temperature's dropping…'

Too many lights; and beeping, constant beeping. The War of the Worlds – that's where we are. I've been taken into the spacecraft.

Now I'm lost.

TRYING TO FIND SOMEWHERE TO LAND

Laura had, at last, reluctantly conceded with regard to the beach hut. 'Well, I suppose I'd better come and have a look at what you've been up to,' was as near as she had got to conciliation, but Martha was pleased all the same. She had visited the bakers in the town centre and chosen a selection of cakes, neatly ribbon-tied in a box, and some quiche from the vegetarian deli, just in case her sister might deign to stay for lunch. The place, already tidy, was being swept and cleaned to surgical standards; even Ted had noticed.

'Royal visit coming up?' he asked, as Martha shook out a mat at the door of the hut. Chairs had already been evicted to the veranda, and a broom stood to attention at the door.

'Might as well be,' Martha laughed. 'My sister's coming, so all hands on deck.'

Ted saluted solemnly, offering his help if needed. As they stood chatting, the buzzing of a helicopter broke the mid-week quietness. They broke off their conversation to follow the aircraft's progress as it ran the length of the shoreline then doubled back on itself.

'Some grockle got themselves stuck on the cliffs no doubt, forgetting that the tide comes in and out at the seaside,' Ted speculated, following its progress back to the higher coastline. Despite its lack of apparent destination, the spectacle of it drew them in, but then Martha noticed it was circling, gradually manoeuvring nearer to the ground. 'It's coming down. Looks like they're trying to find somewhere to land.' And they continued to watch as the bright yellow craft dipped from view.

'Ambulance, that one,' Ted observed. 'Must have had a fall, whoever it is who's got themselves in difficulties.' With a shake of his head at the unending stupidity of those who didn't understand the sea or the coast, Ted called out a 'Good luck with the queen,' as he strolled off along the beach.

Martha put the contents of the hut back into place, and even had time for a herbal tea before a large potted palm appeared round the side of the veranda, followed by a head. 'Thought you might need something to brighten the place up,' she puffed, almost dropping the pot on the decking.

'It's lovely, Laura, thanks.' Martha fussed over the plant, as would be expected by her sister, before inviting her inside. 'Come in. There's not masses of room but it's comfortable and …' She wanted to point out the sense of the place, the feeling, but how to express that to someone who was so matter- of-fact?

Laura stood by the door, as if she wasn't staying. She allowed her head, but no other part of her, to move in a one-hundred-and-eighty-degree sweep of the place. Martha was aware that, ridiculously, she was holding her breath.

'It's certainly got atmosphere,' she announced, turning to smile at Martha. 'I can see why it got you hooked … and the letters of course.' She looked around once more, as if she might spot some additional correspondence which Martha had failed to notice.

The plant was placed, the coffee made, and chairs taken out onto the veranda to admire the view as they drank. Ted sauntered past, trying unsuccessfully to look as though he were on a mission.

'Oh, Laura – this is Ted.' Martha jumped up to make the introductions. 'He's my neighbour, he's been really helpful …'

Ted beamed at Laura. 'I've heard so much about you my dear – and you're every bit as handsome as your sister.' He held out a less than spotless hand, which raised an eyebrow from Laura, but his jollity cajoled her into reciprocating. The cakes were brought out, more coffee made and the fisherman was soon regaling both women with tall tales of the sea. Until Martha's phone rang.

Laura frowned, as if it was Martha herself who had caused the unwelcome interruption. 'Can't it wait?' she huffed, as Martha scrambled inside the hut to find her bag, followed in immediately by her sister.

She glanced at the screen and looked up abruptly. 'It's Martin Andrews – what do you think he wants?'

'Well there's only one way to find out ...' Laura began, but Martha was already answering.

'Oh my god Martin. Oh, no that's awful. No, no, we'll come over there. Just let me get a pen ...' Martha clutched the phone between shoulder and ear as she scribbled something down.

'You've gone really pale – what on earth's going on?' Laura ushered her sister to a seat as the call came to an end.

'I don't ... it's Eva,' Martha announced, still staring at her phone. 'She's ... she wandered off, early this morning, and they've been out looking for her all this time. They'd tried all the obvious places, and then someone out walking their dog called the police. They found her up on North Hill. She must have fallen...' The words dried up as Martha thought about the consequences of what she'd been told. 'That must be why the helicopter ...Oh god, it must be really serious ...'

Laura was quiet for a moment, and then fired into action. 'Well, come on then – where is it they've taken her? Where do we need to go? I've got the car up on the promenade, we can be on our way in five minutes ...'

Martha's head was mayhem. Grateful as she was for Laura's support and keenness to help, she was still trying to make sense of the whole thing. She guessed why Eva had gone wandering, presumably for the same reason she had when Martha had found her previously – to send another letter to Joe; but why had she gone so far this time, if she were just trying to find the post box? Laura had helped Ted to bring in the chairs and crockery, and was now rattling her car keys. Martha came to, grabbing her bag and locking up the hut. 'I'll let you know, Ted – as soon as there's any news,' she said. She had no idea why it was important, but she felt that the old man would want to know.

THE OBVIOUS PLACE

Martha and Martin sat in the waiting room at A&E. Laura had gone off to find cups of tea. The whys and hows of Eva's accident had been wrung dry, and they could only wait to be summoned to Eva's bedside. But the silence stretched their nerves, and Martha felt the need to make conversation.

'So how did Eva come to be living at Moyons Quay?' she asked tentatively.

Martin looked up, as though surprised to find himself in the real world once again. 'Well, I don't really know the details; Eva obviously wasn't a big part of my life for a long time, but Dad always said that she loved this place as a child. They used to come down here as a family, and she couldn't get enough of it.' He looked across to the desk, checking whether there was any sign of news. 'Anyway, when she had some money, and she'd finished globetrotting with her work, she had to settle somewhere, and I suppose this seemed the obvious place…'

'But she never used the beach hut again?' Martha answered her own question.

'Understandable I suppose … all those memories …'

Martin just nodded, his thoughts very much held close.

'One thing that still flummoxes me though,' Martha continued, not wanting them to fall into silence once more, 'Is what happened to the beach hut in the meantime? I mean there were all those years between Eva abandoning it and you putting it up for sale …'

'From what I can gather, the army commandeered most of the beach huts during the war – billeting troops and storage and so on. The beaches were out of bounds anyway, for the general public, so I suppose it didn't really matter that people couldn't use them.' He glanced over again at the nurses' desk, checking that no-one was looking for him. 'I presume after the war they gradually went back to their original ownerships …. But I don't think Eva gave the place a second thought. Even when the solicitor asked me to take over Eva's affairs it didn't seem at the forefront of things. It was only once we started going through all the paperwork … And when I went to look at it, it seemed like some of the local fishermen had been using it in the meantime, just as a casual store …'

'You didn't seem very happy though, that day when you stopped and stared – when I was first moving into the hut.' Martha thought this might be the only chance she got to pursue this particular strand of the story.

'To be honest, I was wondering if I'd done the right thing. It had seemed obvious at first – to put it up for sale, release some money to help pay for Eva's care. But then, when I saw you bringing in boxes, looking so happy to be there, I wondered whether I should have been using it, taking more interest in the place …'

'Mr Andrews?' A nurse called from across the busy room, looking harassed enough to wish that there was no relative to spend her depleted time on.

Martin stood, beach hut forgotten, concern and not wanting to know mixed in equal measure on his face.

'Would you like to come through.'

He looked back at Martha, who shooed him off towards the nurse. It wasn't her place to be there, whether the news was good or otherwise; she would hear soon enough.

Laura bustled back, three large paper cups in a cardboard tray. 'What's happened? Where's Martin?'

'They've called him in. I don't know whether it's a good sign or bad…'

The two sisters sat in silence, sipping at the less than flavoursome tea, drinking it only because it gave them something to do.

After what seemed like hours, but in reality was probably twenty minutes, Martin re-appeared. His face was pale, gaunt. Laura handed him the now-stewed tea. Both women sat sideways on their chairs, looking at his bent head, giving him the time to gather himself before he spoke.

'It's not good news,' he said eventually. 'They think she's had a mini-stroke. She's broken several bones – arm, rib. They're going to check again on her hip, which might also be fractured. And she apparently banged her head as she fell. She's in a coma at present, and …' His voice wobbled; he sucked in air, trying to steady the ship. 'They don't know what the outcome of that is likely to be at this stage, whether she'll come out of it or not, and if she does, what her condition will be …' He took another, longer, inhalation of breath; rubbed his eyes with the heels of his hands. 'There's probably no point in waiting – they've said she could be like this for days …'

They asked if he needed anything. 'We can pop by your house – pick up a few bits and pieces,' Laura offered.

'I'll stay for a while – see how things go,' he said, standing, ready to see them out. 'But they've already said to me that there's not a lot of point in hanging about all night. They'll call me … you know …if there's any news …'

Martha and Laura were quiet in the car on their way home, Martha struggling to get her head round why she felt so intensely involved in the life of someone she had known for only a matter of weeks.

'But then,' Laura began, as if their thoughts were identical and had somehow linked and looped somewhere in the ether, 'You've probably spent more time thinking about Eva, finding out about her, over these past weeks than you have about almost anyone else in your life.' She let that thought settle between them. 'Even…' And Martha closed her eyes at the thought that the barbed subject of Richard was about to be resurrected. 'Even me,' Laura went on. 'Even though we've spent most of our lives together, there are probably things you know about Eva that you don't know about me … if you get my meaning.'

Martha wasn't sure that she did, exactly, but she could take on board the gist of what her sister was saying. She knew the details of Eva's love affair for a start, and now that she thought about it, she knew very little about her sister's early days with Michael; certainly not their innermost thoughts about each other. And Richard. What did she really know about him? Now that Laura had unearthed what had gone on, it was blatantly obvious that she had known absolutely nothing about *his* thoughts and feelings, nothing at all. And that took her back to Martin.

'Poor man,' Martha said aloud. 'If *we're* feeling stunned by all that's happened imagine how he's feeling. I mean, it was only weeks ago for him too, when his involvement with Eva really started, and now she's gone from a distant relative to a mother who's seriously ill …'

Her phone rang. 'Hello Martin.' Martha listened intently for a few moments. 'Okay. Well, it's probably for the best. Do you need a lift or anything? Well, take care. We'll call in the morning.' She turned to Laura. 'Eva's still in the coma. They've told Martin that that's not unusual, and that it's often better for the body's recovery – you know, to be in imposed rest …'

'Let's go to La Speranza,' Laura suddenly suggested, 'Get ourselves to something to eat, and raise a glass to Eva's recovery.'

Martha was about to say she wasn't hungry, that she was tired, wanted to be on her own. But she realised that Laura's suggestion was probably exactly what was needed.

As they sat back, sated by stone-baked pizzas and bowls of salad, Laura, who had been quiet for a few moments, voiced her thoughts. 'You know, back at the beginning I did briefly look Eva up on the internet, but I didn't get anywhere … and then I got sidetracked by my searches for Martin Andrews. Perhaps I should have another look, even if it's just in the archives of the local newspapers? There might be the odd article, mightn't there, even if it was something mundane like membership of the WI or whatever.'

'Worth a try,' Martha mused, tipping back on her chair, trying to stretch out her overfilled belly. 'And something else that's occurred to me – a few times actually …' She drained her glass, poured the last of the bottle of Borolo between their two glasses. 'Is what Eva did when she left the Air Transport Auxiliary. I mean, she obviously didn't stay working for them for ever, did she? And from what

I can gather, she didn't come back to this area for quite some time …'

Laura laughed. 'What happened to just finding out about the letters? Now you seem to want to know every detail of the poor woman's life from beginning to end.'

'True. But you have to admit it is an interesting story …' Martha was aware that her words were beginning to slur. 'And what's *also* just occurred to me … is how we're going to get home, now that you've polished off a good portion of this bottle of red!'

WHY DIDN'T I THINK OF THAT?

Laura was on the phone the next day, far too early, and far more chirpy than the gangs of sparrows encamped in the shrubs beside Martha's back door. 'Now Martha, if you could come and pick me up – say in the next fifteen minutes, we can go and retrieve my car from the restaurant car park, and on the way there I can bring you up to date with what I've found …'

Martha groaned. She didn't care if Laura heard her. Even though her world was spreading its wings again, becoming far more sociable, her unevenly large share of the bottle of wine plus a complimentary serving of grappa the previous evening had left her feeling more than a bit groggy. 'Oh, Laura – can I have a bit longer to get myself going? I need a shower and some toast and …'

'Well, three quarters of an hour then. I've got loads to do – you know, carpe diem and all that.'

The line went dead. No time for negotiating then, Martha smiled to herself. And then remembered Eva. She showered – a brief splash, in and out – stuck some bread in the toaster, then rang Martin's number while she waited for it to brown.

'No change, I'm afraid,' he said, sounding more matter-of-fact than he had yesterday. 'No point in visiting either, they've said, well not for longer than a few minutes, anyway.' He paused for a moment, as if trying to decide whether to vocalise what he had in his head. 'They said that people sometimes respond to music – you know, that they are still aware of it, despite the coma, and that it might help …'

Martha knew he was going to ask her – what she thought, what she would recommend as a good piece of music. 'I don't know what to suggest, Martin,' she pre-empted. 'She never talked to me about music, or dancing or anything like that. Although I'm sure they would have had a gramophone at the castle …' Martha remembered being told that Eleanor Saltrey was a "party girl" and that the woman who had helped Eva with the beach hut – Olivia was it? – had supposedly socialised with the troops. She could imagine them all jiving or lindy-hopping in the main hall of the castle, laughing, enjoying themselves., the lively burst of trumpet notes from a Glenn Miller tune echoing in her head. But for some reason that vivid picture didn't include Eva or Joe…

'We could … oh I don't know, maybe it's not a good idea …' Martha was thinking out loud.

'What? What could we do?'

'Well, I was going to say we could read out the letters – you know, Eva and Joe's letters. Do you think that might help bring Eva back to us?'

'No. Absolutely not.' Martin's tone had suddenly returned to the man Martha had first encountered; the one who'd told her "not to bother me or my family ever again".

'Okay, okay. Just a thought.' Martha sniffed. 'I'll let you get on. Let me know if there's any change.' And with that she put down the phone before she could say anything she might regret.

She decided not to bother Laura with Martin. She allowed her sister just to witter on as she drove them back to La Speranza, and they parked up next to Laura's car.

'Thanks – I'll catch up soon. Let me know as soon as you hear anything about Eva,' Laura breezed, as she opened the car door.

'Hang on,' Martha called out as her sister was about to abandon her. 'Weren't you going to tell me about something you've found out?'

'Oh, yes. Well, nothing coming up on Google or elsewhere regarding Eva specifically, but I did find a website about women pilots during World War Two – the Air Transport Auxiliary particularly. Very interesting actually – I'll give you the details so that you can have a look for yourself, there's so many websites out there …'

'Laura!' Martha attempted to bring her sister back down to earth.

'Yes, sorry, I do sometimes get a bit carried away when I start looking things up. Anyway, the main thing to take from this article was that, despite all the splendid work these women did during the war – and the RAF would really have struggled without them, you know – they were just switched off like a tap, as soon as the war finished. 1945 came round, and that was it.' She splayed her arms out in a position of finality. 'No more ATA.'

'So what happened to them all – all those women who'd done all that work?'

'Well, it seems that it was near-impossible for them to get any other jobs in aviation, especially if they were competing with men, so most of them just went back to their pre-war lives – housewives, mothers, daughters. All pretty drab I imagine, after the experiences they'd had; the fun and the camaraderie as well, I guess - delivering all those planes, living under the same roof. It must have been really hard to make the transition …'

'Especially when women were still treated as second-class citizens …' Martha added.

They both pondered the changes in women's lives – some good, some not so – and the time it had taken for some of those changes to materialise.

'But I can't exactly imagine Eva becoming a housewife, can you?' Martha said eventually.

'Well, I don't know her as well as you – remember, I haven't actually met her – but from what you've said, and from what we've found out, I can't see that she would have taken easily to a life of polish and Brasso and being the "little wife at home" …'

'D'you know, I'd never really thought about her being married.' Martha sat up, looking at her sister, still peering into the car as they discussed the old woman. 'But she must have been, I suppose – at some point anyway.'

'What makes you say that? She sounds like a career woman through and through to me …'

'Well, she's got a different surname to Martin for a start.' The thought had, ridiculously, only just occurred to Martha.

'Now why didn't I think of that?' Laura frowned, standing up and waving a vague goodbye to her sister.

THERE IS SOMETHING ELSE

As Martha waved her off, she assumed that Laura would be headed straight back to her computer, to look up the name "Eva Andrews" instead of Eva Bonfield; to see if there was even a glimmer of more light to throw on the old woman's story. She had no idea what she herself might do. She was obviously persona non grata with Martin for the time being, Laura was off down a new warren of rabbit holes, and Eva was somewhere else entirely. Martha pondered whether, inside the coma, Eva was reliving every volume of the stories from her younger days, indulging in the detail without any interruption from anyone… and the thought brought some solace to her, for the old woman's predicament.

She supposed, as she returned home, that she could go and have a look at some of the websites Laura had told her about, but for some reason there was little appeal there. She had just settled herself at the kitchen table when the letterbox rattled; Martha jumped up, thinking that perhaps a reply to her letter might, at long last, have arrived. But it was just the usual run of bills, plus a large white envelope, filled to capacity, which she guessed immediately would be paperwork from the indomitable Ms Frost at the solicitors. By the thickness of the package Martha guessed that Ms Frost had had some success in sorting out the mess of her life with Richard – the finances at least. But that mountain of potential anxiety had little appeal either at present. What would be would be, she thought, wandering through to the kitchen, putting away the remains of breakfast.

A short time later, the letter box clattered again. Not more post, obviously. She went to the front door, and seeing nothing on the mat, opened it up. A bouquet of purple and pink blooms sat on the doorstep. Martha looked around, but there was no hint of a delivery van or its driver. There was however a card, peeping out from the blossoms, and she lifted it out.

"Can't resist a date with a supersleuth. Dinner this evening?" Was all it said. Followed by a small kissing x. She smiled. Looked up again. And there was Simon, lurking by the hedge of the neighbouring garden. She laughed, beckoning over her shoulder as she walked inside with the flowers, leaving the door ajar.

Simon took an apple from the bowl in the kitchen as Martha reached in the cupboard for the percolator. He had taken a long overdue trip to his sister in Penarth and he related to Martha as she moved about the kitchen how he'd sorted out with her the family affairs which needed to be sorted, and had been able to get home early. 'Anyway, what have you been up to while I've been away?'

'Let me make this coffee and I'll bring you up to date.' They chatted about insignificances, until everything was ready and Simon carried the tray out to the table in the garden. The autumn sun was still strong enough to enjoy, and they both turned their faces to soak up the warming rays.

'So, what's the latest?' Simon asked.

'A lot's been happening actually, while you've been away,' Martha said, turning to look at him. She told him the news about Eva as they drank the coffee. Told him too about her meeting with Martin, and what he'd been told about his parentage.

'My god. Poor Eva – I hope she'll be okay. And poor Martin too, come to that. That must have been an incredible shock to him.'

'I think he feels like he's been living a lie for the last however many years. And of course what he really wants to know now is who his father is …'

'And the one person who could tell him isn't currently in a position to do so?'

'Precisely. He's so annoyed with himself for walking out on Eva – and there's nothing worse than being cross with yourself.' Martha sighed with the weight of experience. She poured more coffee for them both, opened a packet of Garibaldi biscuits. 'There is something else though …' she said, at precisely the same time that Simon was waving a biscuit, commenting that he hadn't had a Garibaldi in years. Presumably he hadn't heard her fully; had demolished the whole biscuit before he stopped and thought about what she'd said.

'Hang on a minute … "Something else" – what something?'

'Well, you remember that I found those pictures at the museum – the ones of the American Air Force? I took some photos of them, and when I came back I enlarged them, first on my phone, and then on the computer. There was one face which had been bugging me; I thought I recognised it, but when I compared it with the photos I'd found in the beach hut it definitely wasn't Joe …'

'So who was it then?'

'It looks remarkably like Martin …'

'Well don't just sit there – go and get the pictures!' Simon had forgotten about the childhood biscuits and was pushing back his chair, ready to follow Martha inside.

It was only when Martha had called the photo back up on the screen, when the two of them, heads together, were scrutinising it, that Simon said, 'Well, of course it would help if I'd seen the man himself – Martin …'

Only then did it hit Martha that she had done perhaps too good a job of keeping the various parts of this unravelling story in so many different compartments, like one of those miniature chests of drawers which you saw in the windows of antique and paraphernalia shops. Neither of the people who had been unravelling the story with her – Simon and

Laura – were in a position to confirm the likeness of the photo to the man in the flesh.

'Who else has met Martin? Who else could you show this to?' Simon was turning his head, trying to assess the face from different angles.

'Well, Hilly …' they both pulled a face at this suggestion, then attempted to stop themselves from giggling at their own childishness. 'And Ted, I suppose. He's seen him a few times at the beach huts …'

'And there is the man himself, of course …' Simon looked directly at Martha. 'Perhaps it's only fair that you show the photo to Martin – let him draw his own conclusions?'

'Hmm.' Martin's abruptness in their last phone call hadn't fostered any enthusiasm in Martha to want to contact him again, any time soon. 'I guess you're right.' She looked again at the screen, zooming in on the face in question. 'This is just as much Martin's story as it is Eva's …'

Eventually Martha put everything away and went to change, leaving Simon in the sitting room, to settle in a more comfortable arm chair. 'Dinner's booked for seven,' he called after her, checking his watch. 'So we've got a bit of time yet.'

She returned, wearing a floral dress that hadn't seen the light of day since long before Richard's disappearance. She arranged herself in the chair opposite Simon, trying to look as though this was the sort of outfit she regularly wore. 'You know I mentioned previously about you perhaps meeting up with Laura? Well, my idea at that point had been to do some sort of "great unveiling" – you know, drawing everyone together to reveal my theories and evidence?' Simon was looking at this different version of Martha, nodding with perhaps a little less attention to her words than she was assuming. 'But that's really not appropriate now, is it? I mean, if I were Martin – and I'd already had my whole life thrown in my face as a lie – would I then want to sit with a bunch of strangers to hear their theories about who my father might be, and how I had come to be conceived? He walked out on Eva; goodness only knows what he'd do with all of us staring at him.'

'Well, all I can say is that I'd hate it if it were me. No, I think you have to go to Martin on his own about this, give him time to digest it all …'

Martha realised, as Simon was speaking – being absolutely fair and correct in his thinking – that what none of the rest of them knew, Simon or Laura or Martin himself – was the conclusion she had drawn about the outcome of Eva's involvement with this man, and the subsequent consequences. And that was the bit she was dreading putting to Martin.

'Anyway, I'll leave you to ponder on that one,' Simon was continuing. 'But you should probably think about doing it sooner rather than later. If I was Martin, I'd really want to know.' Simon looked again at his watch. 'Can I just freshen up in your bathroom, before we head off out?' He stood, anticipating Martha's answer. 'Oh, and you said that the names were on the back of that photo … so who was this mystery man?'

Martha chased the words out of her mouth, before she lost the courage of her convictions. 'Vernon Casey – well that's what it says on the picture, anyway.'

VERY UNEXPECTED

Their dinner had been wonderful. A table tucked in the corner, fairy lights twinkling across the old stone fireplace, and a feast of delicious food. They had talked about anything and everything, the conversation was so easy between them, and had even discussed whether Martha would return to the bookshop, or whether she was ready for some new challenge. They had drifted back along near-deserted streets, still chattering; and Simon had kissed Martha at the front door, but had declined her offer of coffee.

'Probably for the best,' she'd said to her disappointed self, as she got herself ready for bed. And this morning she appreciated his thoughtfulness. She still had so much to sort out – "baggage" as the women's magazines would label it – before her life got back on anything like a smooth path, and perhaps she should take her complications one at a time.

She picked up her phone, found Martin's number. She had no reason to put off the moment any longer, and, she thought, it wasn't her secret to hold on to.

'Hello, Martin?'

'Oh, Martha – how are you?' He spoke as though their last conversation had never taken place.

'I'm fine thanks,' Martha said, pleased that there appeared to be no awkwardness after their previous exchange. 'But how is Eva? Any change?'

'Unfortunately not. I think there's some debate about taking her off the machines – you know, that are doing all the work for her – and just seeing how she responds. But it's really difficult. She's pretty frail at the moment, but you know how determined she was … is …'

'I'm sure they'll do what's best for Eva …' Martha hesitated, '… and if I can be blunt, if the worst comes to the worst, you have to remember that she's enjoyed a long and interesting life …'

'Hmm. I s'pose.'

And here was her moment, take it or regret it. '…And talking of Eva's life – I might have found something else; something which I think you should be aware of …' Martha held her breath waiting for another backlash from Martin. But there was just a sigh, a feather-soft sigh.

'Are you still there? Is everything okay?' Martha knew that the question was stupid, that probably nothing in Martin's life was okay at this moment. But she had to pass on what she knew. 'Could we meet up again perhaps? There's something I need to show you.'

'I'll come to the beach hut ... if that's okay.' No small talk, no "I guess you're spending a lot of time there now" or "it's such a lovely spot". Martha wondered for a passing moment whether he had some instinct about the place, about its relevance in his life story.

'Err – yes, that'll be fine. Shall we say eleven o'clock?'

Martha had just finished preparing coffee when there was a knock on the door. 'Come in, come in.' She was nervous – about the appearance of the place, whether he would have expected her to have changed it completely, or left it exactly as he had handed it over - but more so about what she had to say. 'How are things going?' she started, but she could see that he was tipped on the edge of his seat, leg jiggling, fingernails being picked at. Not a moment for small talk.

She poured them each a coffee, and then picked up her phone. 'This is what I wanted to show you.' She handed it to him with the Air Force photo on the screen, bit her lip as she waited for his reaction.

'Who's this?' he pulled himself upright in his seat, suddenly more alert.

'His name's Vernon Casey – at least that's what it says on the back of the photo,' she paused. 'It's the man I mentioned to you before ...' Martha put a hand to her mouth, all too aware of Martin's outburst at their last discussion on the subject.

Martin looked at the photo again; enlarged the image, tipped it to the light from the window. He looked across at Martha, eyebrows raised. The silence between them was as heavy as a storm cloud. 'So this is the man you think is my father?' he said eventually.

Martha released the breath she had been holding. 'I do. Not just because of the resemblance between the two of you, but because of something which Eva told me…before she became ill.' Martha picked up her cup, looked at the coffee, decided she couldn't stomach it. She was all too aware that Martin could, quite legitimately, demand to know why she hadn't mentioned this before. 'She said … she told me … that on the day Joe left, his departure was very sudden, very unexpected. That the letter he left was his goodbye to her, and that was why she tore it up – she was so angry with him for just going like that, although presumably he had no choice in the matter …'

'But what about this man – this Vernon or whatever his name is. Where does he fit in to all of this?'

'He was the one who brought her the news that Joe had gone, and Joe's letter …'

'But he wasn't her lover, so how come … did Eva just have a fling with him, some sort of consolation, or revenge even, for Joe disappearing…?' And then he sank his head onto his hands, leaning heavily on the small table. The two halves of the story had slid themselves together in his head, without Martha having to say the words. 'He's the one who didn't like her – didn't like the fact that she was seeing Joe, isn't he?' Martin murmured, recalling threads from Eva's stories, but struggling to bring them into some sort of order. 'And so he just came, when he knew Joe had gone, and took what he thought was rightfully his… is that it?' He stared at Martha, an expression of disgust creasing his face.

Martha didn't trust herself to speak. She nodded, putting out a hand to cover his. She had expected him to push her away, but he allowed her hand to stay there as he wiped away angry tears with his other arm. She could only imagine the turmoil that must be in his head; that she had laid yet more unbelievable layers onto the lies he was already struggling with. But it was done.

A GUILT OF HER OWN

Martin didn't want to attend Martha's "get together". She could understand that perfectly, she had told him. He seemed to think that the sins of his father were definitely visited on him, that he needed in some way to take the responsibility, the shame, on his own shoulders. And it didn't matter how many times or how many people told him the same, he would not - could not - accept that this was another man in another life. Or that he was the by-product of that man's actions.

As she wandered aimlessly about the house, half-heartedly attempting housework, Martha still felt that she needed to draw together loose ends – and not least of which was to introduce her sister to her … what was she going to call Simon? Her new friend, she decided. But nevertheless, she felt a guilt of her own about Martin and his story, like making merry in a graveyard, or playing party music when a neighbour was grieving.

Simon had been hauled on board; which just left Laura. And then Martha began thinking that there might be others … Hilly, for example. Did she have a place in all of this, a right to know what had been uncovered? And what about Ted – and perhaps even Carl? Without Ted she would probably have given up on the beach hut barely before she'd started. But it wasn't a party, was it? It was a … Martha had no idea what it was, if she was being honest. Perhaps it was a celebration – of Eva's life, or perhaps it was a closing chapter. And that thought caused her to wobble. That she would have none of this to fill her life any more, once the story was completed, and the cover finally closed on it. Martha forced herself to think of all the things she did now have in her life – of everything that had changed over the past weeks. Simon, for a start. And a better relationship with Laura – probably better than she'd ever had if she was honest. And Eva. If she ever found her way out of the place she'd disappeared into, then the old woman might – would – still need some help and companionship. She couldn't be abandoned, just because her story was completed.

Nevertheless, Martha could feel herself being drawn into that old downward-spiralling vortex. She took a deep breath, pushing aside the duster and polish. 'Laura,' she decided. 'Before I do anything else, I need to sort things out with her.' She picked up the phone, already rehearsing in her head what she would say. But, as if summoned by some otherworld spirit, Laura had appeared at the front window, holding up supermarket bags and nodding towards the front door

'I've tried your phone, I don't know how many times…' Laura pushed her way along the hallway, beginning to unload the bags onto the kitchen table before Martha had barely caught up.

'Yes, I've been a bit busy …' Martha took a loaf of bread from Laura's outstretched hand, surreptitiously discarding a slice from the breadbin which had developed a carpet of green, while her sister's eyes were elsewhere.

'It'd be good to know what's been happening – what the latest is.' There was a formality to Laura's words, as she disposed of an out-of-date tub of yoghurt with a shake of her head. 'You know, one minute I'm your right-hand man, and the next …'

Martha stopped guiltily in her tracks, wondering if Laura had already seen her with Simon - was upset that she'd been usurped, and worse still, not introduced.

'…And the next you've practically done a Houdini act, not a sight or sound from you.' She rammed more tins of chickpeas and tomatoes onto the shelf than was probably good for it, until there wasn't an inch to spare.

'You know you don't have to feed me,' Martha said, taking the empty carrier bags, folding them together. 'I'm okay now – I *will* look after myself.'

'Hhmm.' Was Laura's only response. But she stopped and scrutinized her sister. 'Actually, you do look a lot better … more, I don't know, glowing?' She continued to stare until Martha had to find herself something to do in order to hide her blushing.

'So, what is it you've been so busy with, that's rendered you incapable of contacting your only sister?'

Martha squirmed. Laura obviously *did* know about Simon. Should she say something now – or would that just invoke a whirlwind of warnings and disapproval and "it's far too soon's" from her sister?

'Well, I just thought you'd need some time to catch up with things, you know, after having some time away …'

'But presumably you've now got to the bottom of everything – sorted out the story?' Laura continued, ignoring Martha's attempt at an excuse.

'Well – yes, no … almost.' Martha knew she sounded like the child who hadn't done her homework. 'Look, I was thinking – perhaps it would, well, you know there are so many bits and pieces to tell you …'

'What is the matter with you Martha? If you've got something to say, just spit it out.'

'Well, I wondered if you wanted to come over to supper one evening – you know, to hear the whole story?' She almost got the words out "And there's also someone I want you to meet", but not quite. She decided that presenting Laura with a fait accompli might be easier, although perhaps not for poor Simon. 'Do you think Michael would like to come as well?' she added, thinking it might ease the impact of Laura's bluntness.

'Oh good heavens no. He'd be bored to tears.'

'Thanks a bundle,' Martha retorted, but at least the thought had detracted Laura from asking any more questions.

'I'll bring a pudding,' she said. 'There's a recipe for Walnut Treacle Tart that I've been wanting to try out, and you're always a good guinea pig for anything sweet.'

Martha mentally ticked Laura off her list. And with any luck she might have had some response to her American letter by the time they all got together. That really would add to the story.

'Martha?' Her sister's tone told her this wasn't the first time she'd called her name.

'Sorry, I was just thinking … what were you saying?'

'I was just asking when you're planning on having this meal. I need to know whether I should go shopping again, for more ingredients?'

'Oh, I hadn't really decided,' Martha said, thinking that she needed to check on Simon's availability before she settled on a day. 'Let me just check a couple of things and I'll get back to you.'

'Well, it's not as though your social calendar is exactly bursting at the seams, is it?' Laura laughed. 'It wasn't so long ago that you were doing a very passable impression of Miss Haversham.'

'Well, maybe things are changing.' Martha was aware that her words were more abrupt than she had intended. 'Thanks to you Laura, I think my life is beginning to turn round at last.'

'Well,' she smiled, glowing under the praise. 'But I think a bit of thanks has to go to Eva as well.

If you hadn't started on this project to find out about her life then I think you'd still be pretty much in the doldrums.'

Martha would have described her previous situation more as the depths of despair, but she let it go. Laura was absolutely right, whatever her assessment of Martha's mental state might have been. Without Eva and her life story, she would almost certainly have sunk so far that she would have struggled to heave herself back into the real world. And of course she wouldn't have met Simon.

'You're looking "glowy" again,' Laura said, collecting her bags, putting on her jacket. 'Are you sure you don't have a temperature?'

'Never felt better,' Martha said, giving Laura a hug, which came as a surprise to both the sisters.

WITHOUT A SECOND THOUGHT

'So, hang on a minute – let me get this straight.' Laura was being more forthright than usual, which was saying something, Martha thought.

Amazingly, she'd hit it off with Simon, the minute they'd been introduced. Martha had been dreading the moment, but Laura had surpassed herself. 'Museum Curator – that's an interesting job. How did you get into it?' No probing about him and Martha. And for a moment, Martha thought that Laura hadn't understood the set up – of she and Simon being "friends".

But there was something in her approach to the man, her sideways glances between the two of them, which told Martha her sister knew exactly what was going on, that she didn't need things spelling out. And that made Martha smile.

They'd spent quite some time over dinner, going through the diaries and the photos and everything else that Martha had tracked down over the past weeks. There was much to be absorbed.

'So,' Laura began, taking a sip from her umpteenth glass of Sauvignon Blanc as she attempted to hold all the threads in her fingers and plait them into a cohesive piece. 'Eva has a fling with Joe. Joe buggers off, back to the USA. Eva is furious and upset. Tears up the letters. Flings them around the beach hut …'

'You've left out the biggest part …' Martha started to say. But Laura was ahead of her.

'No, you're right. Joe buggers off; this awful awful man comes along and tells Eva the bad news, gives her Joe's letter … then decides he'll take what he thinks he's entitled to and …' Martha braced herself; the wine had loosened her sister's tongue just a little too much. '…And attacks poor Eva, without a second thought …'

Martha nodded. Simon nodded. 'And so she is even more angry and upset – that Joe could have left her, put her in such a position, that she rips the letters to shreds.'

'That just about sums it up,' Martha said. 'But of course it wasn't really Joe's fault that he went – he was given his orders and had to follow. The US Air force wasn't there to mollycoddle wives and sweethearts, they had a job to do. It was just a shame Joe didn't think to leave Eva a way of contacting him.' Martha was distracted for a moment, thinking of her own unsuccessful attempts to track the man down.

'And then of course she had to deal with the consequences.' Simon took his part in moving the story forward. He topped up their glasses as he glanced at Martha. This was the part of the story which, up until then, Laura really had no idea about

– which she had not been given the route to run along, let alone make the leap to any conclusion.

Laura looked between them. 'Well, you've already told me that Eva had a baby,' she said, picking at the remains of the treacle tart, scooping a dollop of treacly filling into her mouth. And then the thought trickled into her consciousness. 'But what you didn't tell me …' she looked accusingly at Martha, '…Is what happened to the child. Or really what happened to Eva, once the baby had been born…' She stopped playing with the tart, her attention now fully on the conversation.

'Well,' Martha started, 'Eva did tell me she was treated really badly when she had the child. And because of the circumstances of its conception, she didn't want to keep it…'

'But what *actually* happened?' Laura's tolerance was being stretched to the limit. 'After all, the 1940s wasn't a great time to have an illegitimate child, so presumably it was taken for adoption … or are you going to tell me there's a son or daughter somewhere who is suddenly going to come out of the woodwork …?'

'Well, yes and no, but…' Martha took a breath, got more words in before her sister had chance to continue her grilling. '*But*, take yourself back a few steps Laura. We know that Eva had a child, which she didn't want. We know that her brother and his wife were unable to have children …'

'Did we know that? I don't remember …'

'Take my word for it, Laura, or we're never going to get to the end of this story … Where was

I? Oh yes, brother, no children, but suddenly there's a nephew, Martin …'

Laura sat, a look on her face which hinted that at that precise moment there wasn't a single thought in her head; as though she were waiting for some cognisance to be delivered to her before she could continue. And then, the idea seemed to drop into her mind, like a letter into a post box. 'You have to be joking. Are you telling me … you can't be serious … Martin …'

It seemed that the power of speech, usually so dominant in Laura's being, had abandoned her completely.

Simon looked at Martha, nodding, encouraging her to continue. 'It's your story Martha. You have to take it over the line …'

'Martin is Eva's son. She gave him away to her brother and sister-in-law. She went back to her career with the Air Transport Auxiliary. He was brought up by his uncle …'

'So why didn't he say something before now? Why did he let us spend all this time trying to figure things out …'

'Laura!' Martha spoke more abruptly than she had intended, but needed to get her sister's full attention - attention which seemed to have drained away with the wine dregs. 'Martin knew nothing of any of this until about a few weeks ago. As you know, Eva told him the beginnings of the story – about his parents not being his parents. And the fact that she was his mother…' Martha took a breath expecting another outburst from her sister, about why she hadn't been told this earlier, but Laura seemed engrossed, just nodding at her to continue. 'Well, so it was only after me talking to Eva, and finding the photos at the museum – with Simon's help – and by putting all the bits of the puzzle together, that we established who Martin's father must really have been.'

'Which is?' Laura looked up, her face full of questions. The story had gathered so much pace that Martha had forgotten that her sister hadn't been party to this essential piece of the puzzle. She quickly summarised the details of the photograph and the assumptions she had made.

'Does Martin know? Shouldn't he be here now, hearing all this?' It was obvious that Laura's mind was now racing ahead, turning several pages of the story at once.

'I've told him, everything I'd found out,' Martha said patiently. 'And I showed him the photo – of Vernon Casey. He came to the same conclusion pretty quickly…'

'All of which means his father isn't the lovely Joe. That he's the son of that bloody awful man who took advantage of Eva in her lowest moments? God, what a shock.'

'That's why he's not here. I don't blame him at all. He's got so much to come to terms with – not only his family lying to him all this time, but his father – his real father – being at best dishonourable …'

'And at worst, bullying, selfish, callous, brutal … where would you like me to stop?'

Simon slid from the table, went to the kitchen, and the two sisters could hear the sounds of coffee being made. 'Well, it's a pretty dreadful end to a love story,' Laura said eventually, wiping the corner of her eye.

Martha nodded. 'Not exactly what I was hoping for, when I started out on all of this,' she said. 'But there is one other thing, something which not even Simon knows yet.'

'What? Tell me. I could do with some good news… well, some more good news, that is' she smiled, looking towards the kitchen and giving a thumbs up.

Which made Martha smile too. 'Just wait until Simon comes back with the coffee … I'll tell you both.'

Laura couldn't help herself. She had to stack plates and collect together cutlery; carry things through to the sink, anything to expend some energy while she waited for Martha's news. 'Come on Simon, enough shillyshallying! Martha's got more things to tell us.'

Martha raised an eyebrow in the empty room. Since they were children she'd struggled with Laura's bossiness, but her new enthusiastic flippancy was even stranger to deal with. Doors were flung open as Laura made way for Simon with a tray of strong black coffee.

'Come on then, sis,' she demanded. 'Don't keep us in suspense.'

Martha held out until the coffee was poured. 'Well, when we – Simon and I – looked at the details of the memorial to the crashed American plane, and we had what we were pretty sure was Joe's full name, I decided I would try to see if there was any way we could trace him…'

'Why didn't you ask me?' Laura looked indignant. 'You know how good I am at tracking things down on the internet.' She stopped as she realised the significance of what she'd said, the unwanted information this had brought to her sister.

'Yes, I know you might have been able to find things out – but I wanted to have a go myself,' Martha interjected, before they got sidetracked into that particular minefield. 'Anyway, I contacted the Royal British Legion, who gave me details of American services organisations … and they in turn offered to pass on correspondence.'

'Data protection, I suppose…' Laura sighed frustratedly.

'Yes, well, understandable really – I am a complete stranger after all; I could have been anyone. *Anyway*, I wrote a letter – to Joe – and sent it off to them. But didn't hear anything back for ages.' She saw Simon look up, a "you haven't told me this bit" look on his face. Martha smiled at him. 'I wanted to surprise you as well as Laura,' she laughed. 'And I only heard back yesterday.'

'Well, don't keep us in suspense Martha – tell us what they said,' Laura demanded.

'Well, sadly …'

'Oh, please don't tell me Joe's not with us any longer. I thought there was going to be at least a tiny bit of a happy ending …'

'Laura!' Martha shouted in mock-anger. 'Let me finish! Sadly, Joe is not in good health. In fact, he's in a pretty poor way. But it seems that his mind is still okay, his memory is good. Well good for someone who's in their nineties.' Martha stopped to sip her coffee.

'Martha Townsend, I swear if you stretch this out any longer I'm going to …'

Martha laughed, holding up a conciliatory hand. 'Okay, okay. Well, it seems that when the family mentioned the name of Eva Andrews to him, Joe began to cry. He told them he'd never stopped thinking about Eva, that she had been the best thing in his young life, and he'd never forgiven himself – or the US Air Force presumably – for the way he had abandoned her.' Martha stopped, sniffing back a tear.

'Apparently, after he'd returned to the US, he'd been shipped out to the Far East to help in the Pacific against the Japanese, so communications generally weren't easy. But he told his family he had written to Eva, several times, and had no reply.'

'Yes, but …' Laura couldn't stop herself putting forward an opinion, but Martha pushed on.

'Yes, yes, they did discuss the possibility that his letters could have gone astray, as could Eva's replies, but after his fourth of fifth attempt he came to the conclusion that she no longer wanted anything to do with him. Then, once the war was over, he told his family he'd made one last attempt to contact her, but by that time the Air Transport Auxiliary had been disbanded, and he didn't know how else to find her.' Martha rubbed at the corner of her eye. 'Anyway, the first thing he wanted to do after he'd heard that Eva was still around, was to write her a letter.' Martha held up a small envelope. 'And it arrived this morning.'

The three of them looked at each other. 'Does Martin know?' was Simon's first question.

'Yes. I told him straightaway. He's suggested I go with him to visit Eva tomorrow, and read her the letter.'

'But I thought he hated the idea of reading the old letters to her ... wouldn't this be much the same?' Laura said.

'He thought the old letters would just agitate her, bring back all those negative memories. But this letter – well it's got to be more uplifting, hasn't it? Bearing in mind that all Eva seems to have done for the past few months is write letters to Joe which she's tried to send him ... and it's quite likely her fall was because she was trying to do just that.'

THE TINIEST GLOBE OF A TEAR

It felt like a mission – a divine mission. Martha carried the letter in her bag, clutched closely beside her; she had not wanted to let it out of her sight, not wanted the risk of it being lost before it had even arrived at its destination.

She had of course not opened it. It was not like Eva's attempt to communicate with Joe. This one was definitely going to find its intended recipient, and Martha realised she would get to know the contents soon enough, when either she or Martin read it to the still unconscious Eva. When Joe had written it of course, he was under the impression that Eva, although forgetful, would still be able to read and understand his words. Martha hadn't disillusioned him. And maybe … well, just maybe it might be what was needed …

As they entered the critical care ward, Martha retrieved the envelope and handed it to Martin. But he shook his head. 'You read it. I think she would prefer that.'

And so Martha sat on the edge of the old woman's bed. She slit open the letter and pulled the sheet of paper from inside. She had never felt more of an intruder – despite all her previous probing and questioning – than she did at that moment.

"My Dearest Wonderful Eva" it began, and just the mirroring of the words from the old letter, still clinging together in shreds, caught at Martha's throat.

My Dearest Wonderful Eva

It has been so long – so very very long – but I have thought of you every day of my life.

I cannot believe we have lived without each other all this time, that life has gone on without us being together as the single element we were so obviously meant to be.

But that is the hand we have been dealt. I would have given anything not to have had to leave you on that night, to have had one more hour with you, to say good bye – or rather farewell – to you just one more time. But it was not to be.

I hope you have had the most magnificent life, dear Eva. That you have enjoyed every moment, and you have not wasted more than a minute with regrets. We should have been together, and if I could have my life again, we would be together. But it is so good to know that you are still here, and perhaps one day we may meet again.

Until that moment, I remain your ever-loving
Joe

Martha was in tears. Martin was in tears. And there was the tiniest globe of a tear on Eva's cheek, as her eyelids fluttered.

'Eva! Eva,' they both called out in unison, before Martin ran from the room to find a member of staff.

A NEW CHAPTER

They were long days. Eva awake, aware, and then not. There was certainly no chance of a proper conversation – still less of asking about Martin's father.

Martin had persuaded – no, encouraged - Martha to attend the hospital with him. He had definitely wanted her there, and they both sat at Eva's bedside, sometimes together, sometimes one and then the other. There were some glittering moments of awareness; like the time when Eva managed the word "letter", garbled and muddled, but plain enough, and Martha had read Joe's missive to her again and again. It seemed to be the only thing which would command her attention. Martha felt so bad for Martin – that he was virtually excluded from proceedings while she read. She tried to persuade him to do the reading, to get more involved, but it seemed that neither he nor Eva were of the opinion that that was a good idea.

The glittering moments became less. Eva's closed eyes were the more usual sight. Simon and Laura between them maintained the two vigil-keepers with food and hot drinks, and from time-to-time Martin would allow one of them to take over for a while, but he was never far away.

'You look exhausted.' Simon gave Martha a hug as she took her turn to leave Eva's bedside.

'I am. But I really can't see that she's going to hold on much longer … and I would just like to be here, you know, when she takes that final flight …'

In the end it was quick. Both Martin and Martha were there. Eva's eyes fluttered; she held out a hand to each of them, gave the smallest of smiles. And she was gone.

'It's a relief, to be honest,' Martin confessed as he stood with Martha in the corridor while the nurses did what they needed to do. 'There was no way, even if she revived, that she was going to be able to carry on with the life she'd had. And moving from that place and all her memories – well, it would have finished her, in here,' he said, pointing to his forehead.

'You're right, Martin. She would have hated being in residential care. I mean, just look how desperate she was to get out of the house each day…' They both smiled. 'Imagine what she'd be like with no open doors…' The thought of Eva's strong will and determination, the fact that she'd made her exit after doing exactly what she had wanted to do – one last walk – lifted both their spirits.

'I guess I'd better start …' Martin pointed to his phone, indicating the people he would need to inform.

'I'll let Laura know – and Simon. And Hilly of course. She'll want to be kept in the loop,' Martha said, thinking what else she could offer to do. 'Is there anyone else I could contact for you?'

Martin looked at her, and she knew instantly what he was thinking. 'Joe – of course.' She couldn't stop the tears coming to her eyes now. So close, and yet – the two lovers had almost got back together, almost. 'At least it will be easier this time round,' she wiped her face roughly with her cuff. 'Joe's daughter included her email address when she sent Joe's letter, so I can contact her directly now.'

But before Martha could put together her thoughts to Joe and his family, an email from his daughter appeared in her mailbox. She opened it quickly, and saw that there was an attachment – a photo, it turned out, of Joe with his three children.

Children who looked as varied as a football team. The email designated each one, reminding Martha of the uncovered Air Force pictures which now seemed a lifetime away. Isabella was the daughter who had been emailing, and she had something of her father's looks. Fabio had all of Joe's Italian heritage – dark eyes, black hair, olive skin. And Marco. His looks stole Martha's breath away. She had to abandon the screen and sit on the sofa, take a breath to calm her beating heart, unable to comprehend what she was seeing. Marco bore no resemblance to either Isabella or Fabio ... and he looked completely different to Joe too. But the person he did resemble – uncannily so – was Martin.

It took Martha some time, checking and rechecking, re-examining the assumptions about Martin's heritage which she had made along the way, making sure that she wasn't about to make a complete fool of herself. And then she called Martin. Told him there was something she needed to discuss.

'Will it wait?' he'd asked. And Martha thought about the hundred and one things he was probably having to do, in dealing with Eva's affairs, the arrangements he was having to make.

'I think ... probably not,' she said. 'I think you'll want to see this.'

Martin had been as astounded as Martha. 'But, I look so like that other bloke ... Vernon or whatever he was called ...' he muttered as he, like Martha checked and rechecked the picture. 'And what about what you said, you know, about the laws of genetics ... Is this even possible?' The fact that the very varied Moretti faces were all looking back at him seemed to suggest that it was.

'I did a quick bit of searching,' Martha said. 'And even with my very limited knowledge – both of the internet and genetics – it seems that this is not as unusual as you might think. Dark hair and eyes are definitely dominant genes – and so you'd expect all offspring, even in a mixed-parentage situation, to follow that side of their parents' looks.' Martha had also sent a quick reply to Isabella, asking, as subtly as she was able, about Joe's wife and her appearance. Isabella had very helpfully sent another photo, showing Joe and his wife at their wedding, almost by return. Martha showed this too to Martin, and he could see what she had seen – that Joe's wife had had fairer features, but that these had won at least some of the battle with Joe's looks.

'I don't know what to say,' Martin said, looking at the pictures again, zooming in and out, trying to make sense of what he was seeing. 'I mean, we could look at these all day long, could make all the assumptions we cared to, but it doesn't mean a thing really, does it?'

'You mean that Vernon Casey could still be your father – and all that that means?' Martha handed Martin a small glass of brandy. His face was the palest she had ever seen it, and his hands were shaking. 'Well, in theory I suppose that's true,' she paused. 'But I looked something else up.'

Martin glanced at her, looking as though he might not be able to take any more surprises or disputable news.

'DNA tests,' Martha said. 'Apparently it is possible to have your DNA tested, particularly in paternity cases – although it's probably much easier at the moment in The States than it is here; but it's possible none the less. 'We could ask the family …'

She left the thought hanging in the air, not able to guarantee that the goodwill of Joe's family would continue to such an extent, not wanting to raise

Martin's hopes further than could be legitimately expected. 'We'd have to handle it very carefully, of course,' she said. 'It might be a step too far, after only just learning about their father's previous life. But maybe it's worth the risk …'

Martin swigged back the brandy, coughing as it caught the back of his throat. 'Let me think about it,' he said, getting up from his chair. But as he neared the door he turned to Martha. 'Thank you,' he said, his words gentle but heartfelt, before leaving her to look once again at the photos.

'I think you should write it all up – Eva's life story.' Laura was looking through Martha's wardrobe, trying to find something she considered even vaguely suitable for a funeral. 'Lots of people would be interested. And at the very least you should write down something to be read out at the service…' She pulled a navy-blue polka dot dress from the rail, held it up to herself and dropped it to the floor with a shake of her head. 'Martha, you really need to sort out your wardrobe – goodness knows how long you have had some of these clothes …' But she stopped when she looked over at her sister. Martha had held back her tears over the past few days, helping Martin with arrangements, doing what she could, but just the thought of reading something out at Eva's funeral service had suddenly brought the whole story home – and everything which had gone with it. Martha sobbed, as she sat on the bed - hard, gut-wrenching yet silent sobs, until her whole body was shaking.

'She had a great life – Eva...' Laura tried to console her sister, probably knowing that what she was saying sounded crass, that it wasn't just the death of the old lady which was the problem.

'It's not just her – although the story of her and Joe will always make me cry.' Martha eventually got some words out. 'It's Martin's story too – and Hilly, and ...and ...'

'And your own story...' Laura filled in the gap. They sat in silence on the bed, Laura patting Martha's back, holding her close. 'You've come such a long way, in these past few months ... it's been a lot to deal with. But you will, you'll move on.' She handed over a clean tissue. 'And especially now that you have the wonderful Simon in your life,' she said, smiling, giving Martha a playful punch on the arm. 'Definitely a new chapter. No, make that a whole new volume...'

FALLEN PETALS

Martha *had* written some words – hundreds of words in fact, most of which, like the letter she had originally written to Joe, had ended in a hillock of tattered papers at her feet. But eventually a small collection of suitable words had emerged.

She had quoted Shakespeare, which she wasn't sure would have been Eva's cup of tea, but as she said in her speech, 'Never have words been more appropriate "May flights of angels sing thee to thy rest" – for a woman who was brave, determined, and above all a career pilot who loved nothing better than to be flying through the skies …'

She had decided that the whole thing would be incomplete without a few words from Joe. She had brought his letter with her, but had insisted that Laura be on standby. 'It might just finish me off, but it's only right that his words are with her on this day …' She had just got to "…to have had one more hour with you …" when the ponderous oak door of the church rattled and groaned, opening to a flourish of warm air and sunshine, pushing their way inside.

All eyes turn to the back of the church; the vicar is struggling to find his place in the hymnal, taking a moment to look up.

Footsteps clatter on the stone slabs, ignoring the tombs beneath. 'Wait. Please wait.'

Their eyes follow the young woman as she dashes up the aisle, not in funereal black, but in floral summer colours. There is a determination on her face, and relief perhaps. They are all awake now, alive to the prospect of some interest stirring into the grey proceedings.

The vicar steps down, looking disapprovingly at the interruption, hands ready to shoo the woman away, brush her into the churchyard with the fallen rose petals. As he opens his mouth to speak she pre-empts him.

'I'm sorry to be late,' she says. 'But I'm Genevieve - Joe's granddaughter.'

The vicar looks perplexed, unaware of the woman's significance. But the remainder of the congregation gasp - alert, eager.

'He asked that I bring these ...' and she places a posy of roses on the coffin. 'He says he's sorry he didn't bring them sooner ...'

AUTHOR'S NOTE AND ACKNOWLEDGEMENTS

Those who know the west of Somerset will have spotted that most of the story takes place there. Moyon's Castle borrows a great deal from Dunster Castle, Mariner's Weir is strongly based on Porlock Weir, and there are various scenes which are based around Porlock. Much of the wider landscape appears as itself – North Hill, Exmoor and Selworthy. However, I confess to having played "fast and loose" with some of the geography, making some places closer together or further apart; and Moyons Quay takes aspects from Minehead and Dunster Beach and merges them together. However, I hope that the storyline justifies these "cheats".

Similarly, I have taken some liberties with the routes and planes flown by the Air Transport Auxiliary. The airfield locations and aircraft were all used (as noted in the logbooks on the excellent ATA website), but not necessarily in the combination I have suggested.

The original inspiration for the story came from two different directions. I stumbled across some information about the Air Transport Auxiliary, and couldn't believe that I'd never heard of the amazing work which this group undertook during WW2 – and particularly the women, who were certainly venturing into uncharted areas by demonstrating that they could fly on an equal footing with the men. It seemed that most people I spoke to were equally unaware, and I hope I have done just a little bit to bring these servicewomen to the forefront. The other contributory factor to the story was the memorial to the Liberator plane, which did indeed crash on Porlock Marsh. The buckled piece of fuselage, giving the names of the airmen is very moving, and it was another story which seemed to me to need more telling. I have though changed the names of the personnel, and in particular that of the only survivor.

There are many people who have contributed to the finished version of this book, and to whom I owe many thanks. Members of Writers in Somerset have given valuable feedback throughout its writing, and another sterling group gave much time and energy to assisting with the final editing – Christine Human, Fiona Windle, Karen Mahony, Margaret Ingall, and Steve Mahony. It would have been a much poorer book without them. A special thank you goes to Lucia Forte, who supplied vital details regarding her Italian heritage and family characteristics – inspiring a vital plot point.

Printed in Great Britain
by Amazon